A FRIEND IN THE FIRE

AN AUDEN & O'CALLAGHAN MYSTERY

GREGORY ASHE
C.S. POE

A Friend in the Fire

Published by Emporium Press
https://www.cspoe.com
contact@cspoe.com

Cover Art by Reese Dante
Cover content is for illustrative purposes only and any person depicted on the cover is a model.

Edited by Tricia Kristufek
Copyedited by Andrea Zimmerman
Proofread by Lyrical Lines

Published 2021.
Printed in the United States of America

Trade Paperback ISBN: 978-1-952133-30-5
Digital eBook ISBN: 978-1-952133-27-5

Love is friendship that has caught fire.

CHAPTER
ONE

At 12:47 p.m. Rufus O'Callaghan was still in bed, the sheets kicked down around his feet, with one arm hanging over the edge of the mattress to peck at the screen of the burner lying on the floor.

No messages. No calls.

But of course not.

Three months ago, the exchange of numbers had only gone in one direction, leaving it up to Rufus to initiate the conversation. The apology. But he hadn't. And then so much time passed and Rufus was... just *too tired* to try.

He flung the phone across the studio. It narrowly missed the fridge, smacked the floor, and settled in the hall leading to the bathroom. Rufus rolled onto his back and stared at a crack in the plaster that splintered like a spiderweb. Or maybe it *was* a spiderweb. He wasn't exactly domestic. Rufus couldn't remember the last time he'd dusted.

He was having trouble remembering a lot lately.

Because he was tired.

But not for sleep.

Ever since Rufus had checked out a copy of *The Complete Works of William Shakespeare* from the New York Public Library last month and studied Hamlet's famed "To be, or not to be" scene, he wasn't quite tired enough for sleep. Hamlet had raised the question of what dreams may come in sleep, and that, what if our dreams are worse than all of the trials and tribulations in life?

The soliloquy had sent shivers down Rufus's spine.

He hadn't ever considered that sleep—death—could be a cure worse than the disease.

So what was he to do, if he couldn't die and couldn't be happy?

The East Village tenement Rufus called home was old. Over a hundred years, he was pretty sure. The thin walls and thin floors allowed the comings and goings of life to seep into his apartment at all hours. 4B across the hall had adopted a puppy a few weeks ago, and the thing had not once stopped barking. Pauly Paul next door was stoned and singing "Back in Black," but it seemed like he couldn't remember all the lyrics, so every fourth or fifth word was just a really off-key Brian Johnson raspy scream. Below, Mr. Gonzalez was blasting the Game Show Network.

Rufus had considered, for the better part of an hour now, dragging some clothes on and joining his landlord in watching reruns of *Jeopardy!*, but would Mr. Gonzalez notice that Rufus had gotten thinner? Would he notice that Rufus hadn't washed his hair in… he wasn't sure how long? Would Mr. Gonzalez notice the bags under Rufus's eyes—ask the one question that hurt more than all others: *What's wrong?*

Everything.

Rufus returned to his side and stared at the wooden floorboards, visible where the ancient, cheap linoleum had peeled away over the years. If he studied the grains and texture long enough, they began to resemble ink blot tests. Rorschachs, they were called. Did they still use those? Rufus was curious what his results would say about his current state.

There was that one particular image referred to as the "father card." Plate IV. Rufus had read a college textbook, a psych primer he'd picked up for a dollar, and there'd been a chapter on Rorschach tests. It was suggested that any subject interpreting Plate IV as dangerous or menacing would be an indication as to their relationship with men or authority.

Rufus snorted and scratched at the floorboard with his fingernail. What good had men ever been? From Alex Mitchell at PS14, shoving him down a flight of stairs and breaking his arm, to Sam Auden... well, men had been fucking Rufus—literally and figuratively—his entire life, only to then take that metaphorical walk for a pack of smokes and leave him devastated. So, menacing? Sure. Plate IV resembled a man standing over Rufus, ready to stomp his guts out.

Pauly Paul had moved on to "Thunderstruck."

Somewhere outside came the distant *boing* of a basketball being dribbled down the sidewalk. Laughter of young teenagers followed in its wake. Farther—across the street—that screwball who'd taken up residence on the corner for the last week was shouting about the end of the world. Yesterday, the cause had been Hairy Feminist Witches. Today, the world was going to end because of The Lecherous Homosexual.

Rufus cracked a smile. Damn homosexuals.

He thought about going outside to ask if the kook knew which day, *specifically*, the world was going to explode or whatever. Because if Rufus had until, say, Tuesday, he might get his act together enough to get laid one last time.

Pauly Paul was on the "Highway to Hell" now.

Canned audience applause echoed from downstairs. Maybe someone had just won a *Brand-New Car*!

Rufus sat up, his red hair in complete disarray. He climbed off the bed, padded across the floor, and crouched to collect his phone.

1:00 p.m.

Cash Cab would be on soon. Mr. Gonzalez enjoyed poking fun at the tourists as much as he enjoyed trying to beat Rufus at the trivia questions. Maybe if Rufus came bearing a gift, the man who'd babysat him on more than one occasion while growing up would be properly distracted from what a mess Rufus had become.

Rufus picked up a pair of jeans with torn knees from the dirty pile against the wall, checked the pockets, and found a few bucks. Perfect. Margarita had been working the corner near the laundromat, mooching off the gyro street vendor's customers with her little pushcart of enticing mango con chile for the last several weeks. Mr. Gonzalez loved those spicy mangoes on a stick. He'd be too busy munching on that to ask Rufus why he resembled roadkill, and then they could watch *Cash Cab* in peace.

He dragged on the ratty jeans, found a black shirt with the words NO FLAG stamped across the front in white, then spent a few minutes looking for his jean jacket and beanie, the search taking longer than it should have in the tiny studio with little by way of belongings, because Rufus just seemed to... kind of forget what he was doing sometimes.

After tying the laces of his scuffed high-tops, Rufus

was out the door. He slid down the old stairwell banisters, steps barely a whisper on each landing. He tugged the cheap plastic sunglasses from the collar of his shirt and put them on as he walked into the building's vestibule, but he stopped at the wall of mailboxes.

4D - R. O. had a slip of paper sticking out from the bottom of the door. It might have been a menu for a new bougie restaurant in the neighborhood that specialized in free-range potatoes or ethically harvested mac 'n' cheese, or something equally pretentious that would close in six months. Or it could have been one of those "Welcome to the Neighborhood" postcards Rufus had been getting en masse lately, which was a well-meaning exclamation only thirty-three years late. Perhaps it was preapproved credit card junk mail—which, considering Rufus didn't have a credit score, he always found a bit amusing.

Rufus gave it a tug, and out came a sheaf of lined notepaper, folded over several times. Not mail. Rufus furrowed his brows as he hesitantly unfolded the note.

I have information on Daisy
23rd & Ave. C—FDR overpass
11:00 Saturday night
Come alone
-A Friend

Rufus walked along tree-lined East Twenty-Third just before eleven o'clock. Tungsten-orange light from streetlamps filtered through the boughs, casting sharp shadows across his face, discoloring his jean jacket. Then Rufus would step beyond the pool of illumination and briefly lose himself to the dark again.

He didn't wait at the crosswalk. This late at night, so far

from the heart of the city, cars were few and far between. Rufus jogged across the road toward the overpass. Directly ahead was a gas station, the commercial-grade lights of the canopy buzzing loudly and the air smelling of exhaust and benzene. Beyond was the blackness of the East River. And to the right, a makeshift parking lot underneath the overpass.

Rufus hoisted himself over the concrete barrier surrounding the converted lot. The soles of his shoes grated against stray pebbles along the asphalt. That very small sound seemed to echo like standing in an enormous cavern, the scuff of his Cons bouncing off stalactites, the only evidence of life being his own whisper ricocheted back at him.

It made Rufus feel very alone.

A shadow living among nine million people, unable to let go of the past. And not a tangible thing like Peter Pan's, but something more abstract. More hopeless. A shadow that was darkness, resulting from the absence of any light.

Rufus took a shallow breath, dug the folded note from his back pocket, and studied the unfamiliar blocky handwriting.

A Friend.

Daisy had no friends. In fact, the only person outside of the guys and gals in the Ramble who would have even remembered her was Mr. Gonzalez—and he'd have had no reason for this incognito bullshit. And the two people Rufus had reached out to for help—his new NYPD handler, Detective Erik Weaver, and that odd duck working in the Cold Case Squad—they were cops. Good cops, as far as Rufus could tell. But when cops wanted to talk, they used the damn phone.

"*Rufus O'Callaghan.*"

Rufus spun toward the voice, saw the glint of steel, the blade tarnished in the dirty lighting, and jumped backward as a short, stocky man lunged at him. The knife missed Rufus's belly and instead slid into his open coat and ripped a hole through the jean material. Threads tore as the attacker drew back.

"I've wanted to gut you for two years, you fucking snitch."

Rufus stumbled several steps as the man came at him a second time. He avoided the next lunge, managing to knock the guy's hat off in the process. The overhead lights made his blond hair look grimy and square jaw heavy with a five o'clock shadow.

I know him, Rufus realized. *It's a trap.*

Run.

Rufus tripped backward, slammed into a parked car, and set the alarm off. His attacker thrust a third time, and Rufus scrambled to the left to miss the blow. The knife screeched against the car door, and the blond man shouted obscenities.

Rufus pushed off the hood of a second vehicle, vaulted over the concrete barrier, ran across the road, and then made a sharp turn downtown. He heard the heavy tread of his attacker following, but Rufus had survived this long because he knew how to run and how to hide. He pushed himself harder, as far as his long legs would reach without overextending. His lungs burned on the intake of air, blood pounded in his ears, steps hit the pavement like claps of thunder, and the car alarm, now a block or two in his wake, kept the rhythm of the sad, sad song that was Rufus's life.

At the corner of East Eighteenth Street, Rufus cut into the massive residential development of Stuyvesant Town. He ducked around a gazebo, crossed the street, ran up an outdoor staircase that led to one of the many red brick apartment complexes, and disappeared, unseen by his assailant, into the night.

CHAPTER
TWO

The town was called Wahredua, and the club was called the Pretty Pretty, and tonight was twink night. Or so it looked to Sam, anyway. He hadn't intended to be here. He hadn't intended to be anywhere, though, so here was as good a place as any. A guy driving a tractor trailer full of frozen chicken had picked him up on the shoulder of I-70, just outside St. Louis. That ride had ended at Kingdom City. Then the October rain had started, and Sam had jogged south across four lanes to the Petro. Drinking coffee out of a foam cup, he'd made a circuit of the rest stop. The first trucker to say yes was a woman hauling pumpkins, but she wasn't going west. She was going south. Sam grabbed his ruck, and his ride ended at the corner of Market and Jefferson in this town whose name he couldn't pronounce.

Being here, in the club, was an acknowledgment of the central problem of Sam's existence: no matter how far he went, he was still somewhere. Tonight, that meant this club, with the flashing lights, the smoke machine, the smell of too hot bodies and too much cologne. At the bar, two stools down from Sam, a kid wearing a ripped tank, denim booty shorts, and flip-flops was playing with the napkin under his Manhattan. He was pretty, with shaggy hair, although he looked like a hell of a lot of trouble. The dark-eyed bartender was flirting with him. He kept rucking up his shirt and scratching his belly, laughing too loud, trying too hard. *Why not just whip out your dick*, Sam wanted to ask.

In the hour since he'd sat at the bar, Sam had worked his way through two Boulevards—Tank 7s, a farmhouse ale that kicked like a mule. A middle-aged blond in a t-shirt that said CUM WHORE had tried to pick him up, followed by a dark-haired guy who looked fresh out of high school, and then either the dark-haired guy came back for a second try or he had a twin brother. Sam gave them all the same "Not interested." The blond guy took it all right. The first dark-haired guy did too, but his twin didn't.

When the bartender glanced over, Sam raised a hand, and the guy came toward him.

"Another?" he asked.

"Please," Sam said.

When the guy came back with another Boulevard, Sam caught his gaze and held it until the guy swallowed, a flush climbing his neck.

"What's your name?" Sam asked.

"Chase."

"What's the name of the pretty guy you're working on?"

"Nico."

"You know you're wasting your time?"

Chase glanced over at Nico; the shaggy-haired kid was staring out at the dance floor. He'd been doing it for the full hour that Sam had been sitting there, glancing over his shoulder at the same pair of men, following them with his eyes from their booth to the dance floor.

"Is the big, dark-haired guy his ex?" Sam asked. "Or the blond one?"

"Emery," Chase said. "The big guy."

Sam took a long drink.

"They're totally done, though," Chase said. "I mean, totally."

Sam ran his thumb through the condensation on the glass. A steady, house-music beat pumped through the club, interrupted by the swell and fall of voices. A few months before, the heat, the smell, the volume—it all would have combined to send Sam into a tailspin. Sensory processing disorder was a bitch. But the fluoxetine was helping. Some.

"You can see it, right?" Chase said. "I mean, Emery doesn't even pay attention to him anymore."

"You're not worried about Emery," Sam said.

Chase twisted a bar rag in his hands.

"Here's the deal, Chase," Sam said. "I think you've got about a ten-percent chance with Nico. Maybe less, honestly. And that's his loss because you're a nice-looking guy, and you seem sweet. With me, on the other hand, you've got a hundred-percent chance. As long as you stay sweet."

"What's your name?"

"Sam."

"Are you in town for work?"

Sam shook his head.

"Don't tell me you're on vacation in Wahredua," Chase said with a laugh.

"What time do you get off?" Sam said, holding Chase's gaze with the same steady look.

"We close at one-thirty." Chase glanced at Nico, then at Sam again. "Normally I have to stay after, count out, but—" Another furtive glance at Nico. "I could ask Brad to let me go early."

"Do that," Sam said.

Chase twisted the rag for another minute. Then he jogged away, disappearing down a narrow hallway that Sam guessed led to the manager's office. When he came back, he had a huge grin and gave Sam a thumbs-up. Nico noticed and looked over, and then he said something to Chase, and the two of them started going at it like cats in a sack. Sam drank his beer, listening to Nico's voice slowly heating until the shaggy-haired kid left. The poor thing was huffing, his arms folded, his shoulders stiff and square with indignation. Chase stared after him.

"It's a good thing," Sam said.

"It didn't feel good," Chase said. "We're friends, and now he's pissed."

"You don't want him as a friend," Sam said. "You want to fuck him until he screams your name."

Chase licked his lower lip.

"It's a good thing," Sam said again. "You'll be back tomorrow night with a war story, freshly dicked, and he'll be jealous. Guys like him, you've got to make them jealous for them to take you seriously."

Staring over Sam's shoulder, Chase said, "I guess."

Sam shrugged.

"So, what?" Chase said, his eyes cutting back to Sam. "You're like some sort of dating guru?"

Sam thought about a certain redhead, and he just

smiled crookedly.

Chase didn't last until closing. He clocked out early and drove them to his apartment, a second-floor unit in a brick walk-up, and he smiled shyly when he took Sam's hand and led him upstairs. The apartment was what Sam thought of as college-kid-in-a-box: IKEA-style furniture, dirty clothes on the couch, a wobbly pyramid of Budweiser cans on the kitchen counter. The place smelled like day-old pizza.

"No roommates?" Sam said, shutting the door behind him.

Chase shook his head. "Do you want—"

Sam grabbed the hem of his shirt, pulled it over Chase's head, and pressed him against the wall. He kissed him hard, wrapping a hand loosely around Chase's throat, using it to steer him through the tangle of ringer tees and Allbird shorts and a pair of leather chaps. Chase was moaning softly between the kisses.

"Oh fuck," Chase whispered. "Oh fuck."

Sam shoved him backward, and the mattress caught Chase at the knees. Chase fell onto the bed, bouncing once, and his eyes were wide and a little worried. He was trying to cover it with a smirk, one hand moving up and down his chest.

After undoing Chase's pants, Sam tugged them off. Then the bright red jock. Then the socks. Chase was hard, and he reached down to play with himself while Sam stripped, but his eyes were still a little worried. Sam moved onto the bed, kneeling next to Chase, then grabbing him under the arms and hauling him up a few feet until he was fully on the bed.

"Shit," Chase said. "You're really strong. Are you—"

Sam kissed him just to shut him up.

"Lube," Sam said.

"Nightstand."

"Rubber?"

Chase nodded. He looked doped out.

"Where are the rubbers?" Sam asked dryly.

"Oh." The flush crawled up his neck again, and he smiled with embarrassment. "Nightstand."

After that, everything was… basic. Chase was cute, and he was hot, and he tried to make it good for Sam. And once, as recently as a few months ago, a nice, unhurried fuck in a real bed would have been a luxury for Sam. But who was this kid? And who the fuck was Sam? And why did anything fucking matter?

"Oh my God," Chase kept saying. "Oh my God, you're so good."

"No talking," Sam said.

"Oh my God," Chase said, his head rolling to his shoulder. "Yes, Sam. Yes. Please."

Sam yanked his hair once, just hard enough to startle him, and said again, "No talking." Then he slapped Chase's ass. "On your stomach."

That worried look didn't go away, but Chase did it.

When they were finished, Chase lay on his side, one hand trailing up and down Sam's chest. Once Sam had caught his breath, he rolled off the mattress.

"Shower?"

"Oh, yeah," Chase said with that dopey smile. "That sounds nice. Hold on."

"No," Sam said. "I'm going to shower. Where is it?"

"I'll show—"

"For fuck's sake. I'll find it myself."

In the bathroom, he put the toilet seat down. The door was thin, and he could hear Chase sniffling in the other room. Sam held his head in his hands, wondering what the fuck he was doing, and then he turned on the water so he couldn't hear Chase crying anymore. He showered, using Dr. Bronner's Pure Castile Soap, Baby Unscented, and the towel from his ruck. The seam on the towel was giving way, and he yanked off a few loose threads and dropped them in the trash.

When he got back to the bedroom, Chase had pulled himself together, but his eyes were red.

"Hey," he said with a valiant attempt at a smile. "Everything ok?"

Sam grunted, picking up discarded clothes.

"So, if you're going to be in town—" Chase said.

Whatever he was going to offer, the universe spared him the embarrassment of another rejection. Before Chase could finish, Sam's phone rang. He didn't recognize the number, but he was pretty sure the area code was for New York. His heart beat a little faster as he answered.

"Sam?"

Sam sat on the bed because he didn't trust himself to stay standing. He cleared his throat. And then he said, "Rufus?"

CHAPTER
THREE

It took almost two full days for Sam to make his way across the country. The journey occurred in stages, each stage with its own particular brand of asshole. First, Sam had to hitch a ride with a guy pulling a flatbed full of hay, and the guy was so jittery, reeking of weed and meth, that Sam hadn't exactly been bothered when he got dropped six miles south of Kingdom City. From Kingdom City, he hitched west. It felt counterproductive, since he needed to go the other direction, but the westbound lanes had steady traffic, and he could catch a Greyhound in Columbia and take it all the way to New York instead of messing around. That particular asshole was a lady Bible salesperson, as she explained it. Sam wasn't sure if that meant she was a lady who sold Bibles or if she sold lady Bibles, which might or might not have been a thing. She was still pressing pamphlets into his hands when he opened the door at a red light and jogged across traffic. At the Columbia Greyhound station, he bought a ticket to New York, contemplated spending thirty-four hours on a bus with other humans, and told himself Rufus better have a damn good reason for hauling his ass across the country.

He got to the Port Authority Bus Terminal late. Above the haze of light pollution, the sky was dark. *At least the streets are less crowded*, Sam thought, adjusting his ruck before hiking downtown.

New York seemed different. Part of that, he assumed, was that he had the luxury of walking long stretches without bumping into anyone. Part of it was the cool air, unlike the summer heat that had waited for him last time he had been there. Part of it was doubtless the fluoxetine, helping him moderate input that threatened to overwhelm him. But part of it, maybe the biggest part of it, was that the skin on his chest felt too tight and lightning was curled up in his belly, because he was going to see Rufus.

Rufus's apartment building was brick, on a block of brick buildings. Two old oak trees stood near the curb; across the street was a barber's shop with the classic spinning pole and a blue awning that said RAIMUNDO'S. Through the big windows, Sam could see a guy getting a tight fade, and then the barber, presumably Raimundo, said something, and they were both cracking up. *Great*, Sam thought. *Great.* At least somebody was having a laugh tonight. At least somebody didn't feel like his gut were getting zapped every time he took a deep breath.

Shaking himself like a dog, Sam stepped up to the intercom and buzzed 4D.

No answer.

He took out his phone, wiped grit from his eyes, and tapped Rufus's number. The phone rang and rang and rang before clicking over to a recording that simply said, "The voicemail for this number has not been set up. Please try again."

Well, Sam thought, he was about at his limit of try again.

He pressed buttons at random until the lock on the front door buzzed, and then he caught the door and stepped inside. The vestibule had peeling linoleum and dust bunnies the size of terriers. That electricity was really acting up; Sam could barely stand still, and he tried to work a little of it out of his system by tapping the mailbox for 4D. It didn't help. If anything, it made him feel worse.

He took the stairs two at a time. He thought about just turning around, catching the first bus to anywhere, and getting really, truly hammered. Drunk like he hadn't been in a long time.

But he didn't. He kept climbing.

When he was crossing the third-floor landing, a door opened down the hall.

A much older man, with salt-and-pepper hair that'd gone mostly salt, stuck his head out. "You the one making that damn racket?" he asked, loud in a way that suggested he was hard of hearing.

Sam's general impression of New York, based on his previous experience here and a select few '90s films, was that it was now appropriate for him to shoot this old man. Or maybe be his best friend. It was hard to tell. He settled for saying, "I'm here to see Rufus."

The man frowned, sniffed, and pushed glasses up the bridge of his nose that looked to be retro originals. "Brat ain't home."

"Do you know where he is?"

The old man pointed toward the ceiling. "He went upstairs. Richardson blew it on Colorful Words and

Phrases for $200. Brat screamed, 'Everybody knows what a red herring is.'"

Sam didn't understand a word of that except the first bit. "Upstairs?"

"The roof."

"Right," Sam said. "Thanks."

He took the stairs two at a time again. When he passed the fourth floor, the next flight of stairs ended at a reinforced steel door. Sam hesitated, hand on the release bar, taking slow breaths. A light sheen of sweat made his shirt stick to him. He could feel his pulse in his throat. He might have stayed there longer, that lightning coiling in his gut, except he remembered Rufus had told him, once, about coming upstairs. Rufus had told him that he thought about jumping.

Sam shouldered open the door and stepped out onto the roof: tar paper and pea gravel crunched underfoot, and a light breeze wicked heat from him, turning his sweat icy. He glanced left, saw nothing. Glanced right. Rufus was sitting on the raised edge of the roof.

"Rufus," Sam shouted. "Don't!"

Rufus startled, looked over his shoulder, and turned to set his feet on the rooftop. He placed a big book on the ledge beside himself. "Sam?"

"What are you—" Sam took a breath, and his eyes focused on the book. "Oh."

Rufus followed Sam's line of sight, then quickly stood. "Astronomy," he explained. "I was trying to see. Not stars. There aren't any stars here. I mean—" He paused again and motioned vaguely over his shoulder toward the streetlamps. "See the words."

Sam nodded. "The words."

"So…." Rufus collected his book and took a few steps forward, the pea gravel underfoot almost louder than his voice. "You came."

Sam nodded again; his head felt like it was on a string. "You said you needed—" And then he stopped, shook his head, and said, "I'm sorry. You know, about how I left. I should have said that a long time ago, but I didn't have your number, and…." His mouth was drying up. "Son of a bitch, it is really cold up here."

Rufus waited until Sam had finished speaking before suggesting, "Let's go inside." Then he walked past Sam, opened the access door, and started down the stairs.

Sam let a moment pass, the wind pulling his shirt tight against his back, the smell of exhaust mixing with the smell of boiled cabbage from a nearby kitchen. The city looked like glitter that a kid had kicked across an old canvas. He ran back the conversation in his head, ran it forward, listened for the part where Rufus had said he was sorry too. That part of the tape was blank, though. Then he stomped downstairs, his face heating.

He found Rufus inside the apartment, the door to 4D standing open. It was more or less as Sam remembered it: the kitchen to one side, the three stacks of books, the unmade bed, the window. Piles of clothes. The smell of booze that was one step removed from rubbing alcohol. An open clamshell container with the bones from an order of buffalo wings. Rufus wasn't a slob, not exactly; to Sam, this looked like more signs of trouble.

"Well," Sam said, and his voice was deeper than he intended, the words more harshly clipped, "what was so fucking important that I had to come halfway across the country?"

Rufus looked up from where he sat in the middle of the mattress, his elbows resting on his knees, his arms hanging like stunted wings. He wore a very out-of-sorts smile on his face, framed by red hair in disarray from the wind. "My mother was murdered."

In the unit across the hall, some asshole was laughing his head off. Sam shut the door behind him and leaned against it. He wiped his eyes again, finding more grit after the two days on the bus; stubble rasped against his knuckles.

"I'm sorry," he said. "What happened?"

Rufus looked down at his hands and absently tugged on a hangnail. "It was seventeen years ago—that she died. But this past Saturday, someone contacted me. Said they had information about her murder. Everything has gotten sort of… shitty, since then."

Sam tried to run through all of that in his head. Then he said, "Seventeen years ago?"

Rufus wriggled free from his jean jacket before sticking a finger through a hole in the side. "He pulled a knife on me."

Sam came across the room and sat on the mattress, careful to leave enough space between himself and Rufus. "You're ok?"

Rufus folded the jacket but didn't look up. "I'm not dead, if that's what you're asking."

"Not exactly, but it's better than nothing, I guess. I think you should start at the beginning. What happened to your mom?"

Rufus wiped his face with the heel of his hand. "Her name was Daisy."

Sam scooted closer and put an arm across Rufus's shoulders.

Rufus didn't move away, but he didn't lean into the hold either. "You asked me who Daisy was, remember? I said something fucking stupid, like, 'Boy George must like flowers,' or whatever."

"I remember."

"I don't like going to the Ramble because people

remember her. They remember me." Rufus wiped his face again, more agitated this time. He took a soggy breath before continuing. "There'd been a note left in my mailbox—information on Daisy, come alone. I did. I was so stupid. I don't know what I was thinking." He fingered the hole in his jacket a moment longer before setting the coat aside. "A load of human excrement named Devon Kelly set me up."

"Who's he?"

"I told you over the summer that I'd testified against a guy in court, helped Jake put him away for life—that was Kelly." Rufus finally looked at Sam again. "That was only two years ago. What the fuck is he doing out on the street, pulling knives on cute smartasses like me?"

"Ok," Sam said. He breathed out slowly. "How is that possible?"

"Someone paid Devon a visit in prison and smuggled in a pair of spoons so he could dig his way out? I don't know, but it's not kosher."

"He knows—someone knows—where you live," Sam said with a long look. "How are you holding up?"

"I've been dry heaving for two days."

"And I bet you haven't been sleeping," Sam said.

Rufus frowned. "All right. Daisy is dead. I'm falling apart. My most intimate secrets are now revealed. *Whoo hoo*. Please don't step in and act like a surrogate parent. That's the last fucking thing I need."

In spite of himself, Sam smiled. "I cannot believe I missed you. Shoes off. Then get in bed. If you're good, I'll let you brush your teeth first."

"Huh?"

"You need to sleep. For real." He pushed Rufus flat on the bed, grabbed his leg, and yanked off one of the Chucks. "Shoes off. That was step one."

"This absolutely isn't weird at all," Rufus said dryly, watching Sam take off his other shoe.

"Are you going to brush your teeth?" Sam said.

"Bathroom's pretty far away."

With a grunt, Sam rolled Rufus to the center of the bed. He went over to the door, checked the locks, and fished his Beretta out of the ruck. Then he turned out the lights and sat on the floor. A dirty yellow glow filtered in through the window; the muffled sounds of traffic were the only noise.

Rufus exhaled, that one sound filling the darkness like a deflating balloon. "You've got to be kidding. I didn't call you because I needed a watchdog, Sam."

"Great," Sam said. "As soon as I have visual confirmation that you can take care of your own fucking self, I'll be on my way. Tomorrow, we're working on eating. As in, I know you haven't been, so we're going to get real food into you. Now go to sleep."

Rufus shifted on the bed. A moment later he said, quietly, "Fuck you."

In the dark, Sam smiled and listened to Rufus's breathing even out into the rhythm of deep sleep.

CHAPTER
FOUR

Rufus was certain that exhaustion and depression had finally sent him into some sort of psychosis that'd concocted the hallucination of Sam Auden coming to his rescue the night before. A fantasy cooked up with whatever stray ingredients Rufus had left in his memory.

Brown glass marbles. Pumice stone. Shooting stars.

Sam's eyes. Sam's touch. Sam's kisses.

But when Rufus woke, feeling more rested than he had in… a while, there was Sam. Real and solid and ready for breakfast. So Rufus had dragged himself out of bed, had showered and even put on clean clothes, although he turned down the idea of shaving just as quickly as he'd had the thought.

He only had so many spoons, after all, and it was still morning.

Rufus didn't say much on their walk uptown. Even talking had left him feeling drained as of late, but perhaps what was causing Rufus the most distress was that he didn't want to stick his big foot in his big mouth and scare Sam off before he'd gotten a chance to say... something that mattered. So Rufus floated from block to block on his way up to Hell's Kitchen, sidestepping the hustle and bustle of morning commuters, adjusting the collar of his jean jacket so the crisp autumn air whispered on the back of his neck, and periodically glanced over his shoulder to make sure Sam was still there, still following.

BlueMoon Diner hadn't changed. The glass door was still covered in old stickers bleached from the sun. The air inside still smelled of frying meat and old coffee. The television mounted behind the register was turned on, currently playing some generic morning talk show. And it was clean. Well, mostly clean. The first table in the middle aisle still had the remnants of someone's sunny-side up eggs on the Formica top.

Rufus was moving toward his habitual spot when a familiar voice called out, "Freckles!" Maddie was waving from the counter. "It's been a hot minute, baby. Go sit down—I'll be right over."

Rufus raised a hand in acknowledgment before sliding into his booth, the old vinyl cracking under his weight. He took his sunglasses off, hung them from his shirt collar, then shifted to get more comfortable as a spring dug into his ass. Sam sat down across from him, and Rufus couldn't help but stare a moment.

Still built in the chest and shoulders—miles and miles of him, Rufus remembered, when he and Sam shared this booth together three months ago and Sam had been showing off a smidgen. But, and maybe Rufus was waxing poetic here, Sam's pretty brown eyes seemed to soften when they looked at each other now. They weren't strangers anymore. And Sam had come back.

God. Rufus had missed Sam so much. The realization seemed to slam into him, like he'd been hit by a fucking taxi. Hearing Sam's low, smoldering voice again, seeing that very tiny smile he did a bang-up job hiding—it breathed a sense of purpose into Rufus that he hadn't felt in months. Sam was still an enigma, no two ways about it, but just then, in that one suspended second between them, Rufus would have given anything to be *someone* to Sam.

Clearing his throat, Rufus asked, "So. How're you?"

"My back feels like I slept on thirty-year-old linoleum laid down over a rotting subfloor."

Rufus nodded. "That's pretty accurate."

"How are you?"

Rufus tugged his beanie off and tossed it against the dessert display shoved against the wall. He grabbed a packet of sugar and said, "Not so good."

"That's ok," Sam said. "Things are going to turn around, starting today." He reached across the table and snagged the sugar packet. "Real food, remember?"

"Sam. I'm not a carnival game you stick a fucking quarter into. I wish I was. I wish I could come to life and clap my hands and do a somersault for Washington's profile—"

Maddie moved around a table on her way toward the booth, making a *tsk* noise as she approached. "You know I about thought you were dead, Freckles?"

Rufus smiled wryly as Maddie set down two mugs and poured piping-hot black coffee into each.

"It's been almost two months since I've seen your skinny butt," she continued, before giving Sam an appreciative once-over. "Nice to see you again too, handsome. You boys staying to eat? Need a menu?"

Sam shook his head. "Bacon, eggs over easy, home fries, pancakes." He pointed to Rufus. "Whatever will fill him up."

Maddie smiled, looked at Rufus a second time, and put a hand on his shoulder in an almost-motherly gesture. "I remember how you wrecked those pancakes. Is that ok?"

"It's fine. Thanks, Maddie."

"I'll get you some sausage. You look like you need protein," she concluded, before leaving the table.

"Eggs too," Sam said to Maddie. "Does he like them scrambled?"

"Scrambled!" she called back in acknowledgment.

Rufus was staring at Sam. "Thanks for that. Now you both can tag team mother henning me."

"You put off a vibe," Sam said. "You might want to rethink the whole crackhead-chic look."

"You're such an asshole."

Sam just nodded and looked out the window.

Rufus discreetly reached for another sugar packet. "Where were you when I called?"

For a moment Sam's forehead furrowed. Then he laughed, a short, harsh sound, and said, "Who the fuck knows? Somewhere in Missouri. Another shithole."

"Sounds nice," Rufus said. He tore the top off and poured the sugar into his palm. "Been seeing anyone?"

Sam's gaze came back to Rufus, and he cocked his head. That was all. No answer.

Rufus had licked his finger, dabbed the sugar, and stuck it in his mouth. "Whut?" he asked around the digit. "M'm makin' small tuk."

"Oh," Sam said, smiling now. "Small talk."

Rufus took his finger from his mouth. "Why're you

smiling like that?"

"Because I'm going to do us both a favor. No more fucking small talk. Just—just tell me about Daisy, or about this guy Devon, or what we're supposed to do next, or something. But I'm not here to have small talk with you. And I'm not here for you to ask me to my fucking face if I'm seeing someone when you've had my number for the last three months and couldn't be bothered to pick up the fucking phone."

Rufus rubbed his sticky hand on the leg of his jeans. "Christ…. Low-income mental health opportunities are a joke, ok? I'm on a waitlist with an LGBT nonprofit that's backed up six fucking months. I've been trying to keep myself alive." He wadded the paper packet into a tight ball and then smooshed it against the tabletop with his thumb. "I couldn't handle calling you."

"I would have helped you. I wanted to help you. I offered."

Rufus leaned back. The cushion sagged underneath him. Morning sunshine from the window cut a Ziggy Stardust bolt across his face. "Forget it. I don't want to argue about whether or not you were right."

"No," Sam said. "The world would fucking end if we ever argued."

"I almost forgot how charming you were."

Maddie returned, setting down two plates heaped with food. "How about them works, eh?" She nudged Rufus.

"Thanks, Maddie," he said obediently.

"Such a gracious kid," she said in a tone that implied the opposite. Maddie pointed a finger at Sam as she started walking away. "You be good."

Rufus watched her from the side of his eye before he asked Sam, "Did you want to cut my food?"

With a snort, Sam speared some home fries and

shoved them in his mouth. Between bites, he said, "I can understand—I'm speaking in a theoretical sense—wanting to kill you. This guy, Devon, does he want revenge? Why bring your mom into this? Did he—I mean, do you think he had something to do with that?"

Rufus stabbed his stack of pancakes with his fork. "No way. Devon's my age, maybe younger. He'd have been a kid when Daisy was murdered. It's definitely revenge." He glanced up and offered Sam a watery smile. "I was Jake's star witness, after all."

"But the thing about your mom, that's weird. Why use her to draw you out?"

Rufus set the fork down. "I reached out to the Cold Case Squad about Daisy last month."

Folding a piece of bacon in half, Sam frowned. "Why?"

Rufus felt his cheeks warm. His underarms began to sweat. He stared at his food and shrugged. "Daisy... wasn't a good mom. She wasn't even a good person, if I'm being honest. But someone *murdered* her. And no one has ever cared."

"Rufus, I meant—" Sam stopped. "Of course you care. I meant, why now?"

"After everything that happened over the summer, Boy George and Juliana, I realized I wasn't over it. Over Daisy. So I eventually started poking around the NYPD to see if anyone would help me." Rufus picked up his fork again, hacked off a wedge of pancake with the side of the utensil, and shoved it in his mouth. "I'm sure my future therapist is going to have a field trip with me."

"God help whoever has to untangle your particular ball of crazy. Ok. What about Juliana?"

"What about her?"

"I think that's where we should start. The fact that Devon used your mom to lure you out—well, it tells us something. Maybe the Cold Case guys actually did their fucking jobs and went out and asked some questions, and Devon just got wind of it. Or maybe it's something else. Maybe there really is something about your mom's death. So, unless you know where we can find Devon and ask him a few questions ourselves, I want to talk to Juliana. This summer, you used your mom's name to get information out of her, and she clearly remembered who Daisy was. Knew her well enough, in fact, that using her name was an effective way of getting her to trust you."

"Someone from Cold Cases *did* interview me. Uhm… Detective Larkin. So he at least did a cursory read of Daisy's file."

"And?"

"And he's probably a great poker player. I couldn't get any kind of read on him until I'd mentioned Daisy's right arm being missing."

Sam set down his fork. He ran his fingers around his mouth. "What?"

Rufus speared more pancake and repeated, "Her arm was missing."

"Jesus, Rufus. That's some seriously messed-up shit. What happened when you told Larkin?"

"Well, I told him that I'd had to identify the body because I was Daisy's only next of kin. And that when they'd opened the body bag and I saw her right arm had been hacked off at the shoulder, I threw up on the morgue floor. He made me repeat it a few times—like how cops do when they want to catch you in a lie."

"That's… strange. Fuck me. Maybe there really is something, you know, that ties back. He didn't say anything?"

"He thanked me for my time and said he'd be in touch."

"Damn. Now I really want to talk to Juliana; she might be able to tell us what was going on with Daisy when she died." Sam hesitated, the tines of his fork scraping lightly against the ceramic. "It's probably not going to be pleasant. If you'd rather I did this alone—"

Rufus forced down some now-cold scrambled eggs and said, "No way you're going without me, Sam."

Nodding, Sam just went to town on his pancakes.

Rufus ate a few more forkfuls of eggs. Eating became easier after that. It felt sort of like his entire body had been jolted awake, been told that fuel was on the way, and hunger now clawed at Rufus's guts. He'd worked his way through half of the plate before saying, "Daisy and Juliana weren't exactly close. They worked the same area, but Daisy had... hang-ups. About... you know, a lot of people."

"Hang-ups?"

Rufus reached across the table, speared one of Sam's pancakes, and slapped it down on his own plate. "Anyone who found themselves somewhere on the rainbow. Daisy had a fucking opinion."

"I'm sorry. I didn't know that." Sam cut an egg with the side of his fork. "That must have been hard."

Rufus drank some lukewarm coffee, but it tasted sour. He pushed the mug away. "My relationship with Daisy was bad," he said, very quietly. "But she was all I had. And then someone just... took her, you know? It scared the other girls. It scared me." He took a deep breath, cleared his throat, and said with an attempt to sound nonchalant, "Juliana won't be happy to see us again."

Sam rolled his eyes. "I'm starting to remember that this is a pattern with you. If I spend too long here, I'll forget what it feels like not to have everyone want to murder me on sight."

Rufus smiled at that. He glanced up and met Sam's

steady gaze. "I want to tell you a Rufus thing."

"I'd like that."

"My middle name is Monday. Want to know why?"

Sam nodded.

"Daisy had to fill out that parent worksheet before they'd discharge her from the hospital. Baby's first name, middle name, last name. And it was a Monday. Mondays were her best clients."

"Wow," Sam said. "That's messed up."

Rufus nudged his plate aside and drummed his fingers against the tabletop. "From the very beginning, no one's cared about me." He stilled. "It meant something, that you answered my call."

A van drove past, its windows reflecting the sun into the diner, a wave of light cresting over their table and then pulling back, gone.

"It means something that you called," Sam said, his dark eyes steady and serious.

CHAPTER
FIVE

"I think I'll be ok," Sam said when they stepped out of the diner, "if you want to take the subway." He glanced at the sky. The midmorning sun was high and bright; the smell of a hot griddle and onions lingered for a moment after the BlueMoon door swung shut, and then the air was a mixture of crisp, autumn cool and burned rubber. "We need to kill some time. Do you have any overdue books? Fines? Fees? Lusty librarians you've spurned lately?"

Rufus had been halfway to putting his sunglasses on before pausing. "Hold up. *You* on a subway? And what was that about lusty librarians?"

"Fluoxetine," Sam said. "And yes, lusty librarians. If you've been spurning librarians, it might make the next part tricky."

Rufus pushed the glasses up, one light-colored brow arched. "I know which side of my bread is buttered. I'd never spurn a librarian. But are you offering some sort of role-play? Because I'm still a little confused."

"I figure we've got seven or eight hours before Juliana and the others show up. Four hours, if we subtract all the time we're going to spend eating to keep your stomach from devouring itself. That sounds like the right amount of time for a research trip to the public library. Let's see what was going on around when Daisy was killed. Hell, let's see if anybody said anything about her."

"Really?" Rufus asked, and that one word sounded so very uncertain. "The library?"

"What's wrong with the library?"

"Nothing's wrong with the library. I like the library. I only mean, no one goes with me."

"Is that a rule?"

"No. It's just how it is."

"Subway," Sam said. "Library. Newspapers. Or are you going to make me figure out how to get there on my phone? We'll probably end up in Jersey if I try."

Rufus smiled. "Follow me. We need to catch the D to Bryant Park."

The subway wasn't as horrible as Sam remembered. Rufus still made him hop the turnstile, and there were still more people than Sam preferred, but it wasn't nearly as hot as it had been in the summer, and the smell was much more tolerable. Some of that, Sam figured, was thanks to the change in seasons, and some of it was thanks to the medication. He did see three rats before the train came, and there was a woman in their car trying to nurse a Cabbage Patch doll. Rufus must have seen something on

Sam's face because he started grinning uncontrollably, but at least he didn't repeat the bump-and-grind that he had tried the last time.

They got off at 42nd Street–Bryant Park Station, and when they reached the street, Sam had to admit to being a little impressed. The library was built of pale stone with a neoclassical facade, elaborate columns, and statues, complete with a pair of stone lions watching everything to make sure nobody got out of line. To one side of the arched entrances hung a banner proclaiming A-BOO-TIFUL SEASON: CELEBRATING HARVEST AND HALLOWEEN ACROSS FIFTY YEARS, which sounded like the most boring Halloween exhibit the human mind could conceive.

Inside, Rufus led them across the lobby and down a hall. The walls were stone, the floors tile; voices bounced back and forth, echoing, and Sam thought he heard five or six different languages as they made their way through the building. Rufus ducked into a room with a sign that said MILSTEIN MICROFORM READING ROOM, and Sam followed.

In contrast to the main areas of the library, this portion looked like someone had let an accountant in the 1970s go hog wild: green industrial carpet, worn down to the backing, covered the floor, and plastic work tables stood in cramped rows. At the back of the room, several microfilm readers were available for use. To one side was an information desk, where a young black woman was typing something on her computer. The whole place smelled like dust and an air filter that needed changing.

"Batter up," Sam said to Rufus.

The woman raised her head, obviously responding to the volume of Sam's voice, and frowned.

Sam winced.

Rufus shot her what looked to Sam to be a very fake

smile. He tugged his beanie off and approached the desk. "Hi. Sorry. He's just really excited for the Drag Queen Story Hour after this. Can I request a few microfilms? The *New York Courier* and the *Sunday Journal*. February thirteenth to the twentieth?"

The woman's voice was low and smooth. "What year?"

"2002, ma'am."

She pushed back from the chair, smiled briefly at Rufus, gave Sam a warning look, and headed for a door at the back of the room.

"Why those two?" Sam said.

Rufus leaned back against the desk. "*Courier* always writes about the scandals—drugs and rock 'n' roll. The *Sunday* would have come out a few days later, and they're conservative in that way where they derive some sick pleasure out of reporting on everything 'unfortunate' in the city."

"Because it's a cesspool where the combined body mass of the rats is about a hundred times that of all nine million humans?"

"Just give them your pizza crust. You'll be the next Pied Piper."

"The crust is the best part."

A real smile tugged at the corner of Rufus's mouth. "That's why no one has tamed them yet."

Sam rolled his eyes, but before he could respond, the librarian emerged from the back room. She was carrying two small canisters, and she beckoned for them to join her at one of the machines. When they were closer, she held up one of the canisters and said, "This has issues of the *Courier* from February and March of 2002." She held up the other. "This has the last week of January through the end of February for the *Sunday Journal*. Do you know how to use these machines?"

"I know how to use a computer," Sam said. "Why isn't all this stuff digitized?"

The woman, whose name tag said Tiana, was staring at Sam like she wished librarians carried standard-issue battleaxes.

"Because," Rufus piped up, "about eight people, including your mom, read the *New York Courier*." Rufus looked at Tiana. "Brutes. Can't take them anywhere."

"Just show us how to use the machine," Sam said.

Tiana raised an eyebrow.

"Please," Sam added.

That didn't exactly pour oil on troubled waters, but she demonstrated how to insert the microfilm, and then she pointed out the controls for adjusting the magnification and focus and for advancing the film. When she'd finished, she put her hands on her hips and looked at Sam until he started to sweat.

"I think you'd better do this," Tiana said to Rufus.

"That's what I was going to say," Sam said.

Tiana looked at him again.

"I'll just get an extra chair," Sam said.

"Do that," Tiana said.

She said something else to Rufus as Sam was walking away, although he couldn't catch it, but when he came back with a chair, Rufus's eyes were wide and wet, and the tips of his ears were pink.

"I hate you," Sam told him.

They began with the *Courier*, and Rufus sat at the machine, slowly advancing the film and occasionally rotating the image, adjusting the zoom and focus when necessary. Sam could read the screen over his shoulder, and he was impressed by how quickly Rufus could scan a sheet of newsprint.

It was strange to look back at discrete moments of history, even if that history had happened less than two decades ago, while Sam was alive. One page featured a grainy black-and-white photo of Catherine Zeta-Jones and Michael Douglas, with the headline "Will They or Won't They?" A sports page near the beginning of the film was still talking about Super Bowl XXXVI and the Patriots' win—according to the sports writer, a mediocre game barely worth watching. Another section was a full-page advertisement for David Beckham's personal line of underwear.

"Go back," Sam said.

"Ogle British packages on your own time," Rufus muttered.

"The package is nice," Sam said. "But the wrapping is nice too. All those tattoos."

Rufus spared Sam a look over his shoulder. "Huh."

"It's nothing personal," Sam said. "I'm being completely objective. It's a fact."

When they finally found it, it was so small that Sam missed it completely, and Rufus seemed to react to some stimulus that Sam couldn't trace. The redhead rewound the film, and there it was: the bottom of 2B on Sunday, February 24. The article was barely more than a paragraph.

Police hit another bump in their investigation into a string of slayings. A spokesman for the department has asked that anyone with information about the killings contact CRIME STOPPERS or the anonymous police tip line. The most recent victim, a suspected sex worker, was found butchered on Wednesday morning in a portion of Central Park known as the Ramble.

Sam squeezed Rufus's shoulder. "I'm sorry."

Rufus just nodded.

"A string of slayings," Sam said.

"Sounds like Daisy got knotted to the end of that string."

"Why don't I get you a coffee or something?" Sam said. "It looks like we're going to be here a while."

Rufus didn't respond, merely turned the knob and started scanning headlines again. His jaw was set, his eyes bright and focused. He was sitting in the here and now, but his heart and his mind seemed to be somewhere else, somewhere long ago, and he was there alone.

CHAPTER
SIX

When they'd left the library, Rufus mumbled something about wanting that coffee Sam had suggested earlier, and they detoured to one of the food shacks within Bryant Park. In reality, though, Rufus wanted a moment to stand still, because he felt like the nuts and bolts that kept him together were being shaken completely loose, and he didn't have a copy of the owner's manual to his life. The line for food looked long enough that it'd give Rufus the time he needed to pull himself together.

He could remember when girls had begun going missing in the Ramble. And *missing* had been the only consideration they'd been given by polite society. Because New York City, like most cities across the country, would sooner spend taxpayer money to locate an affluent, white-collar family man than they would in searching out young, transient, mostly female sex workers. And that'd been exactly what had happened. The gruesome details had been covered by the *Courier*, and the plethora of articles had jogged memories from when Rufus was a boy.

The year-long search for Joseph Walkerman had ended at the Hudson River. Walkerman's success in banking had been mostly due to mob ties. And when he'd tried to stiff them on money owed, they'd broken Walkerman's knees and fitted him with cement shoes. And while the city had been following the timeline of Joseph Walkerman with bated breath, no one had noticed when the first girl went missing in the Ramble a few years before, setting the wheels into motion for what would, in due time, affect every aspect of Rufus's life.

Rufus looked down at the crumpled, slightly sweaty, Post-it notes that Tiana had given him back in the microfilm room. He'd scribbled the names and dates he and Sam were able to trace through the papers.

Shannon Heaney had been the first, reported missing on November 2, 1998. Her body had been found on December 17, naked and frozen. Rufus had been twelve years old. He remembered Daisy talking on the phone, before she'd stopped paying the bill for their landline. She'd been afraid. She'd screamed and swore at the person on the other end of the line.

Rufus closed his eyes and could dredge up bits of that conversation. If he tried really hard, he could almost hear the words in Daisy's voice, her high pitch just a little scratchy around the edges from years of smoking.

"If I go out there… Shannon's dead! What if Bunny ain't skipping town? What if she's dead too?"

He couldn't recall who Daisy had been talking to. Had she ever said a name? Had Rufus heard the tinny voice of the caller shouting back at her, or was that a manufactured memory? He was honestly a little surprised he'd remembered even that much. By twelve, he'd become fairly adept at blocking Daisy's voice out, if not making himself scarce entirely. It'd been hard in the beginning—little kids want their mother's attention, approval, love. But by twelve, Rufus knew to no longer expect any of that.

He opened his eyes and smoothed out the Post-its.

Bunny—real name Jasmine, according to the papers—had been the second who'd gone missing and was later found naked in the woods of the Ramble. It'd been just before the new year started. She'd gotten the same shrug as Shannon. The same kiss-off. Her name and her story forgotten before the headline had even been printed.

The third to have gone missing in the Ramble was Tiffany Brown. April 4, 1999. She had been found, in the same state as the previous two women, on April 29. That'd been about the time the rest of the girls had become well and truly scared. But due to the catch-22 of their lives as sex workers, they couldn't reach out to the police for help. As far as Rufus was concerned, it'd been nothing but sheer luck that the salacious *New York Courier* had suggested a serial killer was on the loose, and for a hot minute, enough folks had read that subway trash to question why the NYPD wasn't hunting down a dangerous criminal in Central Park before he hurt someone… *more important.*

But according to what scant information Rufus and Sam were able to dig up on the microfilms, the cops had never made any headway on the various cases. Sex workers kept disappearing, kept winding up dead—all the way through 2002, with the last known victim being Daisy O'Callaghan.

"Next," the teenager working the window called. "What can I get you?"

"What do you want?" Sam asked, nudging Rufus toward the shack.

Rufus shoved the Post-its into his jacket pocket and took a step forward. "Hey. How about—?" He paused and glanced at Sam. "Are you spotting me?"

"That's pretty much a given at this point. Although, doesn't spotting imply you're going to pay me back?"

Rufus grinned. "I'm good for it. It's just smarter to never say when." He turned back to the kid. "Can I get that soup and salad combo? And a coffee and a pastry."

The kid sighed. "Anything else?"

"Don't tempt me." Rufus stepped to the side for Sam.

"A Coke," Sam said, "and a hot dog. Oh, and those chips. And second hot dog."

The teenager rang up the order, told Sam the total, and turned to get the items ready with the assistance of a coworker. He slid two cardboard containers through the window a moment later, snagged Sam's money, and dropped a handful of coins in his hand as change.

Rufus grabbed his box. "Thanks," he said, before heading toward a small metal table, one of at least a dozen, situated under the shade of an ancient tree. He pulled the chair out, took a seat, and waited until Sam joined him before taking a bite of the salad.

After demolishing the first hot dog, Sam said, "How are you holding up?"

"I don't know." Rufus moved on to the soup, forgoing the dinky plastic spoon and drinking directly from the cup.

Sam nodded. "Do you want to talk about your feelings? Or is this another bite-my-head-off topic?"

Rufus set the cup down, took off his sunglasses, and gave Sam a leveled look. "I don't want to talk about my feelings, Sam. Don't say it like that. Daisy died a long time ago. I know that. It's not news. It's just… this whole situation is bizarre."

"Right," Sam said with a sigh and then proceeded to

murder a bag of chips.

"*What*? What was that sigh?" Rufus popped the top off his coffee and dunked the pastry in. "Did you want me to cry on your shoulder and get your shirt snotty?"

"Why don't you tell me what you found? How far back does this go? Do you know how many victims overall? How long did it last after Daisy? Did the police ever have any leads?"

Rufus ate the pastry in a few bites, wiped his hands on his jeans, then pulled out the Post-its. He also retrieved a NYPL pen. He hadn't asked Tiana for that. He'd simply pocketed it.

Old habits died hard.

"I'm pretty sure it began in '98 with Shannon," he said. "But the cops didn't put two-and-two together until after the third body was found in '99." Rufus glanced at Sam, squinting a bit from the afternoon sun. "I don't know how many deaths in total, though. One of those articles said eleven women had gone missing by 2002, but it's hard to gauge how accurate that count is, based on the bogus work the NYPD did." He held up one note stuck to his fingertip. "Pretty sure Daisy was the last victim. Because I remember, after she was gone, everything got really quiet. Initially, I'd chalked it up to being so far removed from that life without her there to tie me to it, but the more I think back on it, I'm convinced whoever was doing the killing stopped entirely."

"When you say bogus work," Sam said carefully, "do you think this is similar to what we ran into last time?"

Rufus lowered his finger with the Post-it. "You mean, like, cops being involved?"

"Or being dirty."

Rufus sat back. "I hadn't considered it. But back then, I was a bright young thing, utterly naive of the world," he said a touch sardonically.

"What do you mean, then? They did a bad job?"

Rufus leaned forward again. "Not that they did a *bad* job. Only… that they did *no* job. People don't care about the nobodies of society, Sam."

"People care," Sam said. "Just not always the people in power." He downed the second hot dog, spun the cap on the Coke, and said, "I know we're going to see Juliana, but was there anything in those papers that suggested why your cold-case detective reacted so strongly to that piece of info about Daisy's arm? Or where Devon fits into this? Did the police have a person of interest? Anything?"

Rufus shoved aside the empty wrappers and food containers. He stuck the Post-its on the tabletop in an order that made sense to him, tracing each one with his index finger. "The newspapers said the killer was most likely male, but that's usually a given. The girls were different ages and races, but all were sex workers in the Ramble, so he had a type. I don't know how Devon Kelly gets wrapped up in any of this, because like I said, he was a kid. Someone else must be involved and Kelly's … working for them, or something." Rufus picked up the final note and turned it toward Sam. "Neither paper mentions Daisy's arm."

"If the papers left that detail out of the stories about Daisy's murder, what do you think they left out of the stories on the other girls?"

Rufus lowered the note. "Since those rags live for gore, I can't imagine they'd willingly leave anything like that out. Do you think the police intentionally withheld that information? They do that sort of stuff, right?"

"Right. And judging by how that detective reacted when you told him about Daisy's arm, I think that's exactly what happened. The question now is whether it's connected to Devon going after you."

Rufus blinked a few times. "That's an interesting point."

"Something to think about at least," Sam said. "We'll see what Juliana says." He pushed the wrappers around; the crinkle of waxed paper rode over the sound of a guy practicing scales on his sax. "I know you said this happened a long time ago, and I'm not trying to make any assumptions about you or about Daisy, but... how much did you know about her work? Do you know the people she worked with? Did you know her clients?"

Rufus's throat tightened. He flinched when the memory of a table, thrown across the apartment and leaving a gouge in the floor, echoed so vividly, he swore he heard it with his actual ears. He could feel hard linoleum underneath him, from when he spent the nights in the tenement's hallways, because Daisy had her best clients on Mondays and he had to make himself scarce. And Rufus remembered the smack on the back of his head from that prick, who, upon leaving Daisy's apartment, would always hit Rufus, laugh, and say, "Later, kid," before disappearing down the stairs.

"Yeah," Rufus said, and his voice came out like a choked whisper. He cleared his throat and added, "I mean, I remember some cheapskates in the Ramble and a revolving door of assholes on Mondays. And Mac, of course."

"Who's Mac?"

"Daisy's pimp."

"Was he—" Sam seemed to reconsider the question. "Could he have done something like this?"

Rufus scratched his neck hard, the lingering burn on his skin a promise that he'd dug his nails in deep enough to leave marks. "I don't know why he'd want to kill any of the girls who made him money."

"What about the guys who came around? Anyone that stands out? Even if you don't have a name, anybody who'd know where you live that you've considered?"

Rufus laughed, but it was a forced, breathless sort

of sound. "Considered to be a cold-blooded killer? *No*. But there was this one guy... Jimmy. I used to sit in the hallway on Mondays, you know? Until Daisy was finished. Jimmy used to smack the back of my head when he left. He knocked Daisy around, some." Rufus's chin quivered, and he took a moment before saying, quieter, "It sucks, when you're too little to help your mom."

Sam made a considering noise. "It'd be nice to know what this little cluster of asscrumbs is up to now. Do you think Ophelia could track any of them down?"

"Ophelia doesn't get paid enough to deal with this sort of bullshit. Besides, she's still walking the beat. I don't want to put this on her." Rufus leaned to one side and tugged his cell free from his front pocket. "I can't believe I'm willingly suggesting this... but I can text Erik Weaver."

"Who's that? Your boyfriend?"

"If he was, would you be jealous?"

"Yes."

Rufus's thumbs were poised over the keyboard. He glanced up, his eyebrows raised. "Oh. Uh... he's not. He's my new handler. I'm still hilariously single."

With a snort, Sam gathered their trash and stood. "Then you have my permission to text him."

"Dick."

A little boy ran behind Sam's chair, screaming as loud as possible, "Catch me, catch me!" and a very frazzled babysitter hurried after, calling, "I'm going to whip your butt and then your mother's gonna whip it again!" Rufus tracked the two before he was distracted by a man getting down on one knee in the grass in front of his female companion, who gasped in delight, then stomped her foot and shoved his shoulder when she realized he was only tying his shoe. And a few feet from the unhappy couple, a man wearing a blue Mets hat and a zipped-up, baby blue

Members Only jacket was making a hasty retreat as the woman began to wail about her biological clock.

Rufus shook his head, because New York, baby, and typed out a quick message to Erik Weaver.

Need to meet. In person. ASAP.

CHAPTER
SEVEN

At Rufus's direction, they cut across Bryant Park, heading west on Fortieth. Like so much of the city, it was another canyon of glass and steel, and the wind rushed along it, carrying dead leaves and a flattened Shake Shack cup. At the next intersection, a bus idled at the curb, surrounded by a cloud of exhaust before the hiss of the air brakes announced its departure. On the next block, they passed a twenty-four-hour gym; it was on the second story, but Sam could see people cycling like mad. He wondered if it was like the TV shows, with somebody at the front of the class screaming directions over pounding music. If it were, it might explain the city's homicide rate.

He figured the meet had to be close, or Rufus would have taken them on the subway. He didn't mind walking;

walking was as close to normal as life ever got for Sam, even here, in the concrete jungle. Horns blared. A woman carrying a sheet cake stopped to scream at another woman who had the audacity to be wearing a MAGA hat. A taxi nosed into the pedestrians in the crosswalk, and aside from a few people flipping the bird, nobody seemed particularly bothered by the possibility of death by Yellow Cab.

Rufus glided through all of it. Well, glided was a prettied-up way of describing it, but the idea was right. Rufus slid into openings that Sam didn't see until it was too late. Rufus turned sideways to avoid a bike courier that Sam hadn't noticed, and both of them shouted fuck-yous at the same time without breaking stride. Even on a pleasant October day, Sam was sweating by the time they turned south on Eighth Avenue, but Rufus barely seemed to register the welter around them.

On Eighth, the setting changed slightly: many of the buildings were only two- and three-stories high, many with fire escapes painted an industrial green where rust wasn't flaking off, many of them built from brick before a sixty-foot skyscraper seemed like a more efficient use of the footprint. On Sam's left, someone had erected a billboard on top of a two-story Chipotle; the billboard was advertising NIP-GUARDS TEN PACK NUDE. Thankfully, the advertiser had settled for a picture of the canister.

Rufus headed into a bodega with a red-and-yellow striped awning. Sam followed, watching as Rufus grabbed a short can of sour cream and onion Pringles and then dawdled at the wall of coolers at the back of the store. He was examining the Pepsi Max with ferocious intensity; the guy next to him was pondering the miracle of Snapple Peach Tea. Sam gave the guy a second look; he was thin, midforties, handsome. Refined features that were softened by the hair that had come out of its part and was hanging over his forehead. He was also, painfully obviously, a cop.

A cop in a nice suit. But a cop.

"I assume this guy's picking up the Pringles tab," Sam said.

Rufus grunted in response, flipping the can from hand to hand. "He tries to worm his way out of it."

"Maybe you should go first and just tell the clerk he's getting it," Sam said.

"I don't worm out of it," the man—Erik, Sam guessed—said. "Last time you asked me to buy you a carton of Marlboros so you could, quote, 'Buy off the guy trying to shank you,' end quote, like you were living an episode of *Oz*."

"I don't think that was an unreasonable request," Rufus grumbled. "I was a week late on rent because you wouldn't spot me."

"The trials and tribulations of being a street rat," Erik said with a small smile. He looked at Sam, but he didn't ask. Not yet. He only said, "The Pringles and what else? Make up your mind."

Rufus gave stink eye in the reflection of the coolers, took a step sideways to purposely push Erik out of the way, and grabbed a Sprite. "So impatient."

"What about Iron Man?"

"Unlike some people," Sam said, "like redheads and expectant mothers, I don't need to eat every fifteen minutes."

Rufus muttered another comment under his breath, not caught by Sam, and was already walking to the door. He didn't wait for Erik, and instead he headed south again, jogging across the street during a break in traffic. Sam followed.

"That was a short meeting," Sam said. "Did you get everything you needed?"

Rufus looked over his shoulder. "I still have to talk to

Erik."

"Walking directly away from him is an interesting way of talking."

Sam caught the eye roll before Rufus shoved his sunglasses up the bridge of his nose.

On the next block stood Penn Station, and Rufus headed through the doors without checking back for Erik—or, for that matter, for Sam. Inside, they caught an escalator and went downstairs. A large, open ticketing area waited at the bottom. Sam checked for exits, almost got steamrolled by a little old lady pushing a luggage cart, and finally took refuge with Rufus against the wall, under an IF YOU SEE SOMETHING, SAY SOMETHING sign that was covered in a fine layer of dust.

Two minutes later, Erik crossed the ticketing area toward them. He was carrying his Snapple, and when he saw them, something made him shake his head and take a long drink.

"What?" Erik said when he lowered the bottle. "Your face makes me think this is going to be bad, so let's just rip the Band-Aid off."

"Someone tried to kill me Saturday night," Rufus stated. "So now I need some information on an inmate by the name Devon Kelly, recently MIA. A pimp who worked Central Park throughout the '90s, went by Mac. And some asshole john named Jimmy—I don't have a last name for him either."

"Great," Erik said. "You've always got such reasonable requests. First you want me to single-handedly commandeer the Cold Case Squad for your personal benefit. Now I'm supposed to dig up an escaped inmate, and a pimp and a john with no last names. Jimmy? Really, Rufus? Good thing he didn't have a common name like Michael or David or Christopher. Jesus Christ. That's all you've got?" He twisted the Snapple's lid and said,

"Are you all right? Is this side of beef your bodyguard or something?"

"He's my something," Rufus agreed. He passed the chips and drink to Sam before taking off his sunglasses and hanging them from the collar of his shirt. "And I didn't ask you to *commandeer* the Cold Case Squad, Erik. I asked for your opinion, and you gave me a business card. You're so fucking dramatic."

"How old were these guys in the '90s? White? Black? Latino? Asian? What the hell put you on their tails? And you know what? Back up and tell me about almost getting killed."

"Devon Kelly tried to stab me." Rufus stuck his finger through the hole in his jacket and held it up for Erik to see. "He's currently serving a life sentence, so consider me a little curious as to why he's on the streets again." Rufus pulled his hand free from the tear. "The other two… I haven't seen them in twenty years. Ok, seventeen," he quickly corrected at the change in Erik's expression.

"Fuck," Erik said. "Does this have something to do with work? Because I need to know about it if it does."

"I think Mac and Jimmy might be connected to Daisy O'Callaghan," Rufus said, his voice growing quieter by the word. "My cold case."

"So it's personal. Is this something like what you got into over the summer? Because that was personal too, from what I gather, and that was some serious shit, Rufus. I am not about to get dragged into that kind of fuck-up ass-backwards." Erik looked at Sam. "Jesus Christ. This is the other guy, isn't it? I read the reports, Rufus. I know there was somebody else. And I know he took off while the dust was still settling. What's your name?"

Sam crossed his arms and looked at Rufus.

"What happened over the summer wasn't personal," Rufus retorted. "That was about hunting down a cop killer.

Which, by the way, you boys in blue are welcome for."

"Here's how I see things," Erik said. "You show up. You ask me to dig up info on something that has no bearing on the work you do for me. The whole thing reeks of the same trouble you got into last time, and we all know how that ended: shit sticking to everybody in an entire squad. And you know the thing that really gets in my garters? It's a fucking favor you're asking for, and you're treating me like you scraped me off your shoe."

"Take it down a notch," Sam said. "You passed Drama 101. No need for a fucking encore. Yes, it's a favor. Yes, it's important. You ought to know Rufus well enough to know that he wouldn't ask if he had any other choice." He looked at Rufus. "Do you want to add anything? Or can we tell this guy to go fuck himself?"

"He's the guy who pays me," Rufus answered in a mock whisper. Then to Erik, he said at a regular volume, "There were a few sex workers found dead before Daisy. Maybe… you could find out if they'd been found with amputated body parts."

Erik took another swig of Snapple; the smell of the peach tea turned Sam's stomach. When Erik spoke again, his voice was considering. "It won't be easy," he said, "digging up bodies, figuratively I mean, from twenty years ago. I'm not going to be able to get it by running names through a computer. I'm going to have to ask some questions. I'm going to have to put myself out there."

"Jesus Christ," Sam said. "Just say what you want."

"I want in on this if it turns into something. And I want to be the first one to know about it."

"You're a fucking rat," Sam said. "This isn't about your fucking career or about how you can score points to make the jump from being a dick-hole detective to being a gaping dick-hole sergeant."

Erik looked at Rufus.

"*Fine,*" Rufus interjected. "Whatever you want. But promise me that you'll look into those names so we can call this meeting and I can go upchuck." He motioned across the massive room toward the bathrooms.

"I'll text you if I get anything," Erik said. "If. It's a long shot."

"I'll have my burner for another week," Rufus confirmed before he walked to the bathrooms—no line for men, and an out-the-door wait for women.

"Don't even think about fucking him over," Sam said.

Erik shoved the hair away from his forehead, studying Sam, and said, "You know what? I think I'm going to do some reading about what happened in July."

"Good," Sam said. "Read all about how I shot Anthony Lampo for being a backstabbing, traitorous fuck. If you need any clarification, find me and I'll personally make it perfectly fucking clear."

It was so macho that Sam actually considered joining Rufus and doing a little throwing up himself. But he also couldn't help feeling proud of himself as he stalked away.

CHAPTER
EIGHT

Eight o'clock in the middle of October meant the night sky was black. At least, as black as the sky could be, what with all the light pollution. Rufus led the way across Bow Bridge in Central Park, his hands in his jacket pockets, moving this way and that to avoid other people—mostly couples, he noted, the thought lingering and souring in the back of his mind. They reached the end of the bridge and stepped into a pool of light cast from a lamppost, its erratic electrical hum mingling with the leaf litter crunching underfoot.

Rufus stopped, turned, and looked at Sam. "Sorry I left you with Erik earlier. I guess the reality of what we're doing is sinking in. I really did have to throw up."

"Do you need something else to settle your stomach?

Crackers? Toast? Should I buy you soup?"

"No, no. I'm fine," Rufus said as he removed a hand and waved it. "It's that… anxiety thing. Sometimes it's shakes or dry heaves or… and Erik knows exactly how to push my buttons."

Sam grunted. "He's an asshole."

"He's ok," Rufus corrected. "Honest, at least. No one's going to replace Jake."

"No," Sam said, so quietly that Rufus almost missed it.

Rufus rubbed the bit of scruff on his face. "I hope he wasn't a dickhead to you."

"I can handle a dickhead. And if he comes through with information, it's worth fifteen minutes of Super-Cop pretend time."

Rufus cracked a smile. "Super-Cop in a Super-Suit."

Sam snorted. His eyes raked Rufus up and down, and then his face got serious and he said, "Snake."

Rufus's gaze was already halfway to the ground before he realized he'd been played again. He gave Sam's shoulder a shove. "Stop doing that."

Wearing a tiny smile, Sam just shrugged.

"Still a big dickish brute, aren't you?" Rufus asked over his shoulder as he began walking into the Ramble.

"What was that about a big dick?"

Ok. Rufus walked into that one. The cool air felt nice against the flush on his neck and face. "Ha, ha. Touché." He shoved his hands back into his jacket pockets, and as they passed lamppost after lamppost, all numbered to aid lost pedestrians, Rufus thought about bumblebees. Not that he had any particular interest in bees in general, only that he needed something neutral, something safe, something unrelated to the Ramble, to *Sam*, to think about, and Rufus had checked out a book on insects last winter that had been fascinating.

"Bumblebees scent-mark flowers," Rufus murmured to himself. The path twisted and turned, leading deeper into the oldest portions of the park. "Bumblebee eggs are shaped like sausages." Less and less light filtered through the boughs of the trees. "Bumblebee sperm lives for months inside the queen bee."

"Bumblebees?" Sam asked. "What did you say?"

"Nothing," Rufus quickly said. "Something I read." He stopped as they came upon a familiar boulder to the left of the path. Rufus turned to Sam. "Just up ahead is the gazebo. Assuming she's around."

"Do you want me to wait here? Last time she seemed more comfortable with you."

The question came as a mild surprise, but Rufus wasn't surprised at all by his own response. He didn't even think before saying, "No, I want you with me."

"Good answer," Sam said with another of those small smiles. "Because it was a trick question."

Rufus rolled his eyes. He made his way around the rock face, up the path—man-made from years of sex workers coming this way as a shortcut between locations—and through the dense patch of forest before the trail opened enough that they could walk side-by-side. Up ahead, a shadow against the darker night, was the vague outline of the gazebo Rufus and Sam had visited together months before. Someone sitting on the bench inside startled suddenly when Rufus stepped on a twig and snapped it in two.

"Juliana?" Rufus called, cupping one hand around his mouth. "Is that you?"

The shadow made a move to run.

Rufus swore and broke into a sprint. "Hey, wait! Juliana, it's me, Red!"

She stumbled to a stop in another pair of dangerous kitten heels—one wrong move and, *snap*, there goes your ankle. "Rufus?" she asked instead.

Rufus skidded to a stop a few feet from her, kicking up debris in the process. "It's been a hot minute, hasn't it?"

Juliana pulled her shoulders back, flipped her hair over her shoulder, then pointed one stern finger at Rufus. "Baby boy, what did I tell you about coming around here anymore?"

"It's important," Rufus insisted, raising his hands in defense.

"Oh no. Nothing ain't so important that you need to be stomping around here at night." She stared over Rufus's shoulder. "You brought your hunk of man along too? Don't you boys have anything better to do?"

"Apparently not," Sam said. "We'll try to be quick, though."

Juliana pursed her lips and adjusted the wide belt she wore around her waist. "Come on, what is this?"

"Someone did their best to cut me into ribbons last Saturday," Rufus said. "Because of Daisy. I asked some questions and pissed somebody off."

And that's when Juliana's eyes grew scared. She took a step backward on those damn heels. "I told you: nothing more about Daisy."

"Hold on," Sam said. "This is just talking, ok? We're not asking for anything else."

"We can't talk about this," Juliana answered. "Baby boy needs to stop, and *you* need to keep your nose out of this. It's not any of your business," she told Sam.

"He can't stop," Sam said. "Somebody's already put a target on his back. Now quit bitching about a bad situation and do something to help."

Rufus watched Juliana adjust her belt again, and he

wondered what she kept concealed there. A pocket knife maybe, although with her nails, it'd have to be something that flipped open with ease. "I remember a Jimmy," Rufus prompted, catching Juliana's attention so she stopped fingering the hidden weapon. "He was one of Daisy's clients."

"Red, do you think I'm on a first-name basis with another girl's johns from twenty years ago? Be real."

"Juliana—"

She held up both hands while taking another step back. "No, no, no. I have to go."

"Someone *murdered* Daisy," Rufus protested, his voice cracking on his mother's name. "There's no fucking way on God's green Earth you don't know *something* about what went down."

"Somebody she argued with," Sam said, "somebody whose corner she took, somebody she mentioned, even in passing, who gave her a bad feeling. You wouldn't be freaking the fuck out if you didn't remember something."

"Come on, hunk, it ain't like that," Juliana countered.

"Then what *is* it like?" Rufus interjected. "You're the only connection I have to Daisy. I mean, who else can I turn to—*Boy George*?"

Juliana scoffed. "You could start there."

"What's that mean?"

Juliana looked over her shoulder, studied the dark tree line for a beat, then said as she turned her head back to Rufus, "You were the tiniest thing—maybe you don't remember. Daisy never got on with George."

Rufus exchanged looks with Sam. "Why?"

"Why do you think?" Juliana answered, just shy of spitting the words out.

"Because George is gay," Rufus said without a moment of hesitation.

"He's a user, too. Daisy had her limits."

"What about—" Sam hesitated, glancing at Rufus, and then said, "What about her pimp?"

Juliana smiled a little. It was a lot of emotions for so small an expression, but humor and hurt filtered to the top. "You mean Mac?"

"That's right. What was his deal? Could he know something about this?" Then Sam asked in a rush: "Could he have had something to do with it?"

Juliana's brows drew together. She tugged on her belt some more. Then she looked at Rufus. "He's got no real-world experience, does he?"

"Not about this," Rufus said politely.

"Mac was her pimp. Mac was my pimp," Juliana explained. "He oversaw most of the girls on this side of the Ramble in the '90s. I'm not saying he was Prince Charming, because he could be real mean. You don't make enough cash on a freezing February night, he'd smack you around for it. But he never hit hard enough to make a girl bleed."

"Where is he now?" Sam asked.

Juliana huffed. "Brooklyn, I guess. Come on, boys. I've been waiting for my girl to finish up and she's not back yet. I really should go check on her."

"Brooklyn isn't an answer," Rufus protested. "It's an entire borough!"

"Goddammit, Red," Juliana finally snapped. "Mac up and left by '03. I've been my own damn woman ever since. That shit-for-brains lived out in Bushwick last I heard. Kosciuszko Street. Off the J, a rathole that got condemned. For all I know, that human turd is still there."

"The killings stop," Sam said, "and a year later, Mac takes off. That doesn't exactly sound like a coincidence, does it?"

"It could be," Rufus countered.

Sam shot him a look. "What happened to—do you know if after—" He blew out a breath. "Did another girl take Daisy's clients?"

Juliana bit her lower lip and some of the lipstick stuck to her teeth. "Crystal. Crystal took a lot of them."

"What's the name Crystal's mother gave her?" Rufus asked.

"So you can harass her too?" Juliana shot back. "*No.* Sorry, boys, but we're done. I have to go. Honey's been gone for almost forty minutes, and what john do you know takes forty damn minutes to get off?" Juliana about-faced, walked down the shadowy path, and hugged the tree line as she called in a husky whisper, "Honey? Honey, you zipped up yet?"

"Should I stop her?" Sam asked.

"No," Rufus said on a quiet exhale. "If we push any further, Juliana might actually make good on that pocket knife she was fingering."

They turned in the direction they had come, and after a pair of minutes, Sam asked, "What now?"

"I guess we could always ask Erik if—"

A sudden, blood-curdling scream broke the stillness of the Ramble, coming from the direction Juliana had disappeared.

CHAPTER
NINE

When Sam heard the scream, he pulled the Beretta from the holster at the small of his back and ran toward the sound. It hadn't come from the path, but from farther back, among the trees. He was vaguely aware of Rufus crashing through the brush alongside him. Sam tried to dodge the trees and undergrowth, but it was pitch-black, and the scream had come from an overgrown section of the park. His shoulder clipped a yellowwood, sending its final, feathery leaves fluttering to the ground. Then he had to twist between a pair of holly trees, the leaves scratching his bare arms. A low-hanging maple branch slapped him in the mouth, and the shock of it, the sudden burst of white in his vision, made Sam slow.

He was being stupid. He was liable to get himself

killed. He was doing all the things he'd been trained not to do, and he was doing them because he was so keyed up from being around Rufus that he wasn't thinking clearly.

When he glanced back, he saw Rufus had already stopped. Sam tried to listen over the pounding of blood in his ears; nothing. He wiped the corner of his mouth, and his thumb came away wet. No second scream. No cries for help. No—

But then he heard choked sobs. His eyes had adjusted somewhat to the darkness, and Sam could pick out the trunk of a fallen tree, the gradual slope of the ground, and at the bottom of the gentle hill, a gully thick with bushes. As Sam watched, something moved, and the bushes trembled.

Sam moved counterclockwise so he could come up behind whoever—whatever—was moving. Rufus kept pace, tugging his beanie down, his eyes roving. Sam could smell a hint of Dial soap and wool warmed by body heat. More movement came from ahead, and Sam brought the Beretta up a few inches.

Someone stumbled out from between a pair of bushes. Juliana.

Sam exhaled slowly and whispered her name. Juliana startled and made a noise like a sob, only she had her hand over her mouth. For a moment, she was frozen. Then she seemed to recognize him, and she took huge, stumbling steps that looked even more ridiculous in her heels.

"What happened?" Sam asked in a whisper. "Are you—"

"She's dead," Juliana managed before clapping a hand over her mouth again. She breathed raggedly through her nose, and then she pulled her hand away again to say, "Oh my God, she's dead."

"Take a deep breath," Rufus told Juliana, reaching out to put a hand on her shoulder.

"Who killed her?" Sam asked. "Is someone down there?"

"Honey. My girl. I told you—I should—I should have been looking for her!" Juliana said, her voice shaking and wobbling on every syllable.

Sam turned sideways, doing his best to move quietly through the bushes; when he cleared them, he found himself standing on a narrow, crumbling shelf of dirt that dropped into the gully. He could make out the shape of something lying in the shadows below him, and he waited, counting, until he was reasonably sure nobody else—nobody living—was still down there. Behind him, Rufus and Juliana were whispering to each other, although Sam couldn't make out the words.

"Whoever did that," Sam said when he rejoined them, "they're gone."

Rufus's eyes were big as he looked from Sam to Juliana. "Why did you come tromping through the woods? Why didn't you stick to the path?"

"Honey likes to take guys this way. I was just going to cut across this stretch and come out on the other side, see if she was still working, but then I heard something down—down—" Her lower lip quivered, and the effect was surprisingly childlike on her weary face. "I heard something. And I had to look."

"Did you see anyone else?" Sam asked.

Juliana shook her head.

Sam glanced at Rufus.

Rufus swallowed, and it was loud enough for Sam to hear. He patted Juliana's back and said, "You need to get out of here, so the police don't find you. Still got that girlfriend? Call her. Go home."

Juliana glanced from Rufus to Sam and back to Rufus. With a final nod, she wobbled up the rise, her heels biting deep into the soil.

Sam waited until she'd reached the edge of the stand, and then he said, "I didn't hear breathing, but we should check."

Rufus's hands shook a little as he wiped his palms on his jeans, but he nodded. "Right."

This time, Sam didn't bother trying to be quiet. He forced a path through the bushes, edged along the crumbling lip of the gully, and found where the earth had washed away, leaving a channel that he could slide down into the gully proper. When Rufus followed, Sam caught his arm and helped him to his feet. Then Sam turned on the flashlight on his phone and played it around them to make sure nobody else was waiting.

When he squatted next to the fallen form, he still couldn't hear breathing. She was blond, petite, and too thin; he could tell that much. The wounds, what he could discern in the phone's weak light, were enough that he had to close his eyes and swallow the rush of bile. He checked her pulse and got nothing. Catching Rufus's gaze, he shook his head.

"Did you know her?" Sam asked.

"No. Next generation."

With a grunt, Sam stood again and moved toward the gully's wall. He stepped a pace in either direction, shining the light at an angle, and then said, "Take a look at this. The murdering little fuck rolled her body through the bushes—you can see where the branches are broken." He leaned closer. "He left a trail of blood too. He killed her up there, and then he dragged her to the gully and pushed her in." When he looked over his shoulder, he saw Rufus inspecting Honey's body. "What?"

"He slit her throat," Rufus muttered, having pulled out his own phone and turned the flashlight on. "The wound is full of ground debris." An involuntary shudder seemed to run through him. "Why kill her, make a huge mess, and then disturb more of the surroundings trying to hide her? I mean, if you can even call this hiding…." Rufus jerked his head up and asked, "You don't think that john's into, like… dead people?"

"I guess anything's possible." Sam drew in another steadying breath and pointed. "What the fuck is that?"

Rufus refocused the flashlight and lit up a series of deep, abstract-looking slashes on Honey's shoulder.

Sam moved over Honey's corpse, crouched, and pointed to a deep wound just above the wrist, at the edge of an ivy-vine tattoo. "That's a chopping blow. You can see the vee shape, and the skin around it split from the force of the impact. Why cut her throat and also do that to her wrist?"

Rufus, still crouched, shifted his weight to one foot. He stared up at Sam. "What if it's like before? With what happened to Daisy, and he got… interrupted by Juliana?"

"Jesus," Sam whispered. He gave Honey one last look, then he touched Rufus's arm. "Come on. We need to go, and we've already tramped around down here enough. You're white as a ghost; can you walk out of here?"

"I'm ok." Rufus rose with slow deliberation. "Should I call Erik?"

"Do you trust him? He's not going to hang us out to dry for this?"

"I could make an anonymous call to 911 and give his name to dispatch," Rufus said after a bit of thought. "I don't think Erik would lose his shit, but I'm not willing to chance it, not until he looks into those names."

"Smart," Sam said. "Do it from a pay phone?"

"Good luck finding one." Rufus held up his phone. "I'll put in the call and ditch my burner."

Nodding, Sam said, "Point the way, and you can make

the call while we walk."

Rufus gestured, and Sam caught his hand and held on to it.

"Because I don't want to be halfway across the park and realize you passed out and I left you behind," Sam said.

"You must have me mixed up with another neurotic ginger," Rufus remarked, pushing his fingers between Sam's and squeezing.

"Maybe it was the same guy doing some nervous upchucking in the men's room earlier," Sam said with a small smile, and he tugged Rufus forward.

Rufus called in the murder when they'd put a few hundred yards between them and Honey's body. Then they were alone, moving through darkness, the city's ambient light filtering between the trees to give everything a dusty luminescence. An owl burst from a tree, shooting fast to catch up something—a mouse, a vole—and carry it away. Then, from ahead, a horn blatted for what felt like a full minute, and brakes squealed before the crunch of impact, the tinkle of shattering glass.

They emerged from the park, moving back into glass-and-steel canyons and the twilight haze of the sodium lamps. Three blocks later Rufus wiped down the phone and dropped it in a trash can; Sam let out a breath he hadn't realized he'd been holding.

"Rufus," Sam said as they started down the subway steps. Warm air rose to meet them, pouring out like a gale that smelled of urine and hot metal. "Honey's body? The way she'd been killed? The fact that she's a working girl in the Ramble? You know what that means, right?"

Rufus hadn't let go of Sam's hand, even when he turned on the stairs to stare at the other man. "He's back."

CHAPTER
TEN

Details of the subway ride stuck out in Rufus's mind like jagged rock outcroppings. Sharp and strange. They'd transferred at Fourteenth Street to the Brooklyn bound L to catch the Downtown 6. The asshole conductor had shut the doors half a second too soon, catching the back of Rufus's jacket between them, and he'd had to fight the door to get free. The car had smelled like Chinese takeout.

And all the while, echoing off the serrated edges of Rufus's brain, Sam's question skipped like a needle on a warped record: *You know what that means, right?*

He knew what it meant. And he'd never intended for this. Another girl. Another victim. Rufus had only wanted to move out of the shadows. That meant letting go of the past, and he couldn't forget Daisy the way everyone else had. His only intention, from the start, was to put her to rest.

Rufus had still been holding Sam's hand, had still been standing close enough that he could soak in Sam's body heat, feel the ghost of Sam's arms around him, like a memory that escaped from his Pandora's box. Nestled among the sandstone formations in his mind, Rufus considered how nice it was to touch Sam again. How nice it was that the fluoxetine allowed for it. And how that one passing thought was perhaps the most dangerous one Rufus had ever had—*Sam again*.

They got off at Astor Place, took the stairs to street level, and made for Rufus's crummy shithole apartment. Even this late in the evening, the usual suspects of the tenement were alive and well. 4B was home from waiting fancy tables, and she could be heard through the thin walls, baby-talking the dog that never stopped yapping. Pauly Paul was home from his drumming session. No singing, thank God, but he was probably drunk, as he was banging around the kitchen like a bull in a china shop. And Mr. Gonzalez, God bless, had cranked his commercials up to full volume.

Rufus unlocked his front door and paused in the threshold as he listened to the high-pitched, feminine gasp echo from the television downstairs. He tugged his beanie off and said, "Well... that's not infomercials." He shut the door behind Sam, kicked his Chucks off, and dropped his jacket to the floor. "Ok, now what? We've got another dead girl."

"Well," Sam said. "We could sit on our thumbs and wait for your boyfriend Erik to turn up a name."

"Very funny," Rufus said, deadpan.

"I don't know," Sam said. "Juliana was a dead end; Christ, literally. I guess we can try again—try talking to some of the people she mentioned. The one I really want to talk to is Mac. I know Juliana wasn't convinced he had anything to do with this. You're not either. But it seems strange to me that the killings end, and Mac takes off for Brooklyn. It wouldn't hurt to try to track down Boy George or this other woman, Crystal, but Juliana seemed legitimately scared of talking to us. I don't think we'll be able to get anything else out of her." He rubbed his brow. "What do you want to do?"

Rufus ruffled the back of his head as he walked across the room. He sat on the edge of the mattress and looked up. He felt his hair standing up in a mess. "I want to click my heels together and wake up in a world where there aren't dead sex workers."

"We could look for George's place. He's been around for a long time; somebody must know where he's got a crib. Or we could go to Brooklyn."

"I think we should look into George," Rufus answered. "Because you're right—he has been around a long time. He knew all those girls, those johns, and yes, even Mac. Little tweaker must have *something* to tell us for another Andrew Jackson." He reached into his pocket, remembered his phone was gone, then held his hand out. "Can I borrow your cell?"

Sam handed it over.

Rufus raised his gaze to the ceiling as he recited a number to himself, nodded, then dialed. He put the phone on speaker so Sam could hear. "Darling Ophelia Hayes," he said when the other line picked up. "Love of my life. How are you? Beautiful as ever, I imagine."

"If you're calling for the name of my stylist, you're SOL. She wouldn't give you a shingle bob even if I sent you to her. It's not going to work for your face."

Sam nodded and demonstrated with two fingers as he whispered, "Too thin."

Rufus gave Sam an expression of mock anger while

saying, "My face is just fine, thank you very much. Christ, can't a guy compliment you without getting backhanded?"

"What do you want, Red?"

"Not a fucking shingle bob."

"Goodbye."

"No, no, I need to know where Boy George calls home," Rufus piped up quickly.

On the other end of the call, a horn blared. "Why do you want to know where he crashes?"

"So I can have a bouquet delivered." Rufus added thoughtfully, "I think it's his birthday…."

"Is this… is this something I need to worry about?" Volume dropping, she added, "Like this summer?"

"I was thinking carnations," Rufus continued. "Roses sends the wrong message, you know? Too romantic. We hardly know each other."

"Jesus." The horn blared again. Her voice changed as she shouted, "I'm walking, I'm walking. Yeah, fuck you too." Then, to Rufus again, she said, "He lives in Chinatown. It's a dump over one of the Lucky Noodle joints. I can't remember the number, but it's got a fish market next to it."

"I bet his pad smells great in August." Rufus glanced at Sam and then said, "Ok, thanks, beautiful."

"Call me that again, and your balls are going on sale in the fish market."

"Badass bitch," Rufus purred before hanging up. He gave Sam the phone. "We can go downtown tomorrow morning. He might be home, sleeping the night off."

"Sounds like a plan. Can I say something without being a coldhearted piece of shit?"

"Sure. Knock yourself out."

"I'm hungry. Are you hungry?"

Rufus laughed suddenly and without warning. He tried to get his smile under control as he said, "Since my body was reminded what food was… I'm always hungry."

"Pizza?"

"As long as we order from Frank's."

"I have no idea what Frank's is, but sure. Please don't tell me you like Hawaiian, though."

Rufus got to his feet. "Cheese. It doesn't need anything else."

"A minimalist. I can live with that."

Rufus held his hand out. "I need your phone again."

With a small smile, Sam passed the phone back.

Rufus punched in a number. He stared at Sam while speaking to someone who was, in fact, named Frank. He placed the order, didn't bother with his address, then gave Sam the phone. "About fifteen minutes."

"Look at us," Sam said. "Making progress. You're eating meals, you're sleeping. Hell, you might actually live long enough for this psycho to kill you." He winced. "Sorry. I heard that as it was coming out; I was trying to lighten the mood."

But Rufus was smiling again. "I fight dirty, remember? I'm never above kneeing a guy in the nuts."

"One of the many things I like about you."

Rufus breathed—in and out—then took Sam's hand. He worked the pad of his thumb over big knuckles. "So touching is ok?" he asked at length.

For a long moment, Sam was quiet. Then he said, "Yes. I decided to go back on the meds. For a lot of reasons, I guess. They definitely make a difference."

"Tell me one of the reasons?"

"I didn't like why I went off them. I was… angry when I got out of the Army. The situation was complicated. I didn't want anything to do with them anymore, and that meant no VA. After the summer, when I realized how hard it was to do certain things, I decided I could pull my head out of my ass long enough to get my scrips filled."

"I'm glad," Rufus said simply.

"One of those things," Sam said stiffly, "one of the things that was really overwhelming when I was off the meds, was, well, you. Sex. With you. Sex with you. Just so you know." He exhaled sharply, and when he spoke again, his voice was soft. "What are we doing?"

Rufus could feel his eyebrows reaching his hairline. His face was hot enough to leave a lingering burn. "Uhm... we're talking." He was still rubbing his thumb back and forth across Sam's knuckles. "I'm sorry. I should have said that yesterday, but I've been so... and then seeing you again. I didn't mean to punch you in the face. It was a really shitty gut instinct."

"I can take a punch," Sam said. "What I can't take is not knowing if you're going to wake up one day and kill yourself. I've known too many guys go that way, Rufus. I'm not going to put myself in the emotional equivalent of a shooting gallery. You said something about trying to see someone. Is that for real? Because if it's not, as much as I like this," he raised their joined hands, "then we need to call it here."

Rufus worked his mouth, but each time he opened it to speak, he felt his chin quiver, the lump in his throat getting bigger, and he couldn't—*just couldn't* break down again in front of Sam like before. So Rufus closed his eyes and squeezed Sam's hand tighter. He reminded himself that he *had* reached out, and if he'd fallen low enough to finally be able to admit he needed help, then he *must* want to get better.

I am going to get better.

On his worst days, which were most days, that mantra

was almost impossible to say. But Rufus wanted it, truly, because he feared that cutting his life short might be worse than living through the perpetual ache. He couldn't explain it—maybe his future therapist could without too much psychological mumbo jumbo—but Rufus didn't want to *call it here*.

Not when Sam appeared to want more—not when Rufus finally had the opportunity to be something to someone.

Rufus cleared his throat and worked his hand free from Sam's. He turned to the fridge, plucked a half sheet of paper from under a magnet advertising Big Earl the Locksmith, Call 555-0001, and passed it to Sam. "I really am on a waitlist. That's the date of my first appointment."

Sam looked at it and nodded. Then he looked up at Rufus.

"I don't want to die," Rufus whispered. It took every ounce of strength he had to remain on his feet, to not let his own cowardice bully him, like falling down the flight of stairs and the *pop* and *snap* that followed.

"What do you want?"

Rufus took the paper back and replaced it under the magnet. "Living sucks sometimes, but it's pretty fucking punk to wake up every day, in spite of what's ahead of me." He looked at Sam. "I want to be someone you can trust. I want to be ok."

Sam slid an arm around Rufus and kissed him.

The buzzer to the apartment rang loudly.

Rufus pulled back and stared at the wall intercom like he was ready to cut someone. "Goddammit." He left Sam, moved to the wall near the door, hit a button, and asked who it was.

"Rico, from Frank's! Or did you already forget you ordered a pie, you asshole."

"Dipshit," Rufus replied before buzzing Rico into the building. He opened the door and leaned against the doorjamb, listening to the echo of steps on the stairs. "Frank said fifteen minutes," he called as Rico reached the landing.

"I'm here in twelve—the fuck you want, Freckles?"

"I wanted you here in fifteen." Rufus took the box from Rico.

Rico glanced inside as Rufus moved toward the afterthought of a kitchen. After Rico made eye contact with Sam, he nodded knowingly. "Oh, I get it."

"Great," Sam said. "Now fuck off."

Rico held a hand out. "It's twenty for a full pie."

"Frank has a tab running," Rufus called from around the corner of the fridge.

"Ok, but what about my tip?" Rico countered without missing a beat.

"How much do I have to give him," Sam asked Rufus, "to make him leave?"

"Give him five," Rufus said, already opening the box, which was precariously balanced on the stovetop.

Peeling off a bill, Sam slapped it into Rico's hand and pointed at the door.

Rico saluted Sam as he took the cash. "Have fun." He started down the stairs.

Shutting the door, Sam leaned against it while Rufus was pulling out the first slice of pizza. "Really?" Sam said.

Rufus folded the slice and paused as it was midway to his mouth. "What?"

It looked like Sam was fighting a grin. "Never mind."

CHAPTER
ELEVEN

Waking in bed with someone was nice, Sam decided, even if that someone was a lanky redhead who desperately needed to trim his toenails. Sam's calves were basically mincemeat by morning. With the brief exception of Jake Brower, Sam's sex life had consisted of hookups and frantic, one-off encounters. A morning like this, with someone still in bed next to him, was relatively new. And nice. Definitely nice.

Somehow Sam had ended up pressed against the wall, and Rufus was spread out like an X, one leg sticking out from under the covers. Sam slid to the edge of the mattress, stepped into his jeans, and went to the bathroom. His next stop was the kitchen. If Sam still had any doubts, the refrigerator was proof that this was Rufus's apartment:

a box of Arm & Hammer baking soda with a reminder EXPIRES DEC 2002; a package of shelf-stable ramen noodles with a yellow sticky note that said EXPERIMENT; and a disposable cup of pomegranate seeds, the single-use lid peeling back from where Rufus had tried to secure it.

At least he has coffee, Sam thought as he got the machine going. No coffee might have posed a serious problem.

While the coffee brewed, Sam disconnected his phone from the charger and checked for messages, emails, notifications, and alerts. Nothing. He read the news. Then he started googling, testing out different avenues that might help them track down the woman Juliana had called Crystal.

"*Whuz thad?*" Rufus muttered into the pillow—a very sloppy and tired-sounding "What's that?"

"Coffee," Sam said, glancing up. The X-shaped Rufus had contracted into a pillow-scrunching Rufus. "Are you alive?"

Rufus sighed heavily, made a half-awake noise, and flung himself onto his side. He cracked one eye open and stared at Sam. "Sorta."

"On average, how much time do you spend searching for people you don't know and don't know how to find? In a normal week, for example."

Rufus slowly raised his head. His red hair was askew, and he had marks on his cheek from the sheets. "I'm... *wait*... who am I searching for?"

"Well, we know where George is, and we know where Mac went, and we want to find Crystal, right? Do you have any strategies? I ask because when I needed to find an enlisted guy, for example, I knew his name, I knew his birthday, I knew his social. I could pull up his record. I could talk to the guys in his platoon. I could find out if he had buddies, if he had a girl—or a guy—or kids, or loans, or problems. When we were trying to find out what happened to Jake, it was similar—we had a lot to work with. Now, though, all we've got is a first name: Crystal. And it's probably not even her given name. And she was an active sex worker almost twenty years ago. And our one lead refuses to give us anything. Also, do you have creamer hidden somewhere?"

Rufus kicked the blankets to the foot of the bed and sat up. He scratched his bare chest, saying, "That was a lot of explanations to throw at a guy who just woke up. A lot of the sex workers from the '90s have a record." He stumbled out of bed in nothing but a pair of briefs, walked to the kitchen, and started checking cupboards. "Daisy spent a few months behind bars when I was... ten or eleven, I think. I wouldn't be surprised if Crystal had too."

"Did you know where she was at the time? Daisy, I mean."

"Yeah. Mr. Gonzalez watched out for me while she was gone. He didn't sugarcoat the facts—dammit. I thought I had that powdered creamer." Rufus opened the fridge, then quickly shut it. "I guess it's gonna be black."

"Oh, that's fine. I only take it black anyway. I just wanted you to drag your ass out of bed."

"That was mean."

"Did Daisy ever mention anyone from that time? Did she ever meet up with anyone after? Maybe there's another network of contacts we can try."

Rufus scratched his belly. "Did you do a record or court search?"

"That stuff's online?" Sam tapped the phone screen, navigating to the New York court system's website. He selected the trial courts, and then he searched for Daisy O'Callaghan. He tried not to make it obvious, but he angled the phone away from Rufus as he examined the results.

The search appeared to be pulling results from the full text of the case papers and the decisions, and it offered results that included either only the first name, only the last name, or both. Even for a name as unusual as Daisy O'Callaghan, there was a lot to dig through.

After navigating back to the search, Sam tried again, only this time with the name Crystal. At the top of the results was a yellow bar and a message: *Too many case papers or decisions were found. Only the first 200 will be displayed.*

"Is sex work called prostitution in New York's criminal code?" Sam asked. "Or is it sexual misconduct or something like that?"

"Prostitution," Rufus answered, busily pouring two mugs of black coffee. "Did you find anything?"

"Hold on."

Backtracking to the search prompt, Sam tried again. This time, he included the word prostitution with the name Crystal. Three results appeared.

"Maybe," Sam said, accepting a mug. "Ok, the first one is a bust. It only showed up because the judge used the phrase 'crystal clear' in the decision. The second is… a bust. Apparently Crystal Clean Cleaning Ladies was a front for sexual dust-busting or something of the sort. The third is—holy shit. Crystal Ballard. There's an address. And an address for her lawyer."

While Sam had been reading out loud, Rufus had vanished to the bathroom, running water and toothbrush sounds punctuating in between Sam's words. Rufus returned, looking slightly more alert. "There's an address for her *and* the lawyer?" he repeated, joining Sam and looking over his shoulder at the phone.

"Yep," Sam said, angling the phone so Rufus could see better. "Where are those two? Roughly, I mean."

Rufus pointed at the screen. "Mott Street is Chinatown.

That's where the lawyer is—*was*. I'd have to google that other address, though. Somewhere on the East Side."

Sam typed Crystal Ballard's address into the Maps app. The app displayed a pin not far from Rufus's apartment; the information at the bottom of the screen stated that this was the location of THE PLEASURE BOX, which was, according to the store description, New York City's only combination retailer that offered both 'marital aids' and moving supplies.

"Why do I get the feeling this is no longer Crystal's apartment?" Sam asked.

Rufus stared at the address. "I can get packed and *packed* at the same time. Awesome." He fetched his coffee.

"Very helpful," Sam muttered. "I'm guessing by that reaction that you want to stop by and check it out, or can we head straight to the lawyer's?"

"I've never been one for toys." Rufus took a sip of coffee and then searched his empty cupboards again.

"Definitely the lawyer," Sam said, pocketing the phone. "Did you sleep all right?"

Rufus shut the cupboard and turned, his cheeks and ears that telltale pink. "Yeah. All right. Did you?"

"More than all right. How do you feel today?"

"I don't know. Ok, I guess. Are you going to ask me that every day?"

"Until you kick me out."

Rufus seemed to consider that as he walked to the piles of clothing along the wall. He yanked free a black shirt, its logo so faded that Sam couldn't decipher it, and a pair of Levi's. "Ok," Rufus finally agreed, getting dressed.

As Sam pulled on a clean tee—inside out, because meds or no meds, he still had limits—and asked, "How many breakfast sandwiches will I have to buy you on the walk over to the lawyer's?"

Rufus glanced up from yanking his Chucks on. He had a cute, lopsided smile on his face. "Three. I'm out of gum too."

"Gum," Sam said. "Ok. Gum."

They stopped first at a Duane Reade, where Sam was obligated to buy a pack of Doublemint, and then at a Le Pain Quotidien, where Rufus actually did order three breakfast sandwiches, and Sam followed suit, since it seemed like the polite thing to do. They ate as they walked; the October day was warming up, and a scrim of cirrus clouds offered an inverted topography above the city.

The lawyer's office was in a three-story brick walk-up; the wall was plastered with flyers, at least a hundred of which said RESIST in faded rainbow lettering. There was also an innuendo-laced advertisement for barre classes— GIVE HIM A SQUEEZE HE'LL NEVER FORGET—and a clean, sans-serif page that just said POT. IT'S GOOD. CALL MARK. And then a number. On the next block, Sam could see signage in traditional Chinese characters, and he could smell fresh bao when a breeze picked up.

"She's still listed," Sam said, tapping the placard near the door that named Numa Aguilera Alarcón, Esq., as the occupant of 2B. "Want to see what she remembers?"

"Elephants have ten-pound brains," Rufus said, then caught Sam's look. "Not that Numa is an elephant. Only that the matriarch has a great memory. Never mind. Let's go."

They headed up the stairs; a security gate was chained back, and judging by grooves in the cement, Sam figured the gate had seen a lot of use. 2A was occupied by LUCCHESI LUXURY PROPERTIES: THE NEXT BEST THING TO LIVING WITH NONNA, although to judge by the thick layer of dust in the window and the sun-bleached advertising materials on the shelves, more people were opting to live with Nonna these days.

2B didn't look much better: the bottom of the door was splintered and didn't meet the threshold, the brass finish on the handle had long since flaked away, and the sign that said NUMA ALARCÓN ATTORNEY-AT-LAW was wrinkled from water damage. Sam gave the door an experimental push, and it wobbled open.

The front room was obviously intended as a waiting area, with a desk for a secretary, although the chairs were empty and Sam didn't think a secretary had used the Apple II that was sitting on the desk since the late '70s. A poster hung on one wall; the paper was crinkled with the same signs of water damage, and the plaster behind it bulged ominously. On the poster was written USTED TIENE LOS DERECHOS HUMANOS and it showed a clean-cut Latino man in a suit, smiling beneficently.

"Hello?" Sam called. To Rufus, he asked, "Is this normal for New York? I feel like I'm in *I Am Legend*."

But Rufus was busily pawing through a stack of dusty magazines on a waiting table. "Look." He held up a National Geographic with elephants on the front. "It's seven years old. But I wonder how much new research has been done on elephants in that time?" He opened the magazine and flipped the pages.

"God, how did I ever get you out of that library?" Sam said. Then he called again, "Hello?"

A door at the back of the room opened, and a trim older woman stepped out. She was wearing Beats, and she pulled back one of the ear pads, making a face that belonged on someone about sixty years younger. Her short hair was gray, and she wore a purple velour tracksuit. When she spoke, her accent was pure New York.

"Were you raised in a barn? Shut the damn door."

Sam blinked and pushed the door shut.

"Well?" she said, her gaze flicking between Rufus and Sam. "What do you want? If it's about the drinks at

Tony's, I left the cash under the coaster. It's not my fault if you've got thieves working for you."

"Uh," Sam said, at a loss for words.

Rufus dropped the magazine back onto the pile, took a step forward, and slipped in front of Sam. "You the lawyer?"

"That's right. What is it? Solicitation? It's the big guys who can't ever get it up." She only glanced at Sam before fixing her attention on Rufus. "He hit one of your girls? Well, what is it? Don't you know how to talk?"

Rufus waved a hand absently at Sam. "Don't worry about him. He's a big teddy bear. I am here about a girl, though. A throwback. Crystal Ballard. Does that ring a bell, or do I need to dredge up a date too?"

"I can get it up," Sam said, the words too loud in the small room.

Numa stared at him. Then she looked at Rufus. "Is he simple? I had a cousin who was simple."

"No, he's not—and his dick is fine. Cross my heart. Crystal, does the name ring a bell?"

"I can't tell you something like that. Attorney-client privilege, kiddo. Nobody's going to come to me for help if I go blabbing their business to any cute redhead who drags himself up the stairs."

"Uh-huh. And if it was a twenty-year-old case and I'm just desperate to get in touch with an old friend and completely at wit's end?" Rufus countered.

"Desperate?" Numa's dark eyes narrowed. "How desperate?"

"Fucking New York," Sam said. He pulled the wad of bills from his pocket. "How much is it going to take?"

"Bazooka Joe, unless you've got enough in there for a new pair of tatas, you're going about this the wrong way. Do I look like I need money?"

"Yes," Sam said. "Desperately. For a Dustbuster, if nothing else."

"Ha. All right. A thousand is a good starting place, although the price may go up depending on what you want exactly."

"Counteroffer," Sam growled. "Twenty-five dollars. Fuck the Dustbuster; you can get yourself a fucking Swiffer."

Rufus slapped Sam's chest with the back of his hand. "Calm down, Joe. How about two hundred?" he asked Numa.

"Two fifty."

"Two twenty-five and you've got cash in your hand," Rufus said with a tone of finality.

"Redheads," Numa said. "Cheap, miserable bastards, all of you. Fine. Two twenty-five."

Rufus reached into his back pocket and pulled out his wallet. He opened it, sifted through the bills for what was probably dramatic effect, then offered a few to Numa. "Pleasure doing business."

"Excuse me," Sam said, grabbing Rufus's arm and trying to get a look at the wallet. "You have money?"

"Well, I do pay rent," Rufus explained. "And sometimes I have to buy my own gin when Pauly's got nothing to swipe." He tugged at Sam's grip. "Most of my cash is saved for buying information," he hissed through clenched teeth.

"When you two finish playing grabass—" Numa began.

"Crystal Ballard," Sam said, tightening his grip on Rufus.

"Christ," Numa said. "I don't know. Come on back and we'll take a look. I can't remember my last BM these days, so I write everything down."

"We're going to talk about this," Sam muttered. "At length."

Rufus yanked free and slipped his wallet into his pocket again.

Numa led them into the office at the back, still talking. "Don't do much work anymore. I just keep the place so I don't strangle Aurelio. That's my husband." She flicked a dismissive nail at a framed wedding portrait that had to be forty years old. The office was plainly furnished: a set of particleboard office furniture, a wall of black filing cabinets, and a pair of tubular chairs: chrome legs, fabric upholstery that said Viva Che! The only things that might have been bought after Reagan were the Beats that Numa had pulled down to her neck and a MacBook Air.

She tapped a few keys, frowned, and said, "How long ago?"

Rufus dropped into one of the chairs and crossed his long legs. "Hard to say. She was active in the late '90s. But why don't you look for anything post-2002."

"Won't be on here, then," Numa said, pushing back from the desk, the casters on the ancient executive chair squeaking. She made her way to the filing cabinets and opened a drawer low on the first one. "Christ, my lumbago," she said. Then she worried a file free from the drawer and carried it back to the desk.

After a moment of examining the documents, Numa said, "Pretty straightforward. She got picked up a number of times for prostitution. Like you said, late '90s, early 2000s. Only went to court once, though—ok, it's starting to come back." She tapped the folder. "I remember this girl. She was a working girl, sure enough, but she snitched too. When she got picked up, I'd bail her out, and then she'd call a guy on the force. He'd make sure the charges got dropped—well, except for the one. That's why we had to go to court."

"Why didn't the charges get dropped that time?"

"Lovers' spat," Numa said, grinning ghoulishly. "I think she got out of the life after that. I remember something about, yeah, ok. Here it is." She held up a yellowing envelope from which she extracted a piece of cardstock. "Blessed couple, happy occasion, your presence. She was supposed to get hitched in June 2005."

"Supposed to?" Sam said.

"Well, I didn't attend, and I never heard from her again."

"Do all your clients invite you to their weddings?"

"All the ones who puke while I'm holding their hair and ask me to drive them to Planned Parenthood, yeah, they do."

Rufus leaned forward and snatched the envelope from Numa. He held it out of reach when she moved to grab for it. "What was Crystal's address?" he asked, working open the invitation. "Her real address—with this husband— Norman? She was going to marry a guy named *Norman*?"

"Check the envelope," Numa said. "What I've got on file is—" She read off the same address that had been listed on the court papers. "But I don't think she's there anymore."

"She's not," Sam said. "Rufus's favorite store is there now. Where he spends all his money. The money that he most definitely has."

"God, drop the money thing, Joe," Rufus mumbled as he flipped the envelope around to study the faded penmanship. "Hang on—Park Slope? A working girl was marrying, what, a john and moving to fucking Park Slope? Are you fucking with me?" he asked, looking at Numa again.

"Really?" Numa said. "God damn. I knew I should have gone to that wedding."

Rufus looked at the envelope again, his brows knitting together. "*Son of a bitch.*" He stuffed the invitation back inside and handed it over. "What about this cop who made her prior charges vanish into the wind? Any info on him?"

"I don't know," Numa said. "I didn't want to know, and Crystal didn't want to tell me. I got the sense that there was more to it than just work, but—" She shrugged. "That was a guess."

Sam and Rufus tried a few more questions, but it was clear that they had exhausted Numa's memory about Crystal Ballard—and that they were quickly exhausting her patience. When they left, Numa was pulling the Beats into place again, obviously halfway to forgetting they had ever existed.

On the street, Sam shook his head and said, "I don't like the bit about the cop. That smells funny."

Rufus was nodding as he put his sunglasses on. "We'll have to ask Crystal herself. If she's still living the high life in Park Slope." He looked up at Sam. "But before that, let's visit George. I think there's a fish market a few blocks from here."

CHAPTER
TWELVE

Rufus led the way through the congested, winding streets of Chinatown after their visit with Numa, bringing them to the corner of Hester and Mott. The street was crowded with midmorning shoppers, the area pungent with the stink of fish. Rufus stepped around a few buckets of live crabs, one currently on the lam, and a big ice-covered counter stacked high with whole tilapia—each of the fish seeming to stare at Rufus with their dead eyes. He passed the front door of the noodle shop Ophelia had mentioned last night and came to a stop at an unassuming stoop that led to the apartments overhead.

A punk kid crouched in the doorway, sucking on a cigarette. He glanced at Rufus and blew the smoke upward.

Rufus made a motion with one hand for him to

scram, and when the kid hesitated, Rufus motioned to the cigarette, like, *I'll tell your auntie you're smoking*.

The kid took off.

Rufus tried the knob and it opened. He grabbed Sam's shirt sleeve and pulled him inside. Rufus studied the mailboxes along the wall in the vestibule, then tapped the only one without a label. "This one. I bet it's a revolving door of squatters."

"Good to know," Sam said. "Let's take it slow when we get up there, then."

Rufus started up the steep stairs, quick and quiet on the balls of his feet, Chucks so worn out, there was no tread left to squeak against the flooring. When he reached the fourth floor, the overhead lights flickered now and then, a hum in the wiring just loud enough to make them feel not alone. Rufus stopped outside the first door, angled himself to one side, and knocked. Next to him, Sam had one hand at the small of his back, ready to draw the Beretta if things went south.

The apartment was silent—but the sort of silence where someone with a pulse was pretending they weren't home. Then whoever was inside, they tripped, something skittered, fell, and smashed against the hardwood floor.

Rufus knocked again, louder.

"Who is it?" a voice barked.

"Candygram," Rufus replied.

"*What?*"

"Open the fucking door, dude," Rufus snapped.

Steps drew close, the deadbolt turned, and the door opened as much as the security chain would allow. A dark eye narrowed when Rufus leaned forward enough to be seen, and the occupant asked, "You a cop?"

"I weigh 130 pounds soaking wet," Rufus answered. "What do you think?"

The eye moved to Sam. "He's a fucking cop, then."

Rufus waved at Sam in a nonchalant manner. "He's just pretty to look at. Open the door. I want to talk to you about Boy George."

"Georgie?"

"Did I stutter?"

The stranger hesitated as he looked at Sam again, but shut the door, pulled back the chain, then opened wide. He was considerably younger than Rufus, shorter too, but built in the chest and upper arms. He had a dark complexion and thick, messy hair that'd look nice once a brush was run through it.

Rufus plastered on a fake smile. "Who're you, kiddo?"

"No one. I don't even live here."

"Robbing the place?" Rufus asked, but in a tone that suggested he really didn't care either way.

"N-no! I just came to grab my things. I'm leaving."

"Ok. I'm going to call you Mike," Rufus said. "Let's talk about George for a minute, Mike."

Mike had been holding a backpack in one hand. He slowly set it on the floor. "What do you need to know about Georgie?"

"For starters," Sam said, stepping into Mike's space and crowding the kid back into the apartment, "whatever you know that's making you freak the fuck out."

"Don't kill me!" Mike pleaded, bumping back against the nearby wall. "Oh my God, I don't know anything. I swear, I swear."

"You're going to make him piss himself," Rufus said to Sam.

"It might be an improvement," Sam said, pushing past Mike and grabbing the bag. "This place is a shithole. What do you have in here?"

"That's mine," Mike protested, briefly forgetting his terror and grabbing for the bag.

Sam squatted, yanked on the zipper, and spilled the contents of the bag out onto the floor. A perforated strip of condoms. A skin rag with the imaginative title *JUGGS* (the extra G probably meant to be playful). A dime bag of weed; Sam opened it and got a strong whiff of oregano. And then a white leather wallet—too big to be a man's, and obviously intended to be carried in a purse. He tossed it to Rufus.

Rufus snatched it midair and said to Mike, "This doesn't seem your style."

Mike didn't answer, merely swallowed a few times.

Rufus opened the snap and studied the driver's license inside. "Huh. Cindy Fisher." He turned it for Sam to see. "Looks like Honey, yeah?"

"That is definitely Honey," Sam said, and then he turned his gaze on Mike. "Who, not coincidentally, got chopped up last night. How about that, Mike?"

"That's not mine!" Mike squealed, stumbling along the wall until he hit a swaybacked sofa. It caught him at the knees, and he went down; the old springs groaned under him. "I swear to God, I swear to God, I swear to—"

"God's got nothing to do with this. You'd better come up with something better. Something I'm going to believe."

"It's his! George's, I mean. He didn't come back last night, and I'm sick of this fucking dump, so I thought I'd clear out and take it with me. I swear on the fucking cross, that is not mine!"

Sam glanced at Rufus.

"It's not George's," Rufus said, waving the wallet back and forth. "Unless he got a lot prettier since I last saw him. So when did he swipe this?"

Mike was shaking his head, probably ready to swear to God some more. "It was just here. Last night. And Georgie went to the Ramble. I haven't seen him since. I wanted some cash, please, God—"

"Stop that," Rufus said, closing the wallet. "You sure George hasn't been home?"

"Sure, I'm sure."

"What about anybody else?" Sam said. "Anybody coming around asking for him? Or people he mentioned? Anybody you heard him talking about?"

Mike started to shake his head, then paused so abruptly, it was almost comical. "Well… there was a guy a few nights ago. I thought it was kind of weird they were getting into it because that guy is all about pussy. No way he'd be at the Ramble for Georgie, and yet…." Mike shrugged.

"What do you mean, getting into it?" Sam said. "And what do you mean, all about pussy?" Before Rufus could open his mouth, Sam pointed a finger and said, "No wisecracks. I mean, how could you know what the guy was into? Did you know him?"

Mike was starting to breathe quick and shallow again. "I think he knew Georgie from the old days. Him and Georgie were talking about some of the girls working now, talking about how they aren't shit compared to the ones they used to know, that kind of thing."

"What's Prince Charming's name?" Rufus asked Mike.

Mike licked his lips. "Are you going to kill me if I tell you?"

Rufus cracked his neck. "I'm going to kill you if you *don't* tell me. How's that?"

"Mac," Mike blurted. "Mac Stew—no. Stevens."

Rufus tugged his sunglasses down enough to stare at Mike over the rims. "How certain are you?"

"Hundred percent. *Two hundred percent.* Don't kill

me—you said you wouldn't!"

"I didn't, though," Sam said.

Mike started sobbing. "I just wanna go, I just wanna go, I just wanna go home!"

Rufus glanced at Sam. He tossed the wallet back to Mike, jutted a thumb over his shoulder, and stepped into the hallway.

As they moved away from the unit, Sam was quiet. Then he said, "Where'd Juliana say he is?"

"Kosciuszko Street in Bushwick," Rufus answered, heading toward the stairs. He paused at the landing and reached a hand out for Sam. "Come on, you big lug. We've got two people to visit in Brooklyn."

CHAPTER
THIRTEEN

Getting to Brooklyn was simple, maybe even easy, but not pleasant. Rufus led Sam on a brisk walk east, out of Chinatown, and down the steps of a subway station south of Broadway. Traffic was picking up, and people glared at Rufus and Sam as they hopped the turnstile. One old woman, her hair pinned up under a leopard-print beret, rapped Sam's knuckles with her cane. He swore, loudly, and glared, but the woman turned around like she was going to come after him, so he hurried down the stairs after Rufus, sucking his knuckles.

"You realize," Sam growled as they stood on the platform, "we don't have to jump the turnstiles. We have money. I have money. And, more importantly, you have money."

Rufus leaned forward, staring down the abyss of the dark tunnel. "I don't have money. I told you: I spend it on rent and information." He glanced at Sam. "It's not like I can give the NYPD receipts and they reimburse me. I have to do what's necessary to get the intel so I can get a decent paycheck."

"I'm hearing a lot of complicated excuses from someone I just heard mumble 'F train' to himself and giggle under his breath."

Rufus's cheeks grew pink, and he protested, "Come on—it's such an easy joke! Plus, when I was eight, I really did walk onto the F as a chick was getting plowed and calling her boyfriend *daddy*."

The trip didn't get much better after that; there was construction, or something had fallen onto the tracks, or somebody hadn't shown up to work. Whatever the reason, the trains were running late, and when one finally arrived, it was crammed with people. Meds or no meds, Sam didn't appreciate being crammed into the corner of the car, with a middle-aged man in a bow tie elbowing him every fifteen seconds and frowning at Sam as though it were Sam's fault. Then, halfway across the East River, the train stopped completely, and the man in the bow tie elbowed Sam again and said, "If you don't mind," and opened his briefcase to take out a real, live Chihuahua, which proceeded to bark in Sam's ear and chew his sleeve until they finally started moving again.

When they finally got to the Seventh Avenue station, Sam grabbed Rufus by the arm and hauled him to the side of the platform so the horde could rush past them. Old habits died hard, and Sam tracked the faces moving under the fluorescent lights. He could have sworn he'd seen the guy in joggers and a Members Only jacket back in Manhattan, but sunglasses and a Mets hat pulled low made it impossible to tell. Besides, Sam told himself, this was one of the biggest cities in the world. It'd be strange if he didn't see people who looked alike.

"I hate this place," he said when they emerged into the October afternoon. "In case you were wondering."

"What, the Chihuahua?" Rufus asked with a chuckle under his breath.

Rufus took the lead again, cutting up Ninth Street, his head swiveling as he checked street signs. This part of Brooklyn was clearly expensive—at least, to Sam's untrained eye. The townhouses looked well maintained, some brick and some stone, most with ornamental details. In a few windows, A/C units still buzzed, providing a steady undercurrent to the rush of traffic. Halfway up the block, a CVS and a barbershop marked the beginning of a commercial strip, and then Rufus turned again, heading up another residential street with maples and lindens planted along the verge.

The appearance of the people around them shifted slightly: Sam had been playing Brooklyn Beards, counting all the weird hipster facial hair, including the pedo 'staches, he spotted on their walk, including the treasure trove at the barbershop, but now he noticed women in Lululemons with jogging strollers, dads rocking their dad bods, and a handful of gay and lesbian couples with their gaybies. Everybody looked like they made a lot of money, and the whole place seemed exhausting.

A few blocks later, Rufus stopped in front of a brownstone and nodded up at it.

"This is Crystal's place?" Sam said. "Looks pricey."

"Few hundred thousand, easy," Rufus answered. "But this was the address Numa had a decade ago. If she's moved, maybe the current owners at least have a scrap of information."

"What's our story?"

Rufus pulled his sunglasses down and looked at Sam over the rims. "Want to be my trophy husband? Meet the neighbors?"

"That's a little presumptuous."

"Come on—I think you're pretty."

"Yes, well, trophy husband implies a certain economic arrangement that, I'm going to point out again, I've been deeply misled about."

"You're so fucking dramatic." Rufus grabbed Sam's hand and hauled him up the steep steps. "Stand there and look cute."

"I'm trying," Sam growled. "It's hard when a stranger forced his Chihuahua to lick my ear on a public train."

Rufus rang the doorbell and said, staring ahead, "If you're very good, I'll lick your ear on the ride back to the city."

The door opened while Sam was trying not to choke on his tongue.

"Yes?" The man who stood there had to be at least eighty, and he wore Elton John–style glasses on a beaded chain, a stretched-out cardigan, and slippers that looked like they were glued to his feet.

"Hi!" Rufus said, with a level of artificial happiness that if Sam didn't know him better, he might have fallen for. Rufus took off his sunglasses and said, "You must be Norman Davis, is that right?"

"Hello?" Norman said in a quavering voice.

"My name's Rufus Greene," he continued, grabbing Norman's hand and shaking it. "My prettier half, Samuel," he continued, motioning to his right. "We're moving in. 619, at the end of the block." At that, Rufus turned and nodded his chin at, if Sam squinted, what looked like a Realtor sign stuck in the yard beside the fence. "We wanted to meet all of our new neighbors."

"No," Norman said, shaking his head, his eyes fogged with cataracts as he leaned closer to Sam and Rufus. "No new neighbors. I've lived here thirty years. You're looking for 619. End of the block. Have a nice day." He puttered around in a circle, obviously trying to find the door again.

"Selective hearing," Sam whispered, "completely unhelpful, and a terrible choice in footwear. Is he a relative of yours?"

Rufus raised a hand to his throat in a cutting fashion.

"Honey, who's at the door?" a woman called from farther in the brownstone, her voice drawing closer to the vestibule. A head of blond hair—bleached, but the very expensive sort of bleach—appeared over Norman's shoulder, followed by expensive jewelry, a toned body that spent way too much on yoga and private instructors—and there she was. Crystal. "May I help you gentlemen?" she asked, hand on Norman's shoulder.

Rufus stared for half a heartbeat, cleared his throat, and said with that same fakeness, "You must be Mrs. Davis."

"Charlotte, yes," she said with a note of confusion. "And you are?"

Rufus slapped Sam's chest, a bit too enthusiastically. "New neighbors!" he proclaimed.

Charlotte's eyebrows rose as she glanced between the two. "Oh, you must have bought—"

"619," Rufus answered for her.

Her cheeks flushed a little. "How lovely. It's so nice to have… you know… there's another gay couple on Tenth Street."

Rufus glanced at Sam. "Lucky us."

"We probably know them," Sam said.

"They're looking for the new neighbors," Norman bellowed. "I told them nobody new's been in this house for twenty years. 619, I told them."

"Yes, honey," Charlotte said loudly. "*They* moved into 619."

"619?" Norman said. When Charlotte nodded impatiently, he mumbled, "I don't know about that."

Charlotte looked at the two with a sort of weary expression before pushing the door open all the way. "Please come in."

"Thank you so much," Rufus replied. He gave Sam's sleeve a tug as he walked inside. "Beautiful house," he stated.

"Oh, thank you. It's so messy, I'm sorry. The maid hasn't come by yet," Charlotte replied while guiding Norman deeper into the home.

Rufus is right, Sam thought; it was a beautiful home. Many of the pieces looked like antiques, an eclectic mix of styles and periods broken up by the occasional modern piece, like the glass-and-steel pretzel of a coffee table in the sitting room where Charlotte led them. Apparently messy meant that a stray current of air had moved some of the dust, because the home had a coldly sterile air to it—if it ever got close to truly messy, it was probably because a guest forgot to use a coaster.

In the short trip from the front door to the sitting room, Sam saw only two photographs: one was of Charlotte as a bride, and she was beautiful in it, although he thought he could detect a trace of her hard life in the eyes, perhaps in the way she set her jaw; the other was of Charlotte and Norman together, perhaps taken on an anniversary because both of them were dressed up and they looked much closer to their current ages. That told Sam a little about this woman and about her life. The house itself told him a little more. It was obvious from the furniture, the color palette, and the use of space that poor, befuddled Norman hadn't had a say in the house—beyond his choice of slippers, apparently. If Charlotte had felt any compunctions about spending her husband's money, it was hard to tell from the way she'd done up the place.

Once Charlotte had seen them into the sitting room, she caught Norman's arm, mouthed a silent apology toward them, and nudged her husband back into the hallway.

"I really think I overdid it," Norman was mumbling as they moved away together. "Did I tell you about the Irish hooligan who tried to break down the door today? Redheaded, nasty little thing."

"Well," Sam said, "I feel slightly better knowing he's a horrifying old racist. What's our move here?"

Rufus smacked Sam's arm. "He's like a million years old." He hung his sunglasses on his collar. "This might be radical," he continued, shifting to watch Charlotte leading Norman farther away. "I might tell her the truth."

Sam thought about it for a minute and then grunted. "Do you feel up to it?"

"Not really, but if I cry a little, she might feel bad for me."

Reaching down, Sam took Rufus's hand and squeezed it once.

Then Charlotte's heels clicked back toward them, and when she appeared in the opening, she said, "I'm very sorry about that. Norman gets tired so easily these days. I don't even think I got your names."

Rufus smiled brightly, stood from the seat he'd taken on the sofa, but his expression dissolved a little as he spoke. "It's… Rufus O'Callaghan. My mother was Daisy."

Charlotte froze midstep and clutched the gaudy, expensive necklace she wore. "E-excuse me?"

"Daisy," Rufus repeated. "Do you remember—for fuck's sake!" He lunged, grabbed Charlotte's arm as she fell backward, and struggled as she stumbled forward into his hold. "Sam, holy shit, I think I killed her!"

"For the love of God," Sam said, launching off the sofa to help him. Together, they maneuvered her onto the sofa, where Sam stood, eyeing her pale face and closed eyes and shallow breathing. "What the fuck happened?"

"I don't know. She pulled a Southern belle," Rufus protested. He left the room, ran down the long hallway of the brownstone, a door slammed against a wall, and a moment later, Rufus appeared with a wet washcloth. He put it on Charlotte's forehead and waved a hand in front of her face. "Lady, come on. Wake up. Jesus Christ, even *I'm* not this dramatic."

Charlotte's eyes fluttered a little and slowly opened. "Wh-who are you?"

"If I say it again, you might actually stop breathing," Rufus remarked.

Charlotte sat up in a rush, the soaking wet washcloth falling into her lap. She pointed at Sam and asked, "You're not Daisy's little boy. Who're *you*?"

"My name's Sam. I'm the pony in this dog-and-pony show, I think. More importantly, who are you? Charlotte or Crystal? Which one is it really?"

Her jaw went slack. "C-Crystal... my God. No one's called me that in twenty years."

Rufus made a so-so motion with his hand. "Seventeen."

She looked at him and then Sam again. "Where did you hear that name?"

"Juliana," Sam said. "And don't go fainting again just because she's another blast from your past. You might not realize it yet, but you're in a leaky boat on an ocean of shit. You help us, we help you. You—" He turned to Rufus. "What was the expression?"

"Southern belle," Rufus supplied.

"That's right: you pull another Southern belle, and we're out of here. You can deal with this psycho by yourself when he catches up to you."

Charlotte's face blanched.

Rufus crouched beside the couch and put a hand on her back. "Don't worry. Take a deep breath. Sam isn't much of a people person," he said, turning to glare up at him.

Charlotte realized, after a moment, her pressed slacks were soaking wet, and she picked up the washcloth. "Juliana... Jesus Christ," she swore, sounding very unlike her Park Slope persona. "What the—heck—is going on? What psycho?"

Rufus patted her back while asking, "This might be a stretch, but think real hard—I'm talking back to the late '90s when Daisy was still—"

Charlotte turned in her seat and grabbed one of Rufus's hands. "Oh my God. *Daisy*. And Rufus. Look at you, all grown—"

Rufus stopped patting. "Yeah, all grown up and too skinny, I know. Look, we need to ask you some questions. About Daisy. About who you think might have had reason to hurt her."

"You must be kidding."

"Do I look like a stand-up comic?" Rufus retorted before he ground his teeth and took a deep breath through his nose. "Please think about this. It's important."

Charlotte furrowed her brows and began to shake her head, then her expression faltered, like an old television stuck between stations. "I don't know who killed your mother, Rufus. I really don't. Not her or—or any of those girls. But...." She glanced at Sam. "Mac wasn't someone you wanted to be around when he was in a mood. You know?"

"He was a mean fucker?" Sam said. "Got rough?"

Charlotte nodded. "Sometimes, yes."

"I don't remember him hitting girls," Rufus replied.

Charlotte's gaze darted to him. "In private. Daisy hid you from the worst of it."

"I'll be sure to put her in for the Mother of the Year Award."

"What about any of Daisy's clients?" Sam said. "You picked up some of them, right?"

"Do you remember Jimmy? He was a customer," Rufus added.

"Jimmy?" She said that name like she was tasting it for the first time. "*Jimmy*. Yes. I mean—a hundred years ago. I remember him," she answered.

"You probably need to tell her all of it," Sam said. "Start at the beginning."

"Start at the beginning?" Charlotte echoed while she cast Sam a look. "What is going on?"

Rufus laid out the bare bones of their investigation, starting with Daisy's death and filling in enough pieces for her to understand why the two of them were standing in her brownstone with a wet washcloth. When he'd finished, Rufus glanced at Sam.

"And the clock's ticking," Sam said. "This guy is starting to kill again."

Charlotte was dabbing the corners of her eyes and seemingly fighting back something worse that was lodged in her throat. "Daisy was a sweet girl," she said at length, voice wavering a little.

Rufus didn't reply.

"But I simply *don't* understand what any of this has to do with men from a lifetime ago."

"That's one of the things we're trying to figure out," Sam said. "Which pieces of the puzzle fit, and which don't. Jimmy's one of the names that's come up in our investigation. Mac's another. A hustler named George. You recognized Jimmy's name, though."

"I remember Jimmy," Charlotte confirmed, setting a hand against her chest. "But I remember a lot of johns. I wish I didn't, but it's not something I've ever been able to erase from my memory, you know?"

"Jimmy used to see Daisy on Mondays," Rufus prompted.

Charlotte rolled her eyes. "I wouldn't know that. But when she—well, I took on some of her clients. Jimmy included. But I met Norman soon after that."

"So talk about Jimmy," Sam said. "What did he look like? How did he act? Did he bring you presents? Did he get rough? Did he smoke a particular kind of cigarette? What kind of weird stuff got him off? At this point, any detail might help, so let's hear it."

Rufus met Sam's eyes. "I really could do without hearing what got him off."

"Jimmy wasn't some kind of sex freak," Charlotte interjected, looking up at the two of them. "Do I need to remind you this was twenty—"

"Seventeen," Rufus corrected.

Charlotte's cheeks were finally regaining a bit of color. "*Seventeen* years ago. I don't recall what the hell got him off, but it wasn't anything worth remembering. And you say rough like that wasn't the norm. A working girl who didn't go home with a black eye had a good boy for a client."

"All right," Sam said. "We'll do this the hard way. Hair?"

Charlotte puffed her cheeks out like some sort of animal on the defense. "Blond. Jimmy was blond."

"Height?"

"He was usually on his back."

"Estimate," Sam growled. "How closely did things line up?"

Rufus was frowning a little. "Daisy was just over five feet. He towered over her. So I'd guess Jimmy was at least six feet."

Charlotte rubbed at the wet spot in her lap from the cloth. "Sounds right," she grumbled.

"Eyes?" Sam said.

"It was dark," she protested. Then a startled look overcame her features, like a long-lost memory suddenly dragged to the surface. "I remember he smelled like Misty Lights. That cigarette with the rainbow package? Gosh. This was so long ago—Rufus, you were a tiny thing when those were popular. But I remember it always made me laugh, and I told Daisy, because those were ladies' cigarettes. He'd share them with Daisy when he came around."

"Good," Sam said. "Good. Any clues about where he lived?"

"No idea," she said, although her tone had changed. "I assumed he was local to the Manhattan area. No reason for a john living in Brooklyn or Queens to come all the way to the Ramble for a bit of action, you know?"

Sam wasn't entirely sure that was true, especially if the john liked to chop up the trade, but he didn't press the point. "What about his work? Callused hands? Bad back? Complained about being on his feet? Smelled like a butcher's shop?"

"Oh my goodness," Charlotte said, and she tittered a little. "No. He smelled fine. Looked fine, too. The girls were always jealous that Daisy got the lookers."

Rufus rolled his eyes to the ceiling. "And I get the one sperm donation that looked like this," he said, motioning to himself.

Charlotte glanced at Rufus, to Sam, and back at Rufus. "Well… anyway. Jimmy was… nice to look at. Fit. Built." Her face grew bright red, and she tugged at the sleeves of her expensive blouse. "The only time he ever got… mean was when you didn't do what he wanted. It could be anything. You were too slow answering the door. You got him off too fast or too slow. Once, he brought me some cigarettes; when I told him I didn't smoke, he slapped me. Split my lip right here."

Nodding, Sam looked at Rufus. "Anything else? Did he wear a ring? Did he mention family? I'm not just talking about a wife. Christ, did he say anything at all?"

Charlotte slowly got to her feet. She awkwardly placed her hands on the wet spot of her pants. "No, I never saw a ring. He never talked about family, either. Sometimes he'd tell me that he wanted a girl like me. But… do you know how often we heard shit—crap—like that? The only man who ever meant it was Norman."

They tried for another fifteen minutes to get something else significant out of Charlotte, but the time was wasted; Charlotte became steadily more and more focused on "a little glass" of chardonnay, which Sam refused to let her get. Finally, though, Sam realized he wasn't going to get anything else out of her that was useful, so he conceded. He and Rufus let themselves out while Charlotte clip-clopped toward the kitchen.

"Christ," Sam muttered, listening to the racing footsteps. "You'd think it was the Kentucky Derby in there."

Rufus was rubbing the lenses of his sunglasses with his shirt. "What the fuck did we glean from that, Sherlock?"

Sam blinked. "Not a whole lot, unfortunately. Mac got rough. Jimmy got rough. The world is full of guys who like smacking a girl around, but I'd still like to talk to those two shitbags. What's next? Bushwick?"

Rufus hopped down the brownstone stairs in response.

"Lead the way," Sam said as they set off. He was already playing Brooklyn Beards again, and he was up three French handlebars by the time they got to the end of the block.

CHAPTER
FOURTEEN

Rufus wasn't happy about hunting down Mac Stevens. Not because Mac was a violent pimp who'd had a long-standing history with Rufus's murdered mother. No. At that particular moment, the most frustrating goddamn thing about the fucker was that they had to take the G, and connecting anywhere in Brooklyn was always *an event*. Because when the G promised to get you to your destination in thirty minutes, you'd better plan to be walking down those subway steps over an hour and a half later.

"You know what I'd kill for?" Rufus asked as they walked toward Kosciuszko Street. "One of those soft-serve cones. Vanilla. Covered in chocolate sprinkles. The rainbow ones are good too, but Daisy never let me have those." Rufus glanced sideways at Sam. "You know, a few years ago a bunch of ice cream truck drivers got busted in this multimillion-dollar scam? Long Island City, I think. The fucking cops called it Operation Meltdown."

"So let's get a cone," Sam said.

Rufus waved one hand. "I doubt we'd find any out and about. It's too cold."

"Ok," Sam said. "So no cone."

Rufus looked at Sam again. "Can I borrow your phone?"

"Are you going to search for ice cream trucks?"

Rufus stopped walking and smiled. "No. I like that idea, but I need to call Erik. I should have done it last night, to be honest."

With a grunt, Sam unlocked his phone and handed it over.

Rufus tapped in the number he'd memorized months ago, put the phone to his ear, and touched Sam's arm as he counted the rings. Maybe it was the novelty of being able to touch without fear that he was stressing Sam out, or maybe because Rufus found it comforting, but he had no intention of stopping unless he was told to.

"Erik?" he said the minute the line was picked up but before anyone could get a word in. "Guess who."

"I'm guessing it's my fucking good-for-nothing fuckup CI who can't be bothered to pick up a fucking phone when a fucking hooker gets fucking chopped to bits right after he starts talking about a serial killer from twenty fucking years ago." With what sounded like a massive effort, Erik drew in a breath. "How am I doing so far?"

"Christ, Erik. My ears. I'm practically innocent." Rufus pushed the knot of tension in his chest down to his gut. "Sounds like the right guy, though."

"Explain yourself."

"Do you want the build-up or just the denouement?"

For a moment, the only answer was the thunder of Erik's phone hammering against something. A desk, probably.

"Every. Fucking. Detail. Right now, Rufus, or you're gonna find out real fast how well suited you are to the food-service industry."

"I didn't do anything," Rufus protested. "I mean, I sure fuck didn't *kill* anyone. I went to Central Park last night to—to talk to an old friend. That's all. And then we found her—Honey—dead. I called in the anonymous tip and ditched my phone."

After a moment, Erik said, "You're literally talking to me on a phone."

"It's not mine. But call this number if you need me."

"Are you still with the living mountain?"

Rufus hesitantly smiled. "Yeah. I sure like him."

Sam frowned at him.

"I don't want to hear about it," Erik said. "Don't ask, don't tell was a wonder-worker. Don't know why we ever got rid of it. Where are you?"

"He's got abs you could scrub laundry on," Rufus said without missing a beat. "Hands so big, he can hold my entire ass."

"A Tickle Me Elmo has hands big enough to hold your entire ass. Where are you?"

"Tickle Me Elmo can't reach deep enough for my itch. I'm in Bushwick."

"What are you talking about?" Sam asked. Then he pointed a big finger at himself and raised an eyebrow.

Rufus waggled his eyebrows over the rims of his sunglasses. "By the way, did you find anything in your search? You said you'd look into it for me."

"I'm working on it. The pimp, I might have his record. If he's the right one—hard to say without a last name. Nothing special, though. The john, Jimmy, I'm not getting anywhere with him. I got my nose whapped for Devon Kelly, so thanks for that. He escaped, but you already knew that." Erik grunted. "People are pissed. Heads are going to roll."

Rufus was frowning as he listened. "The fuck are my tax dollars paying for if all you found out was intel I already had? By the way, Mac's last name is Stevens."

"Fuck this. I've got a very important appointment to go piss into the wind."

"Baby, you gotta stop sweet-talking me. My mountain is listening."

"I don't know what that means," Sam said. "I don't think I want to know. I'm going to buy a Coke in that CVS; no, don't say anything. I'll get you something too."

"What do you have so far on those killings?" Erik said. "I want an update."

Rufus watched Sam cross the street and open the door to the CVS. "I got some intel from a woman who left the scene in the early 2000s. Violent pimps and violent johns smacked some girls around, but no one she thought would cut someone up."

"Who's your girl?" His voice sharpened. "She's in Brooklyn?"

"Yuppie-central," Rufus answered, still watching the pharmacy. "But don't harass her. I already did that, and I almost killed her by mentioning Daisy."

"Well, I'm going to need her name, whether it kills her or not. I've got some six packs from the good old days. I want her to take a look; maybe she'll be able to point out Jimmy."

"Charlotte Davis. When she was working, she went by

Crystal."

Another grunt. "I'll try to get out there in a day or two."

"Thanks, babe." Rufus pulled the phone back, hit End, and looked up in time to watch Sam return. "Good timing," he called. "What'd I get?"

"Jalapeño Cheetos and Squirt. That'll be two fifty-nine."

"I.O.U.," Rufus answered, offering the cell in exchange for the snacks.

"You're lucky you're cute," Sam said as he opened his Coke.

Rufus shoved his bottle into his jacket pocket and opened the Cheetos as he began walking again. "Pretty sure Mac's place is either on this block or the next," he explained. They crossed the street, and a Manhattan-bound J train rumbled overhead on the elevated platform. A customer exited a pizza place, and the heat and smell of yeast and marinara sauce followed him as he hurried to his double-parked car.

"Did he give you anything?" Sam asked.

"Not really. I think I had more than he did. But he's pretty pissed at me. I think I owe him." He looked at Sam, ate another handful of Cheetos, and asked, "What should I get him? A sweater or something?"

"Yes. You should get him a sweater."

"You're being sarcastic, but in that way that makes it hard to read." Rufus finished the Cheetos by the time they reached the end of the block, and he tossed the bag into an overflowing trash bin. "It's kind of hot," he continued. "A turn-on."

"I'm so happy to hear that."

"Ok, stop it," Rufus said before jogging across the street.

The next block was residential, made up of single-family homes, new apartment complexes still gleaming with clean brick and bright chrome, as well as hundred-year-old brownstones. He pointed to a dark-colored building about halfway down the block. The yard was overgrown, the fence long neglected, and there were posters on the front door that suggested the building might have recently been condemned.

"I think that's the one," Rufus said quietly.

"Any chance you'll let me go first?"

Rufus took his sunglasses off. "Didn't we have this conversation once before?"

"Yes, and as I recall, that didn't go particularly well." Sam studied the building. "Which unit?"

Rufus blew out a big breath. "Fuck me. I don't know. We should check them all."

"Ok. And if I tell you to stay put while I check them?"

"I will disobey."

Sam rolled his shoulders a few times, nodded, and said, "Then I'll try not to shoot you in the back."

"Oh my God, fine. If it'll make you feel big and manly, you go first." Rufus yanked open the rusty gate and motioned for Sam.

Sam took the steps two at a time and gave the door an experimental push; it opened easily, and he headed inside, Rufus on his heels. The interior of the massive home was completely dark, with sunlight only poking through a partially opened curtain of one window and another that'd been broken and boarded up with plywood that had a fallen-out knot in the middle. The floor was littered with debris and dust, and the surrounding rooms had closed and locked doors like each floor of this once single-family residence had been revamped into apartments or rooms-to-rent over the last few decades. A few pieces of furniture had been left behind in the move-out, broken and discarded in the corners. The dust on the floor was undisturbed except where they had walked, and when Sam cocked his head, Rufus pointed up.

"The notice said this place is going to be knocked down," Rufus whispered. "Be careful of rotten floors or stairs."

"Ok," Sam said. "You're definitely going first."

"Are you serious?" Rufus gave Sam a shove from behind. "You wanted to impress me."

Flipping the bird, Sam moved ahead, testing each step before trusting his weight to the next section of floor.

Rufus followed closely behind Sam, taking the same steps and wincing every time something creaked and groaned. He couldn't help but imagine falling through the floor and having his body found after winter when the brownstone was bulldozed in favor of another one of those swanky new complexes.

But despite the handrail wobbling under his grip and the final step of the next staircase easing down like Rufus had stepped on a marshmallow, they reached the second floor without killing themselves. These doors were all locked too, and when Rufus gestured up again, Sam took the lead on the stairs.

At the third floor, Rufus wiped the dirt and grime from his palms onto his jeans. "Fuck this, I'm taking the fire escape on the way down."

"Fire escape might be even worse."

"I'll take my chances," Rufus muttered, before grabbing Sam's arm and pointing to the closest door on the left. "This one. Look at the lock plate—the wood around it is splintered."

Drawing the gun from its holster at the small of his back, Sam set himself near the door. He didn't do anything that Rufus could see for a moment, and then he shouldered into the room, moving hard and fast, the pistol coming up as he swept the room. His steps were measured but quick. He moved out of sight, and Rufus heard another door open and *thwack* against a wall.

"Clear," Sam called back.

Rufus slipped into the room. The dust was heavy in the air, there was a mattress on the floor, a chair beside the window, the backrest broken and hanging awkwardly near the floor. He tiptoed to the second door and poked his head into what was a bathroom. "No Mac," he stated, turning toward Sam.

With the toe of his sneaker, Sam knocked over the chair; it cracked against the bare boards, and the sound echoed through the house. He crouched and inspected the bottom of the chair and then said, "Mattress?"

Rufus leaned against the bathroom doorjamb. "*Yeah…* I'm not getting near that thing. Who knows what it's seen."

"Baby," Sam said, but he did snap off the chair's already dangling backrest and use it to raise the mattress by one edge.

Rufus pointed as a spot became visible when Sam lifted the mattress. "Sure hope that stain is just pee."

"Maybe it's rat juice."

Rufus made a face and slipped into the bathroom. "You're gross." He checked the medicine cabinet—a blister of Tylenol probably a decade old, an opened box of condoms, and a bottle of Aqua Net that looked retro. "Hear me?" he called. "*Gross.* Who says that—rat juice?" He shut the mirrored door, finagled his knuckle under the toilet lid, and raised it. Nothing but discoloration and no water. Rufus unbuttoned the cuffs of his jacket, pulled the fabric over his hands the best he could, so as to limit the possibility of leaving prints, then picked up the tank lid.

"Ah, Sam?"

"I think I found more rat juice."

"Ok, Rat King. But I found a knife."

Sam's heavy, hurried steps came toward him.

Rufus balanced the tank lid on the sink and pointed inside at a four-inch folding knife with black matte coating on the blade. "I don't think that's rat juice on the blade."

"Do you have gloves?"

"Why the fuck would I be carrying gloves?"

"We need something to lift it out without getting prints on it. And without smudging any prints that might already be there. What about your beanie? Shit, never mind. Hair."

"How dare you even suggest that," Rufus said with a dead-serious tone. He yanked open the medicine cabinet again and suggested, "What about an old condom? You can stick your fingers inside, not me."

Sam held out a hand. When Rufus passed over a foil-wrapped Trojan, Sam ripped open the package and slid two fingers inside the condom. The latex looked dry and brittle, and he grimaced as he reached into the tank. Then he hesitated and handed over his phone.

"Pictures," he said. "Lots of them. Flash and no flash. Every angle you can think of."

Rufus took the cell, turned the camera on, and started taking photographs. "This is like an art installation—the condom and the knife." He turned on the flash. "We could sell this collection for a cool mil. Call it something like *Love Hurts*."

Lifting the knife by the joint, Sam said, "Maybe then you'd be able to pay for your own fucking Cheetos. Did you get the serial number?"

"*Oui, mon capitaine*," Rufus said as he swiped through the pictures. "There's no less than a hundred, I think we're good." He glanced up. "And I like when *you* buy me Cheetos."

"Good, because we're too far down that road to stop now. Why is there blood on the blade?"

"I don't know. I didn't put it there."

"I mean, why not clean the blade? Hell, why not get rid of it somewhere you're not squatting?" Sam frowned. "Jesus, I mean, Honey was cut up pretty bad. Do you think this is our guy?"

Rufus bit his lower lip. "It's a little too coincidental, finding a bloody knife the day after Honey's all cut up, isn't it?"

Sam nodded. "Do you want to call Erik again?"

"Do I have to?" Rufus whined.

"I think he'd like to know. Consider this your disgusting cat-hair sweater or whatever you were going to give him."

Rufus rolled his eyes. "Cat-hair sweater…." He picked the most recent number in the call history. He put the phone to his ear as Erik picked up. "Hey. I found a thing you might want to know about."

"Christ have mercy. What now? Did you track down a hooker's sister's dogwalker's neighbor's weed dealer's best friend who happened to also live near the Ramble twenty years ago?"

"Are you questioning the way I get you information? Because I can stop." Rufus watched as Sam carefully returned the knife to its hiding spot in the toilet tank.

"And buy those disgusting sour cream and onion Pringles how? With what money? Don't bullshit me. What do you have?"

Rufus made a sucking sound between his teeth, high-pitched enough that it would carry, *and hurt*, through the line. "I went looking for the pimp. Mac. He's not home, but I found a knife and there's blood on it."

Erik groaned. "Christ, you didn't touch anything, did you? Stay there. I'm on my way. And in case I wasn't clear: do not fucking touch anything. Just grab on to each other's peckers and hold tight."

"You're so sweet." Rufus supplied Erik with the exact address and hit End. "Erik's on his way to grab the knife. He told me to hold your dick while I wait."

"Pass."

"You don't think it's romantic?" Rufus continued. "The condemned building, the stink, the bloody knife?"

"And the rat juice. Don't forget the rat juice."

Rufus stepped into the bedroom again. "I'm turned-on. I can barely contain myself."

CHAPTER
FIFTEEN

Whatever Erik had meant by *I'm on my way*, it apparently didn't signify *right now*. Or maybe that was a New York thing. Maybe, for all Sam knew, everybody in this whole fucking city was *on their way*, all of them emerging years later from those goddamn subways. And when Erik did arrive, snapping for them to talk quickly before the crime scene unit got there, it wasn't exactly an improvement.

From the bathroom doorway, Sam watched as Erik took several photographs of the knife still inside the tank.

"You didn't touch it, did you?" Erik asked for what had to be the twelfth time.

Sam gave Rufus a very pointed look.

"Does it fucking look like we touched it?" Rufus asked.

"Go wait in the hall," Erik said. Probably the twelfth time for that too.

"Does it look like it could be a match?" Sam asked.

"Oh, sure," Erik said. "Let me just compare it to my photographic memory of the victim's wounds and then access my perfect internal database of forensic pathology."

"It's because you all spend so much time breathing in particles of dog shit," Sam said to Rufus. "That's the only reason I can think of for why everybody in the whole city is like this."

"Don't be mean," Rufus murmured.

"Hall," Erik said. "Now."

Sam followed Rufus out of the bedroom. They listened while Erik moved around inside: footsteps, the crinkle of plastic, the squeak of rusted hinges. Then the sound of the mattress hitting the floorboards.

"What the fuck is this?" Erik asked from inside the room.

When Rufus looked at Sam, Sam said, "He's a smart guy; he'll probably figure out the rat juice on his own."

Finally Erik emerged from the bedroom carrying a sealed evidence bag, the bloodstained knife visible inside the plastic. The detective stripped off his gloves, pocketed them, and eyed each of them before his gaze settled on Rufus.

"This Mac Stevens guy," Erik said, joggling the evidence bag. "Anything you want to add to what you've told me so far? One minute you're asking me to look up records on an older-than-fuck pimp, and the next thing I know, you're here, and you just happen to find a bloody knife where this guy's been known to squat."

"It's not a fucking coincidence," Sam said. "We're

investigating, and an investigation follows a line of inquiry. We're not doing fucking magic tricks."

"And who the fuck are you?" Erik said, moving into Sam's space and drilling a finger into his chest. "I looked you up. What was that shit at Benning right before you left?"

"Don't touch me," Sam said.

"I asked you a question," Erik said, jabbing a finger into Sam's chest. "You walk away from Benning and people are dead. The last time you were here, cops ended up dead. What the fuck are you doing back in my city?"

"I said don't touch me."

"Hey, hey!" Rufus pushed Erik back and moved to stand between the two. "He's here because I called him, Erik. *I* called *him*. Get it? Back off and talk to me."

Shaking his head, Erik started to answer. Then his hand dipped into his pocket and came out with a phone. He held it to his ear, said, "Weaver," and listened. His expression tightened, and after a moment he said, "Shit balls. Again? Ok. Ok. No, I'm all the way up the inner sphincter of Brooklyn; I'll get there as soon as I can, but I've got to wait for the techs before I can—no! Don't let anybody fucking move the body—no, dipshit, not anybody, not even the ME. Yes, 'that kind' of anybody." The last was delivered in a tone of pure scorn, and then he disconnected. His eyes narrowed as he studied Sam and Rufus and seemed to replay what he had said.

Rufus plastered on the most sickeningly sweet smile he seemed to have in his repertoire. "Was that your mom? She seems nice."

Erik shoved his phone back in his pocket. "You boys did some good work. Let's leave it at that. Stay away from this case."

Rufus grabbed Erik's shoulder before he could bully his way past them and to the stairs. "That call was in relation to this case, wasn't it? This might have started off as me asking for a favor, but it sure as fuck isn't going to end that way. You need my help, so spill," he demanded.

"Not that it's any of your information, but that call didn't have anything to do—"

"Bullshit," Sam said.

"—with what you've been doing, and—"

"Extreme bullshit," Sam said.

"—and," Erik said, his face reddening as he tried to keep control, "when I tell you that I want you to back off from an investigation, it's for your own safety—"

"Arrogant, head-up-your-own ass bullshit," Sam said.

"—and also your obligation as a confidential informant—"

"Petty bullshit."

"—who has agreed to—Jesus Christ! Will you let me finish one fucking sentence?"

Sam looked at Rufus.

Rufus drew his hands to his chest and said, "Erik… you really do care. Want to go steady? We can share a soda pop and stay up past our bedtime and you can tell me everything about who the fuck was just found dead."

"Stay away from this case," Erik said, pointing a finger at Rufus. "Stay away from it. Stay away from it. Am I being perfectly clear? That's an order, by the way. If I see your ass anywhere near Central Park, I'll drop both your asses in the closest cell and forget about you for a week."

Rufus shifted his hands into a defensive posture and said in a colorful accent, "Wouldn't dream of buttin' into your case, copper."

"Don't," Erik said. "And don't let the BFG change your mind. Now get the fuck out of here before I have to explain who you are to somebody who matters."

When Sam and Rufus had reached the street, the brownstone's front door still closing behind them, Sam said, "He reminds me of that actor I want to punch in the mouth all the time."

"Ryan Gosling," Rufus supplied without missing a beat.

"That sounds right. Central Park?"

"Just can't stay away, can we?"

CHAPTER
SIXTEEN

Rufus and Sam crossed along Bow Bridge, once again heading in the direction of the Ramble. The sky was dark by the time they'd reached Central Park, and lampposts cast harsh lines of color across them as they passed underneath. The air was crisp and the wind stirred up the smell of dead leaves. Rufus hunched his shoulders and tucked his chin against his chest as a particularly cold gust came off the water.

"Every time we've crossed this bridge," Rufus started, only raising his head as the wind calmed, "it's not been for romantic reasons. Ridiculous, don't you think?"

"That's an easy thing to fix."

Rufus caught Sam's look. "From your lips." He slowed

and inclined his head toward a gaggle of uniformed officers barricading the routes into the forest. The whole area was a mess of shadows and orange tungsten against a northeast autumn backdrop. "Is that Ophelia?"

"Could be. Yeah, it is—look how she's ripping that guy a new asshole."

Rufus made a sound under his breath before rushing ahead. He slid up behind Ophelia as her request to be let on the path was denied and she looked about ready to brute force her way past the other cops. Rufus slipped his arm through one of hers and gave a yank. "And you call me a pain in the ass," he chastised.

"What the—" She turned to shove Rufus before pausing. "Red?"

Rufus waggled his eyebrows and tugged her arm again. "Come with me. Leave these nice boys alone." He looked at the police standing at the barricade, who seemed relieved by his intervention, before adding, "Before they piss themselves."

"Partners in crime," Sam said when he saw Rufus holding Ophelia's arm.

"Oh, what the hell," Ophelia groaned as she was dragged toward Sam. "You too? Did you move here? Do I need to start mentally fucking prepping myself for double-trouble?"

"Based on those shoes," Sam said, "you need to start mentally fucking prepping your wardrobe first. Boots when you're off duty, Officer Hayes?"

Ophelia gave Rufus a shove to free herself of his hold. "You got a problem with my choice in footwear, Mr. Auden?"

Sam rolled his eyes. "Never get into it with a New Yorker," he muttered to himself. "Why can't I fucking remember that?"

Rufus rocked back and forth on the balls of his feet. "I can't believe you haven't figured that out yet." He gave Sam a cocky grin.

Ophelia put her hands out. "Both of you can it. The fuck are you doing here, Rufus?"

Rufus shrugged. "I'm on a walk. Bow Bridge is very romantic. Isn't it romantic, Sam?"

"You said something about my lips."

"There, see?"

Ophelia ran a hand through her short bob of black hair. "Just once, just fucking once, I wish you'd be straight the first time around."

"Too easy," Sam said, shaking his head at Rufus.

Rufus's face grew pink, but he said nothing.

The vertical crease between Ophelia's eyebrows deepened. "Why're you here?"

"Heard someone died," Rufus said, lowering his voice.

"It could have been a heart attack," Ophelia said.

"Sure," Rufus answered. "Could have been an allergic reaction to a Nutri-Grain bar they had in their pocket. Could have been a freak bolt of lightning. Except someone died in the *Ramble*. So I don't think it was a heart attack or an allergy or an act of God. And you're here, which says something."

"And Erik," Sam said.

Ophelia's eyes darted to Sam. "Erik who? You mean, Detective Weaver?"

Sam grunted, scanning the cordon, obviously hoping to spot Erik deeper in the Ramble.

"I heard on the scanner," Ophelia said after a beat. "Another girl was found in the Ramble."

"You don't work around here," Rufus pointed out.

"No. I know that. But a second girl dead? I mean, was

she killed during the day or just found in the daytime? I haven't heard from Juliana all week." Ophelia crossed her arms and looked at the other uniformed officers. "I guess I wanted to make sure it wasn't her."

"Yeah, well, when you find her, tell her thanks for a shit-heap of nothing," Sam said. "What did those guys on the line tell you?"

"You've seen her?" Ophelia asked, eyes brightening.

"Saw her," Rufus confirmed. "Talked to her. Got reprimanded by her. She was ok, as of last night."

Ophelia nodded automatically. "Look, if you say Juliana is ok, then thanks. That's what I needed to know, and it's a relief to hear. The guys on the line are keeping everyone out—Weaver's in there with the ME and someone from CSU." She looked at Rufus. "Why was Juliana handing you your ass?"

"I don't know."

"Rufus—"

"Don't get all twisted up, Ophelia. It's nothing. Don't worry."

"It's nothing," she echoed, jutting a thumb at Sam but keeping her gaze locked with Rufus's. "I don't think it's nothing when he's here."

"It's a personal thing," Rufus said at length.

"Don't be a dick," Sam said. "Tell her and ask for her help."

Rufus felt like a chastised child. He stuffed his hands into his jacket pockets and said, "My mother, Daisy, was murdered in the Ramble seventeen years ago. I was asking Juliana for some help figuring out... you know, who did it."

For the first time since she'd been dragged away from the barricade, Ophelia's features softened. "Oh. All those girls in the late '90s?"

Rufus nodded.

"I'm sorry."

"Yeah. Thanks. I sniffed around Cold Cases a month ago, and suddenly it seems like girls are dropping dead again."

Ophelia drew in a breath and let it out slowly. "So you're not letting it rest."

"I can't. Not now."

She looked at Sam. "And you're helping him figure out… so this is related?" Ophelia turned and pointed toward the officers.

"That's about it," Sam said.

Rufus looked at the tree line as voices broke the relative quiet. He could make out Erik first, then who he guessed were personnel from the City Medical Examiner's office hauling a gurney across the uneven ground. "He's gonna break a kneecap if he sees us."

"Wait," Ophelia said, taking Rufus's jacket sleeve. "If I hear anything from my girls in there, about Daisy or about who might be in that fucking body bag, I'll see what I can forward your way."

Rufus took his sunglasses off and narrowed his eyes. "Really?"

She nodded.

"Sam," Rufus said. "Give her your number. Call him, ok? I'm down a phone at the moment."

Ophelia added Sam's number to her cell, pocketed it, and said, "I'll do what I can, Red."

"Appreciate it," Rufus answered.

"Shit," Sam said. "Body bags. Plural. Look."

CHAPTER
SEVENTEEN

They were halfway across Bow Bridge when Rufus turned and leaned against the parapet. Sam followed; the stone was cool and slightly porous where he rested his elbows on it. The sky was hazy with light from the park lamps. Where Sam could make out the leaves, he could see that autumn had already claimed some of the trees, orange and rust-colored and crimson, but there were evergreens too, a spruce like a flicker of blue-green flame. The wind had died, and ahead, the lake was cut glass except where a pair of guys were kicking rocks into it. Both of them were in all black—black t-shirts (Metallica, of course, and Cannibal Corpse), and black jeans, and black Chucks—with stringy hair and features accentuated with dark makeup. On the opposite bank, a pair of girls in

Pikachu cosplay were blasting something from a portable Bluetooth speaker.

"Good Christ," Sam said.

"AKB48 makes me want to take an ice pick to my eardrums," Rufus growled, looking in the direction of the Pikachus and pop music.

"Somebody should tell them to show some fucking respect."

Rufus said, "This reminds me of high school cafeterias, though. They're the cute cheerleaders at one table and those d-bags are, in all likelihood, probably drama kids. I was at the dropout table."

"I don't remember anybody in my high school dressed like a Pokémon. It was bad enough just to be one of the kids who liked Pokémon."

Rufus shuffled sideways and asked in a low voice, "Did you catch 'em all?"

Sam snorted, but he could feel his face heat.

Rufus smiled and nudged Sam's shoulder with his own. "What're we going to do?"

"Ophelia says she's going to call when she knows who was killed. If she finds out, I guess I should say. But it's probably a safe bet that it's another working girl. Two of them, this time. Christ, is he accelerating? Or was one a witness? Or is he changing his pattern? We could wait, ask around when some of the trade shows up, but I think everybody's going to find somewhere else to be until the cops finish processing the scene. That could be hours. It could be days."

Rufus nodded. "I agree. What about the knife, then? Maybe there's something we can learn without having to wait for techs and labs and Erik to hem and haw over sharing details."

"We already know one thing: this asshole didn't use

that knife to kill today. So much for continuity. It's weird as fuck that Mac had this knife hidden where he likes to squat, but it's even weirder that he'd go out and kill without it." Sam drew out his phone, pulled up his photos, and tapped on the first picture of the knife. Angling the screen toward Rufus, he said, "What do you see?"

"I see a nasty knife in an even nastier toilet." Rufus pursed his lips before adding, "And one guy's sexy, condom-sheathed hand."

"Right. Well." Sam swiped forward. "Who carries a knife like this one? First thing that comes to mind."

Rufus was thoughtful for a moment. He studied the early-evening crowd that'd gathered near the police barricade in order to watch the action. "It looks scary to me. So I'd hazard a guess that it's not common?"

"I'm not exactly an expert either." Sam hesitated, and then he zoomed in to display different parts of the knife. "Right here, on the pommel, that's to break glass. And here, on the back of the handle, that looks like it's another edged surface—maybe for cutting something that the full blade couldn't get to. The matte coating on the handle and the blade, that's a finish that's specced by the US military. Not necessarily Army issue, but a lot of manufacturers follow those specs so that a military guy can buy their gear without getting ripped a new asshole by his CO. So what does that tell us?"

Rufus returned his attention to the phone, standing shoulder to shoulder with Sam, and Sam could smell his Dial soap and sweat. "Tells me," Rufus started, "that you know a lot more than you care to admit. Also that maybe this guy either served or… wanted to? Maybe had a hard-on for military-style weapons but not the balls to get sent overseas?"

"Lots of guys like that. Cops. Hunters. Human jerk-off tissues who never moved out of Mommy's basement.

Here's another thing about this knife: it was probably expensive. You can get a decent folding knife for twenty bucks at Walmart. This was probably somewhere in the hundreds of dollars. That's a lot of money for a knife you're going to leave in a toilet, and honestly, that twenty-buck knife you could have gotten at Walmart? It would have done the job just as well. If you need this kind of knife, genuinely need it, then why dump it? And if you've got a boner for military stuff, why dump it? And if you didn't need it, why lay out the cash for it in the first place? Hell, if you're going to kill again, why dump the knife at all?" The questions were rolling now, and Sam couldn't stop himself. "And does any of that sound like Mac Stevens?"

Rufus used his finger to swipe through the photos as Sam held the phone and hypothesized. "It doesn't seem like a Mac-thing," Rufus admitted. "But it's not like I really knew him either. Could someone be framing him? Is that too over-the-top?"

The boys in black were now chucking hunks of broken asphalt at a styrofoam lid floating on the water, laughing manically at each miss. The Pikachu girls cut off their music and started screaming abuse across the lake. Sam was pretty sure he was hearing poorly accented Japanese, and he was equally sure Rufus could have identified the insults. And, probably, said them with a better accent.

"He was squatting," Sam said. "Mac, I mean. He was squatting in that place in Brooklyn, right?"

"Sure. I mean, I hope he wasn't paying rent for that condemned dump."

"But it must have been decent at some point, and he must have liked it, or he wouldn't have gone back. So that narrows down the people who might have planted the knife; they'd have to know he was crashing there first."

"I think we should research this knife angle a bit more," Rufus concluded. "It sounds unique—not something you can grab from a shelf and slap down some dollar bills for. Maybe someone with more experience with knives can point us in the direction of where a guy could purchase this."

Sam closed the photos on his phone and opened a search. "How far is it to Midtown from here?"

Rufus shrugged. "Depends where in Midtown. How in a rush are you?"

"Oh, not much. Just trying to save your scrawny ass."

Rufus squared his shoulders and prodded Sam's chest. "I'm sorry, you were saying something about my *wonderful ass*?"

"Yes. All two ounces of it. Midtown, please. We need to get to Eighth Avenue and… Forty-Third. We're going to see what the people at Holtzman Army and Navy can tell us about this knife."

Rufus corrected politely, "Forty-Third and Eighth." He started walking before mumbling, "Two ounces… you asshole."

The Pikachu girls had started throwing rocks at the boys in black, and the boys in black were alternating between trying to shield themselves, crane-like, by pulling one leg up to their chests and covering their heads with their hands, and screaming back at the girls.

"Do you have any idea what they're saying?" Sam asked.

"*Watashi wa subarashi Momotaro desu,*" Rufus repeated. "It's nonsense—something about being the Great Peach Boy…." He looked toward the girls one last time. "Shouldn't you have to have an ass to be called Peach Boy? You know, like the emoji?"

They walked south and west into the dark, the air smelling like boiled meat when the breeze shifted, the occasional joggers thumping past them, the leaves swept up by the wind and skittering across the pavement. At Seventy-Second Street, they took a subway, and Sam was proud of himself for only shoving one person while getting off the train. He was less proud of himself that that one person happened to look ninety years old and was wearing shopping bags for shoes, but to be fair, she tried to bite him first.

When they came up from the 42nd Street–Port Authority station, Rufus turned north along Eighth and then cut west again, following the flow of traffic on Forty-Third Street. The illuminated sign for a discount electronics store flickered and buzzed. The smell of fresh bread and frying falafel wafted out from the simply named DELI. They kept to the south side of the street, where temporary construction scaffolding threw shadows under the streetlights, and Sam was surprised to find that in October, in the evening, he was chilly.

On the next block, Holtzman Army and Navy was squeezed between a white awning that said $2 PIZZA - FAST, HOT, CHEAP and a black awning that said THE BLACK BOX - NIGHTMARE DREAM EMPORIUM AND PERFORMANCE ART THEATER, SPECIAL THANKS TO THE ETHEL MERMAN FOUNDATION. In contrast to both, Holtzman Army and Navy had only a printed cardboard sign stuck in the display window with the name, the hours, and two phrases: IN GOD WE TRUST, ALL OTHERS PAY CASH; and, below it, CONCEALED? NO BIG DEAL.

Glancing at each of the three storefronts in turn, Sam said, "Title of your autobiography?"

Rufus snorted, collected himself, then without warning, burst into the first truly authentic laugh Sam had heard since he arrived in the city. "Fast, hot, and cheap," Rufus said between wheezes. "Just call me Ethel!"

Sam couldn't help it; a smile slipped out.

Inside, the air smelled like oiled canvas, cheap rubber, and machismo. A pair of skinheads were examining military-style fatigues from the discount rack, and behind the counter sat a middle-aged man with a huge black beard. Sam took out his phone as he approached.

"Hi," Sam said. "We were hoping you could help us with something."

Beardy dragged his fingers through the ZZ Top–style he had going on. "Ask me anything you want, son. It's a free country."

"What can you tell me about this knife?"

Beardy took Sam's phone and held it up at an angle that suggested he needed bifocals. "Nice blade. Looks like a custom job."

"Custom means a paper trail," Rufus said quietly.

Beardy glanced away from the screen and let out a breath. "Sure, sure," he said in response to Rufus. "Wouldn't be that easy, though. I'd have to look into this a bit more—confirm the smith and whatnot to get accurate details." He offered Sam the cell. "Why do you ask? In the market for something similar?"

"Maybe," Sam said. "How custom are we talking? Is this unique? Or does it have some personalized details?"

Beardy crossed his arms over his barrel chest and puffed his cheeks. "Oh, it's unique, son. Looks like it started as a standard-issue military blade, but those additions to the handle and pommel? You wouldn't see your average enlisted man with a knife like this."

"Any idea who might have done the work?"

Beardy cast his gaze from Sam to Rufus and back again. "Sure, I got an idea or two. But I'm wary as to why you're asking for the details of another man's purchase. Could be you should just fuck off."

"Could be," Sam said, tapping the screen to advance

to the next photo. "And could be that, another day, I'd be happy to sit here and listen to you fist yourself while you talk about the Fourth Amendment or the right to privacy or whatever the fuck gets you off. But today, I'm a little short on time, and I've got a full plate. See that? That's blood, and it's all over this fucking knife. So, yes, I'm asking for the details of another man's purchase. I want to know who bought this knife. I want to know where he got it customized. I want to know where it got delivered or if he picked it up. I want to know everything you can tell me about it. Now. How fucking wary are you feeling?"

Rufus had prodded Sam when the other man started in on one of his rants, but Sam ignored him. Rufus pushed harder, even elbowed him in the ribs at one point, but Sam didn't acknowledge Rufus until he'd finished taking Beardy to task. When Sam looked at him, Rufus murmured, "Not everyone thinks it's cute when you're an asshole."

Beardy made himself look real big behind the counter. "Listen here, son. I don't know who you are, but I don't like you. I don't care what kind of trouble you or your *pal* here have gotten into—but if you're trying to pass the buck and frame some other god-fearing, law-abiding citizen for your mistakes, you can about-face and see yourself right out the front door. I got a loaded pistol under this counter, and I ain't afraid of defending myself against crackpots like you. Get me?"

Rufus was already yanking on Sam's arm before he could respond. "Let's go," he ordered. "Sam, come on."

Sam was still formulating a response when Rufus dragged him out of the store.

"God-fearing," Sam said, marching ten feet and spinning back to point a finger at Rufus. "Pass the buck. Law-abiding. No. No. No fucking way."

He was halfway to the door before Rufus caught his

arm again.

"Come on," Rufus tried. "The only thing you're going to accomplish is getting yourself shot by a nutcase."

With a grimace, Sam let himself be guided away from Holtzman Army and Navy, and at the end of the block, he shook himself free of Rufus's grip. On the other side of the street, a twink was wearing a child-sized rainbow leotard, stretching it to its limit and, in the process, committing a list of misdemeanors that started with indecent exposure.

"You know a lot of random stuff," Sam said. "Knives. Talk."

Rufus held both hands out and gave Sam *The Look*. "I'm flattered, but you need to narrow the scope a bit. Knives have been made out of flint, copper, iron… have been used for both table utensils and weapons. Some of the most famous are probably the Swiss Army knife or bowie knife. There's apparently a whole knife community these days too. They use forums to complain about the most ridiculous shit, like whether a maker's mark or serial should be allowed on the knife or if it destroys the integrity of the blade… thanks for that novel-length post, Brad in Wisconsin."

"Fuck off, Brad," Sam muttered, not really listening. Then his attention swung back to Rufus. "Wait. What about serial numbers?"

"*What*?" Rufus repeated. "Brad said they shouldn't be allowed, because it meant his blade wasn't one of a kind and it somehow belittled the artistry or something. I don't even remember how I ended up on that forum, but I left after reading his butt-hurt post."

"Are the serial numbers ever unique? Like, each blade gets a different number? Because that's some personally identifying shit right there. Or is Brad just being a whiny bitch?"

Rufus appeared to be registering the gravity of the

question. "Oh. I don't think there's a national registry, but makers who do slap serials on their designs usually supply a certificate of authenticity. Brad didn't like that either. So it's at least unique to the individual maker."

"Well," Sam said. "Let's figure that the fuck out. How do you feel about another hot dog?" Then Sam frowned. "Don't."

Rufus smiled. "You went there, not me. What's the hot dog for? Did I do good?"

"The hot dog is to keep you from dying of hunger while we figure out where this knife came from. Plus, I liked that park."

They hiked east a few long blocks, returning to Bryant Park, where they'd been only the day before. Instead of approaching the library this time, though, Sam headed directly for the same food vendor where they had eaten on their last visit. Even at this hour of the evening, there was a line, but it moved quickly. The girl in front of them was demanding princess 'roni, which Sam translated into some sort of highly processed orange pasta.

"Are you really getting a hot dog?" Sam asked as they approached the window. "Or was I projecting?"

"I'll have a hot dog," Rufus confirmed. "Since I'm pretty sure you've got an intense desire to see me deep throat something."

The girl who wanted princess 'roni was staring at them.

"This is how it ends," Sam muttered. "Arrested for corrupting a child."

Rufus glanced at the kid and stuck his tongue out.

She began to scream.

By the time the girl's father had gotten his food, hoisting her to one shoulder and bellowing to make himself heard over her screeching, Sam's ears were ringing. He ordered for himself and Rufus, and they carried the four-course meal—Rufus had added nachos, a milkshake, and cotton candy to the original order of one hot dog—over to an empty bench.

Sam held out an empty hand and coughed.

Rufus sat and stared at Sam. "I'm either going to high-five you or spit in your hand. Do you want to take your chances?"

"I want your part of the bill," Sam said, but he did move his hand back. Just to be safe.

While they ate, Sam pulled up the photos of the knife. He checked each photograph, selecting only those in which the stamped serial number was at least partially visible. Then he went through the smaller set of photographs again, double-checking the serial number and looking for any additional marks that might indicate who had crafted—or at least modified—the weapon. He borrowed a stub of pencil from the vendor and scrawled the serial number on the back of a foil hot-dog wrapper, and then he typed the number into a search engine.

The results weren't promising. The search engine informed him, with what read like sadistic glee, that there were no good results to his search. Instead, it offered him a series of white page entries with phone numbers that came close to the serial number Sam had entered.

Rufus had already downed the hot dog and was halfway through the Oreo milkshake, all the while watching Sam fiddle with his phone. He finally slid along the bench until his hip bumped Sam's, then watched over his shoulder.

"Any ideas?" Sam said.

Rufus pointed at the screen. "Hit the 'see more results' option. All these pages are bogus."

Sam tapped the screen. Halfway down the next set of results was an entry for TalkKnife, apparently a forum for knife fanatics. When Sam touched the result, it opened a forum discussion where people were posting details about their favorite knives, with several of them including screenshots of the blades and accompanying documentation.

"Certificate of authenticity?" Sam said. "That's what you were talking about?"

Rufus made a noise around the straw in his mouth before setting the cup aside and saying, "That's the same site I found Brad on! Yeah, these are the certs the makers give out—the ones who add serials, anyway. Did the search ping on a specific post? Maybe our serial matches one of the posters. If it does, we could have Erik file a search warrant for the IP address."

"I think it hit on this one," Sam said.

The post in question showed a picture of a knife that looked similar to the one they had found in Brooklyn. Also attached was a certificate of authenticity. In a burst of enthusiasm, the poster had also transcribed the information, which was probably what the search engine had identified as a possible match: a serial number that was only two digits different from the number Sam had entered into his search, and the name of the company that had sold it: Out of the Forge. A second search turned up a phone number and address for Out of the Forge, which was apparently an artisan smithy located in Butte, Montana.

"Getting closer," Sam said. He wagged the phone. "What's our play now?"

"I'll call them," Rufus offered, meeting Sam's gaze. "We tried it your way and you got feisty."

"The redhead is the even-keeled, charming one," Sam said. "What could go wrong?"

"No reason to be a jerk about it. I can be fucking charming," Rufus said defensively. "Give me your phone."

Handing over the phone, Sam said, "You're very charming. You're also kind of proving my point."

When Rufus placed the call, he set it to speakerphone. It rang once before a woman's voice came on the line. "Out of the Forge. This is Miranda. May I help you?"

Rufus looked at Sam and said, "Well, hello, Miranda! I sure do hope you can help me—I'm in a heck of a pickle. You see, I was blessed to purchase a gorgeous custom knife from y'all, but I have completely misplaced my certificate of authenticity after a cross-country move, and long story short, I'd be mighty gracious if a copy could be emailed to me. Is that something you might offer your customers?"

"Mighty gracious?" Sam mouthed.

"I think we can do that, Mr.—I'm sorry. What's your name?"

"Carmichael," Rufus said. "Rufus Carmichael. Now, I should warn you, since that purchase and this whirlwind journey across our great country, I've had a name change. Mother was remarried, a second cousin got wrapped up in the immediate family… it was ugly. So I got it legally changed—a fresh start, you understand? Yup. Same last name as my great-great-grandmother. She came to America in 1901. Anyway. I have a serial, if that's an easier way to look up the cert." Rufus grabbed the hot dog wrapper from Sam.

To Sam, the note in Miranda's voice sounded like desperation. "Yes. Fine. That'll be just fine, Mr. Carmichael."

Rufus smiled and read out the serial Sam had scribbled. "Sure do appreciate it, Miranda," he concluded.

"What kind of country bumpkin are you?" Sam whispered.

On the phone, Miranda was typing furiously, probably afraid—*afeared*, Sam corrected—that Mr. Carmichael would launch into more conversation. Then came mumbled words, Miranda's voice confused. A moment later, she said more clearly, "All right, I've got it right here, Ms., I mean,

Mr., um, Carmichael. I'll send it to the email we have on file for you—"

"Oh boy," Rufus said with a shake of his head. "I'm damn sorry about that. You see, this knife was a beautiful gift from my darling baby sister, but even though it was for me, when she placed the order—bless her heart—she accidentally registered the blade in her name. I thought I'd corrected that, but I must have plum forgot. I'll give you my personal email, though," he continued without missing a beat, giving Sam a pointed look.

Rolling his eyes, Sam recited the address.

Rufus repeated the email for Miranda. "Get that, Miss Miranda?"

"Yes," Miranda said breathlessly. "All sent. And if that's all, Mr. Carmichael, I'm going to wish you a good day and—"

Sam disconnected the call. When Rufus raised an eyebrow, he said, "You tormented her enough."

"*Tormented?*" Rufus repeated while Sam opened his email. "I was being polite and pleasant."

"Huh," Sam said. "I guess I just plum didn't notice." Without waiting for a response, he tapped his way to the mail app and refreshed it. A moment later, an email from customerservice@outoftheforge.com appeared in his inbox. He opened it, downloaded the attachment, and swore. Then he angled the screen toward Rufus so he could see the certificate of authenticity naming Charlotte Davis as the original purchaser.

CHAPTER
EIGHTEEN

Rufus shut the front door of his apartment. He turned the deadbolt, yanked off his beanie and jacket, then said, "Charlotte Davis, aka Crystal, bought the knife found in Mac's pad." He dropped his attire to the floor, kicked off his shoes, then made for the fridge. "What the fuck is going on?" Rufus retrieved a slice of cold pizza from the night before and took a bite, despite being full from a dinner of junk food at the park. "Do you think she's exacting some kind of revenge on her former pimp?" he continued around mouthfuls of bread and cheese.

"Well, we know Mac has history with those girls, including Charlotte. Beyond that, I've got no idea why the knife would be there. Fuck, for that matter, I've got no idea whose blood it might be."

Rufus gnawed on the crust. "It could be Charlotte's blood. Although, she didn't appear to be favoring any kind of wound. It could be Mac's, for that matter. Or maybe it's pig's blood and the knife was left there to frame him."

"Maybe," Sam said, already shaking his head. "Seems like it'd be easy for a lab to tell that it's not human." Crossing the small apartment, Sam copied Rufus and pulled a slice of pizza from the fridge. Between bites, he said, "Do you think Ophelia knows Charlotte's history with Mac?"

Rufus grabbed the gin bottle from atop the fridge. "I doubt it. Ophelia is my age. Juliana might be her contact in the Ramble, but there's no reason she'd be telling Ophelia juicy details of days long since passed. Do you want a glass?"

"Gin?"

"Yeah," Rufus said, giving the contents a shake. "It's Pauly Paul's. As long as you don't drink too much, you won't want to cut your left eye out in the morning."

Sam's mouth twisted. "How could I say no?"

Rufus opened an overhead cupboard to fetch a mug. He poured a bit of gin into it and offered it to Sam.

Sam took a drink, coughed, and held the mug away from him. "Jesus Christ. It might as well be paint stripper."

"Don't waste that," Rufus said. "Sooner or later, Pauly's going to catch on to who's been swiping his bottles."

Frowning, Sam took another drink, his lips peeling back as he finished. "Yeah, well, if I have any enamel left on my teeth after this, it'll be a miracle. So what are we supposed to do now? Talk to Charlotte? Confront her? Talk to Mac if we can track him down? Shit, I'd rather have my balls chopped off in a turnstile than get dragged to Brooklyn again."

Rufus let out a bark of a laugh while shaking his head. "Tell me how you really feel about Brooklyn."

"Did you forget the beards?"

Rufus rubbed his own chin and the bit of scruff he had in response. "You saying you don't want me to grow this out?"

"Come a little closer," Sam said, and then he threw back the rest of the gin, his pupils dilated, something—a smile? a smirk?—pulling at the corner of his mouth. "I've got to make an informed decision."

Rufus leaned forward. "Informed. Is that what you call it?"

"I said closer."

"Jesus Christ, are you blind?" Rufus took a step to close the distance between them.

Sam moved faster than Rufus expected, catching him around the waist with one arm, manhandling him up against the wall. His stubble scraped Rufus's cheek as he pressed against him and whispered, "What don't you understand about closer?"

Rufus felt Sam's phone buzz in his pocket.

"Ignore it," Sam said, forcing Rufus's head to one side, kissing a line down the side of his neck.

Rufus's eyes practically crossed, but then he felt the buzz again, indicating a call and not some sort of social media notification. "What—*God, yes*—what if it's Erik?" He grabbed Sam's hips, yanked their bodies together, and let out a desperate little sob as he added, "Or Ophelia?"

"I pay twenty-eight bucks a month," Sam said, teeth nipping Rufus's collarbone through the thin tee, "to some Walmart bullshit cell service for voicemail. They can earn their fucking blood money."

"Fuck, *yes*. Wait, Sam… it might be important." Rufus weakly pushed back so they could make eye contact. "Just check."

Eyes narrowed, Sam ripped the phone from his pocket. He examined the screen and answered with a grunt.

"No, it's not a fucking good time, Officer Hayes. You can call back in," a gleam in his eyes, "an hour—"

"*An hour*," Rufus laughed, grabbing the phone. "You're going to kill me," he told Sam. "Hello? Ophelia? You hear that? I'm going to die. This news better be big."

"Red, what the hell is going on?"

"I'm about to get laid for the first time in three months."

"God, your scrawny ass in some kind of sex sling. That's an image I could do without. If you can slow things down without getting your willy stuck in your zipper, I've got an update."

Rufus felt himself deflate a little. He groaned like a chastised boy. "*What?* What've you got?"

"You know our two victims from the park today?"

"Gosh, how could I forget."

"A girl who went by Chantalle, legal name Juanita Esquivel, and a guy named George Goodman." The call was staticky with Ophelia's exhale, and she added, "I think you knew him as Boy George."

"Wait, *what*?" Rufus looked at Sam. "The second body was George? How certain are you?"

"Holy shit," Sam muttered.

"Well," Ophelia said, "fingerprint ID, so pretty certain. Want to tell me what's going on here? I thought this guy was after working girls. Is he branching out?"

"I'm not a behavioral analyst," Rufus said. "I don't know why he took George out. Maybe because the guy is a pain in the ass who stuck his nose in the wrong place at the wrong time?"

Voices in the background of the call. Then a noise,

like a hand moving over the phone, and Ophelia's voice, quieter. "Red, this is serious. What is going on?"

"Don't worry, all right? Detective Weaver is handling things—he'll figure this out." Rufus took a fistful of Sam's white shirt, and repeated, "Don't worry."

"And what do you know about Weaver?"

"He's gotten me paid, looked after my ass, and hasn't let me marinate in my own juices, despite my attempts to the latter," Rufus answered.

"Yeah, well, three months isn't very long. I think it's time you stepped back from this. People are getting killed, and you're in danger. Keep your head down for a little while. You say Weaver is working on this, fine. Let me see what I can shake out on my end too."

"Are you serious?"

"Two dead girls in two days, plus a dead hustler? That's serious."

"That's not what I mean," Rufus replied. "After everything that happened in July… are we cool?"

"We're cool." Ophelia hesitated. "I'll see what I can turn up." More voices on her end of the call, and then, "I've got to go. For once in your life, do what somebody tells you and keep your head down."

Rufus couldn't help himself. He glanced at his crotch and said into the phone, "Keep it down. Right." He hit End, tossed the phone onto the countertop, and said to Sam, "Ophelia says Boy George is the second vic. She's going to dig around for anything of interest."

"Picked up some of that. Maybe I should turn the volume down on that phone."

"I was *not* expecting that other body to be George." Rufus put both hands on Sam's hips and pulled him close again. "Maybe we should look into who Chantalle, aka Juanita, was."

"Is that what you want to talk about right now?" Sam said, his hands closing around Rufus's wrists—not forcing him away, just holding on to him.

"No, but I was trying to bring my thoughts to a reasonable conclusion."

"Reasonable," Sam murmured, and his hands slid to Rufus's waistband, twisting to undo the button and then jerking hard to force the zipper down.

Rufus's hands mirrored Sam's motions. "It's not my fault Ophelia called." He swore while fighting the fastening on Sam's pants. "Are these padlocked or something?"

Sam's face was disturbingly intent as he reached down and undid the button, never tearing his gaze away from Rufus. Then he yanked down Rufus's jeans and briefs. Sliding one hand under Rufus's shirt, he spread his fingers over Rufus's belly, pinning him to the wall. Then he took Rufus in his other hand.

Rufus made a sound in his throat and knocked the back of his head against the wall. He abandoned Sam's jeans, wrapped his hands around Sam's neck, and brought their mouths together. "Sam," he whispered over and over between kisses. "I missed you so much."

"I missed you too." Sam gave a few more quick flicks of his wrist, and then he stumbled back, taking Rufus with him toward the bed. "Christ, I missed you. Christ, I missed you more than I thought possible." He was kicking his way free of his jeans, his dick poking Rufus in the thigh. His breathing accelerated, and as they fell onto the bed, he released Rufus suddenly. "Shit, shit!" He let out a slow, whistling breath, arm over his eyes. "Fuck. I thought I had this under control."

Rufus had been touching Sam, touching anything he could reach, but he stopped abruptly, Sam's words akin to laying his palm on a hot stove burner. "I thought you had your meds."

More of those slow, controlled breaths. "I do. But this is—fuck, I don't know what this is." His arm flew out suddenly, his fist hammering the wall. "For fuck's sake."

"Hey." Rufus grabbed Sam's hand. "Come on. It's all right. What would you prefer? No touching? No kissing? Whatever it is, I'll do it."

For what felt like a long time—maybe only a minute, but it felt so much longer—Sam lay with his arm over his eyes. Then, blindly, he reached out, groping until he found Rufus's arm. He took him by the wrist and guided Rufus's hand on the center of his chest.

"Just give me a second," Sam said. "Fuck, I feel like I'm falling apart. Just give me one second. No, stay there."

Rufus shifted a bit, keeping his hand on Sam's chest as he asked, "It doesn't hurt, does it?"

Sam didn't answer. Pauly Paul's laughter, shrill and drunken, exploded in the hall outside, and Sam jerked. He pulled his arm away from his face, his pupils huge as he stared up at Rufus. "Kiss me."

Rufus wanted to oblige more than he wanted air to breathe, but he didn't move. "I don't want to make it worse."

"Kiss me. I feel like I'm coming out of my skin, otherwise I'd kiss you myself."

Rufus hesitated, almost said *no*, but Sam had asked. Rufus wasn't forcing him, wasn't making it worse, if Sam was asking, right? He leaned close and gently, chastely, kissed Sam's mouth.

Sam grabbed him, pulling him down the rest of the way so that they lay together. When the kiss broke, Sam kissed Rufus back, and then he kissed him again. He was hard, sliding against Rufus's thigh, his breaths sharp and panting. His hand found Rufus, stroking again.

"I want you to fuck me," Sam whispered.

Rufus's brain nearly short-circuited. He pulled back to meet Sam's gaze. "Really?"

"Yeah. Yes. It's probably going to fry my brain, but I want you so bad."

Rufus stroked the side of Sam's face briefly, then leaned in again to press their foreheads together. "In any other circumstance, that request would have me preening, but… are you… sure?"

That intense focus was back as Sam studied Rufus. "I'm sure."

Rufus sat up, yanked his shirt over his head, and climbed off the bed. "Let me see if I have any condoms."

"In my ruck."

Rufus stopped midstep on his way to the bathroom and turned around. He went to the stacks of books along the wall, Sam's ruck pushed up beside them. He crouched, opened it, and focused on the hunt for condoms and lube, not studying each and every little item Sam deemed important enough to carry cross-country with him. "Were you a Boy Scout?" Rufus asked as he got to his feet.

Eyes half-closed, Sam watched him, taking those same slow, controlled breaths.

"Because you're prepared," Rufus explained, holding up the foil-wrapped condom and travel-sized bottle of lube. He climbed onto the mattress before adding, "Never mind. Dumb joke. I don't do this a lot, so… I'm a little nervous I might suck."

Sam resumed stroking him, pausing only for Rufus to roll down the condom. From beneath those hooded eyes, Sam whispered, "I'm ok," but Rufus couldn't tell if he was reassuring Rufus or himself. "I'm ok. I'll be ok." Then, clearing his throat, he added, "And you'll do just fine." A tiny smirk pulled at the corner of his mouth.

Rufus pushed Sam's leg back against his chest, helped

him get comfortable, and said, "Don't tell me if it's bad, but if you need a minute, say so."

Sam whimpered when Rufus entered him, the sound small and vulnerable from the big man. He squeezed his eyes shut and shook his head, saying, "I'm ok. It's just a lot." Then his eyes came open, and he said, "And don't get a big head; you know what I mean." His legs crossed behind Rufus's back, the hair coarse, the muscles dense, drawing Rufus closer.

The heat between their bodies, clenching muscles, rasp of body hair, the gasps and quiet moans that punctuated the rhythmic creak of the old bed frame—Rufus compared having Sam here again, vulnerable and his for the taking, to an out-of-body experience. His spirit had snapped free of his physical body and was exploring the universe without limitation. There was no fall, no *pop*, no *snap*. Rufus just kept flying, and when they'd both peaked, he was left sated, sweaty, and blinking back the stars from his vision.

Rufus was distantly aware of the damp mattress underneath them, the blankets kicked to the foot of the bed, and one leg twined around Sam's, but he was still out in the solar system somewhere, floating, like a buoy, and it was incredible. "You ok?" he eventually asked.

Stretching, Sam smiled and nodded. His dark eyes drifted across Rufus's face as though searching for something, and then he said, "Ok. Better than ok. But it's so intense, when I get like that, that it's scary. Lucky I've got you, huh?" One hand came up, following the line of Rufus's thigh. "You know what?"

"What?" Rufus asked, countering Sam's movements by running his own hand along his jaw.

"I'm falling in love with you." From the street below came the shriek of brakes, the blare of a horn. "I guess people don't say cheesy stuff like that here."

Rufus felt the lurch in his gut, the warning of his

inevitable fall. The tips of his fingers against Sam's face grew cold. Tingly. His heart raced as he grabbed at stars, desperate to remain above the world a moment longer. "Rufus thing?" he whispered.

Just a nod.

"I've *been* in love with you."

Rolling onto his stomach, Sam kissed Rufus's leg and said, "That's nice."

The panic ceased suddenly, almost comically. Rufus asked, "That's *nice*?"

Sam laughed and kissed his leg again. "It's fantastic. It's amazing. It's wonderful." His fingers smoothed down the hairs on Rufus's thigh. "This isn't really my thing. I've never—I've never had anyone like you before. I guess I'm trying to say I'm happy."

And like that, Rufus was happy too. He felt his eyes well up, but he blinked them clear and said, "Ditto."

Sam rolled his eyes. Then he slapped Rufus's stomach. "Now, since I've officially put out for you, will you please buy me dinner?"

Rufus sat up on his elbows and held a hand out. "Sure. Loan me a twenty?"

CHAPTER
NINETEEN

It wasn't sleep, but something close, Sam skimming the edge of darkness. The farthest west he'd been was Hood River, Oregon, in the Columbia Gorge. He remembered water the color of slate. He remembered the brown scrub oak and the dense, bristling pines on the canyon's walls. The windsurfing capital of the world; he had sat on a floating dock, jeans rolled up to his knees, the water fifty degrees and numbing his feet, while men and women passed lightly over the water, their shadows on the water like shadows on stone.

Then his phone vibrated, and he woke.

It was Erik Weaver. "Did I interrupt bedtime?"

Sam rubbed his eyes. Rufus, next to him, had somehow

managed to stretch out like a starfish, his skinny frame taking up most of the mattress. Elbowing him, Sam said, "I'm awake."

"Must be nice," Weaver said, "not having a job, not having responsibilities, not having a care in the world."

"Fuck off, Weaver."

"Must be nice not having anything to worry about but how to fuck up my life."

Sam elbowed Rufus again.

"I swear to God," Rufus muttered into the pillow, "I don't care how much I like you, if your elbow finds my ribs one more time, I'm killing you."

"What do you want?" Sam asked into the phone.

"Is Rufus there?"

Sam put the phone on speaker. "He's here."

"It's about that knife," Weaver said. "I want to talk."

Rufus raised his head and stared at the phone through one eye. "Talk when?" he asked, his voice gravelly with sleep.

"Well, I know you boys need time to pluck off the cucumber slices and wash off those restorative clay masks."

"Fuck off, Weaver," Sam said, hearing the aggravation in his voice and unable to control it. "Just say when and where."

"There's a place called the Striped Bottle."

"Wow, Erik," Rufus teased. "I never would have thought you, with your movie-star looks, would step foot into a dive like the Bottle. When do you want to meet?"

"An hour, unless the princesses—"

Sam disconnected. He flopped back on the bed, rubbing his eyes again. "How far is this place?"

"Only a few blocks," Rufus said. He sat up and ran

both hands through his thick, fiery hair. "It's on St. Marks."

"Time to shower, then."

"Don't use too much hot water. I'm on a budget."

After digging out his Dr. Bronner's soap, his towel, and a clean tee, Sam headed into the bathroom. It was approximately the same size as the old footlockers in the enlisted barracks. Sam showered, grateful for the sting of the hot water, the soap scrubbing away the smells of sweat and sex. Meds or no meds, the intensity of being touched by Rufus, of being fucked by him, had left Sam feeling like every nerve was raw. But that had been the point, in a way. Jake had liked to top sometimes. A few other guys, although that was rarer. The level of vulnerability was different for Sam, higher. He had wanted to give that to Jake. He had wanted to give that to Rufus.

When he finished, he dried himself and dressed and swapped places with Rufus. He hung his towel to dry on the back of a chair, and then he caught up on the news while he waited. When Rufus emerged, Sam put on socks—inside out—and boots, and Rufus pulled on his Chucks. They headed out.

The city had settled into the restless thrum of the streetlamps. Rufus took the lead, guiding Sam down one street and then another until they turned onto St. Marks. Two storefronts down, Rufus stopped. This storefront had no awning, no windows, no obvious signage. The door had a simple wooden placard that said The Striped Bottle; when Rufus opened the door, muffled music and the smell of hops escaped into the street.

Inside, the Bottle was like so many other dive bars: dim lighting, duct-taped upholstery, neon COORS and BUSCH signs, and decades' worth of grime accumulating on every surface. An unadorned wooden bar ran the length of the room on the right-hand side; on the left-hand wall, generations of patrons had stapled flyers, tagged their names, gouged hearts and penises, and otherwise left their mark. Cocktail tables, most of them stabilized by matchbooks or Sweet'N Low packets, filled much of the space, although there were booths in the back. Through an opening, Sam could see a stage with loose cables and an abandoned amp.

The clientele was geriatric punk, but without any irony and without losing any of punk's edge. Men and women in studded-leather jackets, men and women with piercings and mohawks—often dyed purple or pink or bleached white—men and women with tattoos and cigarettes, their Doc Martens held together with tape. At the back, in one of the booths, Erik looked surprisingly inconspicuous in a black tee and jeans and boots, although he still stood out a little. Too handsome. Too young. Too clean-cut. He also looked exhausted.

"Drink?" Sam said to Rufus.

Rufus was smiling as the overhead speakers began to play a low bass followed by a sick guitar riff. "Dead Kennedys, all right. Yeah, a beer. Erik's buying for us."

The bartender was a stout, older woman desperately in need of a new bra. *No*, Sam corrected himself on closer inspection, *in need of any bra at all*. In response to his look, she adjusted her leather vest and said, "Yeah?"

Holding up two fingers, Sam said, "Buds. The pretty guy back there's getting them."

She opened two bottles and slid them over. Sam passed one to Rufus, and they carried them back to the booth where Erik was nursing a bottle of his own.

"Thanks," Sam said, saluting Erik with the bottle before taking a long drink.

"Jesus," Erik said to Rufus. "It took you one day to corrupt him? He's as bad as you are. What kind of fucking Pringles am I going to have to buy him?"

Rufus clinked his bottle against Sam's. "Sour cream

and onion, because I'm going to steal them."

"Taking the night off?" Sam said. "Three murders on your plate, and you have time for a beer?"

"Fuck you. I haven't slept in twenty hours, and I needed to shower and change clothes. I wanted to talk in person, and it was either here or at the love nest."

Sam made a face, taking a pull of his beer as he glanced away.

"You want to reconsider anything about what you told me earlier?" Erik said. "Fill in any details? Provide the director's cut or the actor's commentary or the fucking unabridged version of your little field trip to Brooklyn today? Because I'm cooking in shit soup, and I'd sure like a better explanation than what you gave me."

Rufus drummed his fingers on the tabletop. "And the Academy Award for Best Original Drama goes to…."

"We told you all of it," Sam said. "If you rushed us down here for this bullshit, I'm going to be pissed."

"You didn't tell me that Charlotte Davis just happens to be married to Norman Davis, who happens to be a top donor of the Fraternal Order of Police. Jesus Christ, the kind of money they give, if they wanted the commissioner to give them a pedicure, he'd just ask them if they liked Rose de Seville or Cotton Candy Pink. And you sure as fuck didn't tell me there was some kind of connection between that woman and Mac Stevens."

Sam glanced at Rufus.

Rufus leaned back against the saggy booth. He spread his legs, knee knocking against Sam's under the table. "I told you her name. I didn't realize I was supposed to have a Magic 8-Ball on me at all times." He motioned shaking the toy. "Is this old geezer important? Worth bothering Erik over him? Oops—try again later."

"When we called you," Sam said, "we didn't know

there was a connection."

"Bullshit," Erik said.

Sam shrugged.

Erik took another drink, his movements quick, almost violent. When the bottle thumped down, he said, "You said when you called me."

Sam nodded.

"So you figured it out after you called me?"

Sam glanced at Rufus again.

"Maybe," Rufus answered. He picked at the label on his beer bottle. "I'm pretty good at *Jeopardy!*, after all. But why don't you tell us about Charlotte and Mac's connection."

"Charlotte Davis is the one who bought that knife," Erik said. "Did you know that?"

"We made some calls," Sam said.

"Fuck," Erik said, and then jerked the bottle up to his lips again. When he set it down, he was practically shouting over the music. "Could have saved me some time."

"Why are you so steamed about this?" Sam said. "You took the knife. You're the detective. It's not like we're on call."

"I'm steamed because I've got three dead bodies and a lunatic running around." He banged the bottle. "Fuck. You knew that too?"

"You have a bad poker face," Sam told Rufus.

"Poker?" Rufus repeated, a mock-surprise expression passing over his face. "Fuck me, I thought we were playing Old Maid." He leaned over the tabletop. "George is dead and I'm weeping for the tweaker. What else you got, Erik?"

Erik ran one hand along the table's edge; to Sam, it

looked like a good way to get hepatitis. Then Erik pointed his bottle at Sam and said, "You're in town. I don't like that. You rack up body counts. I don't like that. But you're not my CI." He pointed the bottle at Rufus. "You, on the other fucking hand, are supposed to be getting me what I need. It's not supposed to go the other way around." He blew out a breath. "The blood on that knife? A-negative. We put in a request for the ME's office to fast-track the DNA, but Christ knows how long that's going to take. Typing is easy, but the DNA…." He shook his head. "Want to take a guess how many people have A-negative blood?"

"Little over six percent of the US population," Rufus answered, deadpan. "Ask me another one."

"Ok, genius. In a city with more than eight million people, that's still almost half a million with A-negative blood, so this isn't open and shut. But that rent boy, the one they found with the second girl? A-negative."

"George?" Sam said.

"That's right."

Rufus tore free part of the beer label from his bottle. It curled around his finger. "Doesn't make sense—the blood being George's."

"Why?" Erik said, his eyes sharpening as he turned on Rufus.

Rufus glanced up as he flicked the wet label to the tabletop. "Charlotte bought the knife, right? And Mac had it. But that knife wasn't used to kill this new girl or George. I say that because you were called to that scene while you were busy ripping my asshole in two an entire borough away."

Erik rocked the bottle back and forth. "Maybe. But if Mac's prints come up on that knife, it might not be that simple. Maybe he killed the first girl, and then the next time he used something else. Lots of ways this could have gone." He pushed the bottle away and slid out of the booth. "This thing is serious now, Rufus. Whatever you get, I want it. And I want it right away; I don't want to have to come around kicking down your door just to get an update. Understand?"

"Sure," Rufus mumbled.

Stopping briefly at the bar to pay for the beer, Erik made his way out of the Bottle. Sam watched him go, and after the door closed, he sipped his beer and counted to sixty. Then he said, "Stay and drink? Or get out of here?"

"Let's get out of here." Rufus got to his feet. "Go back to bed and turn the phone off."

"I like the way you think."

They left, heading back the way they had come with Rufus in the lead. In the skyscraper canyons, the sodium lamps hummed, their light a dirty orange. Sam thought about the empty miles of Iowa and Kansas and Missouri. Nebraska, hell. Just the broken asphalt on the interstate's shoulder, the smell of trampled timothy, the stars.

He was so far gone that he didn't see the man until he'd cleared the shadows of a recessed doorway, and then it was too late. Sam barely had time to process the essentials: short, muscular, knife. And then the guy was on them.

CHAPTER
TWENTY

Rufus had very nearly reached his apartment building when he heard that quick, cool, slick sound of a blade slicing the night air, followed by footsteps moving away from him. Away from Rufus and toward Sam, who'd been trailing a few steps behind. Spinning on one heel and nearly overextending, it took Rufus an extra half a second to take in the stuttering details: short, stocky figure, lunging at Sam, *knife*.

Sam reacted faster than Rufus could believe. The big man moved forward instead of back, as though rushing to meet the knife. The blade missed him by inches, and then Sam closed the remaining distance, barreling into the attacker and driving him toward the closest wall. Both men's hands were a blur, Sam grappling to control the hand with the knife, the attacker trying to free himself.

Rufus had been momentarily frozen in fear, watching Sam move into danger as if he actually were a tank. Then Rufus's reflexes kicked in, telling him to run, to hide, to stay safe until the danger had passed. After all, that's how he'd made it this far in life. But the knife wasn't coming at him. It was coming at Sam, and that woke some sort of primal rage inside Rufus. He ran to the curb where piled garbage bags and discarded furniture, including a standing lamp with a broken base, awaited trash pickup.

As Rufus wrapped a hand around the lamp, he heard a low cry behind him. Turning, he saw the attacker pull the knife back. In the orange-tinged shadows from the sodium lamps, the blade was dark with Sam's blood. Rufus couldn't see where Sam had been stabbed, but he could see the shock in the big man's face. Sam tried to grab the other man's wrist again, but the attacker slashed at his face, and Sam stumbled back, pressing a hand to his leg. The attacker came after him. The knife zipped through the air, slicing at Sam's neck, his belly, his leg. Then Sam hit the curb and stumbled. The attacker pulled back the knife. The squat little fucker was grinning.

Rufus screamed wildly before picking up the lamp like a bat and swinging it directly into the attacker's arm. The base cracked against the guy's body and the energy behind it caused the pole to snap in two, the base end hanging awkwardly due to the coiled cable inside. The man yelped, dropped the knife out of reflex, and clutched his arm.

It might have been the blood loss, but Sam stared at Rufus, mouth hanging open, apparently beyond words.

Rufus ripped the cord free from one end of the lamp and raised the makeshift weapon again as the stocky attacker turned around and his face was finally illuminated.

Devon Kelly.

"You little snitch," Devon growled.

"Get the fuck out of here!" Rufus screamed, moving at Devon, swinging the lamp again, cutting off the other man's chance of retrieving his weapon.

"Why won't you fucking die?" Devon crouched and nonetheless tried to grab for the knife.

Rufus hit him with the lamp. "I'm like a goddamn roach. Nothing kills me or Keith Richards." He swung again but missed as Devon dodged, cut his losses, and ran down the block. The pounding of his steps echoed off building facades.

Rufus watched Devon retreat and then his hands began shaking so hard that he lost his hold on the lamp. It hit the sidewalk, bounced, and rolled. Rufus's extremities felt numb as he stumbled toward Sam. He dropped into a crouch. "A-are you…?"

"Fine," Sam grunted, but his hand was still pressed to his thigh, and his fingers were dark with blood. He tried to stand and landed hard on one knee. He tried again.

Rufus grabbed Sam and managed one shoulder under his arm to help him stand. "Do you need an ambulance?"

Sam grunted again. "I'd rather go murder that prick. Shit, this is going to need stitches."

Rufus moved Sam to the curb and helped him sit more comfortably. He tugged his jean jacket off and pressed it against the blood seeping from between Sam's fingers where he still gripped his leg. "Give me your phone."

Sam passed it over.

It took Rufus a few tries before his shaking hands were able to tap out 9-1-1. He requested an ambulance, gave the cross streets, then hung up, despite the dispatcher telling him to remain on the line. Rufus crouched again and put more pressure on the wound, his jacket now a bloody mess.

Sam grunted; then, with what looked like effort, he relaxed and laid a hand over Rufus's. "Thanks. Christ, talk about being out of practice. That guy almost had me for dinner."

Rufus was shaking his head as tears poured down his flushed cheeks. "That was Devon Kelly."

Shushing Rufus, Sam used his free hand to wiggle the beanie, in what he probably thought was a comforting gesture. "That was him?"

Rufus wiped his nose on his bare arm and repeated, "That was him." He looked over his shoulder as the wail of an ambulance echoed from a block or two away.

"Well, fuck."

Rufus stood when the bus turned the corner and its headlights lit up the dark street. He waved for the driver's attention, and when the siren was turned off and two EMTs exited the vehicle, he returned to Sam's side.

A trip to the ER was always a crapshoot if one wasn't complaining of head or chest pain, but Rufus had figured because Sam was actively bleeding, they'd be in and out real quick. He was half right, anyway. Sam was seen almost immediately, but after he'd disappeared through the automatic doors, Rufus had been left sitting in the waiting room, sans bloody jacket he'd chucked into a garbage bin, for almost two hours. A grandmother a few seats away was staring at the muted television mounted to the wall. She smelled like chicken noodle soup. A young black girl across from Rufus held an ice pack to a bump on her forehead that was the size of an egg. Somewhere behind him, a mother had been having a real shitty night, crying about her baby Alejandro, since Rufus had taken a seat.

When Sam came limping out, Rufus helped him outside and flagged a taxi to take them home. He didn't say a word on the drive, only held Sam's hand and tapped the mute button on the television mounted to the back of the passenger seat, but it wasn't working, so they listened to the same thirty second sound bites of New York late night news, upcoming Broadway productions, and shopping commercials for flagships in Herald Square. On his block, Rufus had the driver pull over just past his tenement so the cabbie wouldn't know which building was his. Rufus paid with cash, told the guy to keep the change, and then aided Sam out of the car and into his building.

"I'm so sorry," Rufus said as he shut and locked his front door.

"Because you have cash for a taxi but not for a hot dog and chips?"

Rufus tugged his beanie off and dropped it to the floor. "I'm not kidding around, Sam."

"I'm fine. We're fine. That human-sized scrotal sac, however, is not going to be fine when I find him." Sam breathed out softly, his breath warm where it grazed Rufus's neck. "You've got nothing to be sorry for. I'd be dead if not for you."

"If not for me, you wouldn't be here at all. You wouldn't be hurt. You wouldn't be sucked into this train wreck of a life I live."

Sam shushed him and pulled him into a hug. One big hand moved slowly up and down Rufus's back. Sam was still favoring his leg, and he leaned heavily on Rufus. "Your hair smells like beanie."

"Is that good or bad?"

"It's you. That means it's good. And I like this very much, but I'm going to fall over if I stand here much longer."

Rufus jerked back. "I'm sorry," he said again. "Did they give you any pain meds? I think I might have some Tylenol, but I can get something good from Mr. Gonzalez."

"They shot me up with lidocaine, and I've got extra-strength Tylenol. They offered something stronger, but I've got enough shit in my body already. I just need to sit. Or lie. Lying down sounds really good."

Rufus once again aided Sam to the bed. Then he got down on one knee and began untying Sam's boots.

"Thanks," Sam said, dropping back onto the mattress. Then he patted the bed next to him. "So who's Devon Kelly? Besides yet another convict you helped put in prison."

Rufus dropped the boots to the floor and then climbed up beside Sam. "I robbed him. My exit strategy out of his apartment wasn't one of my more graceful attempts, and Jake, who'd been staking the place out, caught me red-handed. I didn't know who Kelly was, didn't know what he was wanted for, or that Jake had been trying to get evidence on him for months in order to make an arrest. So that's when Jake offered to drop the robbery charges and give me the CI job, if in turn, I testified in court against Kelly."

"That's why Kelly knows who you are: he saw you in court."

"Right," Rufus answered. He raised his head when he felt Sam's phone vibrating in his pocket. "Do you mind?" he asked, reaching in.

Sam rolled his eyes and shook his head.

Rufus looked at the screen and swiped to accept the call. "Hi, honey. Can't sleep? Want me to sing you a lullaby?"

"Red, what happened to tall, dark, and stormy?"

"You'd rather talk to him?" Rufus glanced at Sam. "Ophelia's got a thing for you now. Thanks a lot."

Sam rolled his eyes again.

"Exclusively," Ophelia was saying. "I would

exclusively prefer to talk to him instead of you."

"Tough shit," Rufus answered.

"I ran Juliana to ground."

That made Rufus sit up. "Yeah? Did you get anything out of her?"

"She didn't want to talk. Said something about a certain nosy redhead who had turned her life upside down. I told her that sounded familiar."

"Well, that's simply not true," Rufus said in a tone of nonchalance.

"I tried getting some background on the victims, names of family, if she knew anything like that. She didn't have much. Or didn't want to say much. About all I could get out of her was complaining. Honey got mouthy with johns. Chantalle couldn't keep an accurate count. Shit like that. Juliana wanted to tell me about George beefing with a guy named Mac a few days ago, some shit like that."

"Hang on," Rufus interrupted. "Juliana confirmed that George and Mac were getting in each other's face?"

"Well, apparently it wasn't uncommon. She makes it sound like they had history. He was a pimp or something?" Ophelia blew out a breath. "This is the chickenshit stuff I have to dig up. It'd be nice if I could get a decent lead for once."

"Mac was a pimp," Rufus confirmed. He climbed over Sam, off the bed, and got to his feet. "I found where he's been squatting too—Bushwick. A beef with George could definitely explain the bloody knife Weaver took into evidence from Mac's place…. Must have been a hell of a scuffle they had."

"That's a nice idea, but I'd like some forensics to back up Juliana's story."

"Yeah, yeah, forensics. Science is sexy and all that. Did Juliana say anything about Daisy ever being a point of contention between them?" Rufus asked in a rush.

"Look, I tried the Daisy angle and got jackshit. Juliana clams up when I even think about asking her."

Rufus's brow furrowed. "How hard did you try?"

"I've never seen Juliana running scared like this."

"Fuck," Rufus said on the exhale. "All right. Thanks for the intel."

"If I can squeeze anything else out of her, I'll let you know."

"I owe you," Rufus answered before hanging up. He looked at Sam. "Ophelia says George and Mac fought a few days ago."

"Ok." Sam thought for a moment. "So how does Devon Kelly get the idea that you're asking about Daisy?"

Rufus shook his head while running his thumb over the rubber case on the phone. "Don't know. He escapes, I guess, jail and comes at me... using Daisy as a lure. But he's too young to have ever been involved in her murder, so... he's working on behalf of someone, right?" Rufus's eyebrows were drawn together as he looked up. "And we still don't know why Charlotte bought that knife. I think we should talk to her again. About the knife, Mac, and even Devon Kelly."

CHAPTER
TWENTY-ONE

The next morning, Sam's leg was worse. He had slept poorly, with the Tylenol a paper buffer against the pain, and although he hadn't wanted to give up the bed with Rufus, the redhead had taken over most of the mattress halfway through the night. Moving around helped with the stiffness, and after leaving the apartment and hobbling for a couple of blocks through Manhattan, Sam found himself able to move at an acceptable pace.

His temper, though, might have been stretched thin. He realized this after yelling for two minutes when Rufus asked about getting a bagel.

"Sorry," Sam said when he finally managed to rein himself in. "It's my leg. Yes. You're right. A breakfast bagel would make me feel better."

Rufus had stared at Sam with a *fucking duh* expression, but refrained from actually using the words, which was a blessing. He'd stopped at the first food cart they'd come across, waited in line with the rest of the morning commuters, and paid with his own money.

Sam was too tired to comment on the last part.

Bagels in hand, they descended to a subway platform covered in pink glitter. Covered. It was not an exaggeration; it reminded Sam of sparkling sand, dunes of it shifting in the air stirred by the trains. An individual—Sam couldn't tell if they were a man or a woman, and perhaps that was the point—wearing a flowing white caftan was rolling and heaving on the glitter while a pair of uniformed police watched, waiting for the performer to tire themselves out. A pair of tourists were elbowing their way through people, trying to get a selfie. An older woman in support hose spat on the platform.

"Like a fucking beached whale," Sam said, watching more of the heaving and bucking and rolling.

Rufus licked a bit of cream cheese off his thumb and tossed his wrapper in a big trash bin. "I think it's kinda pretty."

The subway ride wasn't easy. The seats in their car were full, and when Rufus offered to check the next car, Sam shook his head. He clutched the overhead rail and tried to keep the weight off his bad leg. The pain stayed at a manageable ache until the train screeched to a halt, or until Sam unthinkingly shifted his weight, or until a middle-aged man rammed his shopping cart full of books into it.

Medication and long experience had helped Sam build up barriers against the world, against the way it overloaded and overwhelmed him, but the pain had eroded those barriers down to cobwebs. The shriek of the brakes. The smell of liverwurst. An elbow in his ribs.

When they got off at the Seventh Avenue station, Sam stepped to the side, letting the horde flow past him until the platform was mostly empty again. He was sweating, and it had nothing to do with the warmth inside the station. Rufus threw him a few glances, but Sam shook his head again. When he trusted himself, he limped up the steps.

He didn't even have the energy to play Brooklyn Beard, even though he spotted two guys with identical, old-fashioned waxed mustaches, like the kind on a cartoon strongman.

They made their way into the den of bougieness, Park Slope, passing stroller mommies and gaybies and a man in a polka-dot piratical blouse—Sam didn't know what else to call it—pouring bottled artisan water that appeared to be branded specifically for dogs into a tiny plastic doggy bowl. When they got to Charlotte's brownstone, Sam had to lean against the wrought-iron railing at the bottom of the steps. The day was cool. The wrought iron was cool. The sun, where it made its way through the London plane trees, made him feel feverish. He bent over the rail and upchucked and felt marginally better.

"Jesus Christ, Sam." Rufus moved close enough to put a hand between his shoulders. "Sit down. You stay here. I'll talk to Charlotte. Real quick—in and out."

Shaking his head, Sam wiped his mouth. "It's just the antibiotics. I should have eaten more. Or less. Who the fuck knows? Help me up the steps, would you?"

Rufus exhaled. "You are such a butch man."

But he offered Sam his arm, and Sam leaned on him—maybe too much, judging by how Rufus grunted— and managed to get up to the door. Like the rest of the brownstone—like the rest of the street—it looked quietly expensive: polished dark wood with a large glass insert, the glass ornamented with a stainless steel design that probably was intended to provide the illusion of security.

A privacy applique rendered the glass translucent instead of transparent, and when Sam knocked, he peered through the glass to see if he could make out anyone approaching.

No one came to the door.

He knocked again and glanced at Rufus. "Charlotte was pretty freaked last time we were here. What are the odds that she split and took her pet fossil with her?"

"Maybe Norman was due back to the Museum of Natural History," Rufus agreed before banging on the door himself.

The hallway on the other side of the door remained dark.

"If we took the subway for nothing…."

"It wasn't for nothing," Rufus said. "We got to see that art installation, didn't we?" He took a step back to look up at the second-story windows. "Maybe they're sleeping. Or in the shower. Or… do you think Norman can still get it up?"

"God bless his ancient prick. Come on, let's go. Is it worth checking Mac's squat again?"

Rufus made a *tsk* sound, reached into his back pocket, and produced the lock picks he typically carried in his jacket. "What're the odds of an alarm system being engaged?"

"Looks like they've got money. I'd guess the chances are good. Why? Did you see sensors last time we were here?"

A blush crept up Rufus's neck and cheeks. "I didn't think to check. Come on, block me for a second."

"Why?"

"So I can break in." Rufus crouched in front of the lock.

Sam limped into position. "This is the best I can do; somebody's still going to wonder what's going on if they look closely."

"Hush," Rufus grumbled as he tinkered. When the tumblers fell into place, he stood with a triumphant grin. "There, see? Piece of cake." He pushed open the door a little and waited, but no house alarm sounded.

"Nice," Sam said, laying a hand on the door. Then he hesitated. "I'm guessing you're going to be muleheaded about waiting until I've had a look."

Rufus stuffed the tools in his back pocket while raising a light-colored eyebrow. "Says the guy with a stab wound. Like fuck I'm waiting outside."

"Maybe they'll let us share a cell," Sam grumbled as he pushed the door open fully. In spite of his best efforts, Rufus slipped inside first, and Sam limped after him.

The house was silent, the kind of stillness that Sam associated with emptiness. An accent table lay on its side, and what had once been a piece of crystalline art that Charlotte might have bought at Columbus Circle or Brookfield Place now lay shattered across the tile. Sam groaned when he saw the stairs in the foyer.

"Whatever happened here, whatever we're looking for," Sam said, "if it's not on the ground floor, fuck it."

"Shh...." Rufus waved his hand at Sam and hurried deeper into the home, silent on the balls of his feet. He returned a moment later, pointing over his shoulder, whispering, "Nothing in the kitchen." He glanced at the stairs and said, "I'll go look."

Grimacing, Sam said, "Brooklyn can fucking eat me," and followed Rufus upstairs. Slowly. Rufus had already checked the room at the top of the stairs, and as Sam reached the landing, Rufus backed out of the doorway. His face was pale as he looked at Sam and shook his head.

"I found Norman." Rufus swallowed and tapped the side of his head like his thumb and index finger was a gun. "He's still in bed. I didn't see a pistol anywhere."

Sam nodded. "Did you touch anything?"

Rufus vehemently shook his head. "No." He rubbed his bare arms as visible gooseflesh rose on his freckled skin.

Sam thought about easing the Beretta from its holster. "How long ago, do you guess?"

"It's hard to say without touching or uncovering him. But the blood is definitely dry."

He left the Beretta where it was; whatever had happened here had happened, and the killer hadn't stuck around. Sam made his way down the hallway; the temptation to prop himself up with one hand was strong, but this was now a murder scene, and he and Rufus had already left prints on the front door. No reason to make things worse.

The next room was also a bedroom, and Sam studied it from the doorway. The room was clearly Charlotte's, with a canopy bed draped in light, rosy silk and a chintz-upholstered fainting couch. The furniture was all white and doubtless expensive; through an opening, Sam could see an en suite bathroom. The bed was empty, but more signs told the same story that had begun downstairs. Wild tracks in the high-pile carpet; maybe someone had been kicking and dragging her feet. A drawer hanging open. The duvet pulled askew, as though seized in a final effort.

Sam glanced at Rufus, who had moved ahead to the next door down the hall. Rufus used the hem of his shirt to grab the knob and open the door. He cautiously poked his head in, was still for a moment as he studied the surroundings, then slipped in through the crack of the doorjamb. He reappeared before Sam could count to sixty, shaking his head. "Just an office. Nothing looks disturbed."

With a tilt of his head to indicate Rufus should follow, Sam moved into the bedroom. He found himself straining to listen, but the brownstone's thick walls muted the outside world. The only noises were Sam's and Rufus's steps, accompanied by the hiss of blood in Sam's ears.

When he got to the bathroom, Sam smelled it before he saw it: piss and shit, sure, but also something else. The beginning of rot. A hint of death, like an oil slick floating on the perfume of verbena soap and crushed rosemary.

Charlotte was in the tub, dressed in a lacy teddy that poor Norman had probably never seen her wear. Under other circumstances, her pose might have been funny. She lay perpendicular to the tub's length, her head at an uncomfortable angle, her legs hanging over the edge, one unshod foot dangling almost coquettishly. The other foot was gone.

"Jesus Christ," Sam whispered.

Blood covered the enameled tub, the tile, the lace teddy. Spots of it marked Charlotte's toned cheeks. In her struggle—or perhaps in her killer's carelessness—a bottle of body oil had been knocked over, and Sam's mind automatically tracked it to the scent of verbena and rosemary he had noted earlier. The oil had mixed with the blood, a pinkish pool spreading almost to the door. Sam looked over to Rufus to warn him not to step into the mess on accident. When he saw the look on Rufus's face, he forgot what he was going to say.

Rufus was staring at the body, his face ashen, and then he slowly raised a hand and pointed at Charlotte. It took Sam a moment to understand what Rufus was indicating: a mess of cuts high on Charlotte's shoulder.

"What—" Sam began.

But then he saw it.

It wasn't just a mess of cuts. It was a pattern. No, a design. A flower, carved into Charlotte's shoulder. And not any flower either.

A daisy.

CHAPTER
TWENTY-TWO

Rufus convulsively swallowed the acid and bile coming up his throat. He sank into his habitual position of knees to chest, arms wrapped around his legs, a nasty habit he'd never been able to break—protect himself, make himself as small as possible. Rufus's head swam, his skin broke out in a freezing sweat, and his fingers and toes were tingling as his breathing quickened to near hyperventilation. "Is… is that a daisy?"

Crouching next to him, Sam laid a hand on his back. "Come on. We need to get out of here."

Rufus shook his head. He couldn't get up. He couldn't move. He couldn't leave Charlotte looking like that. Rufus broke into a sob. "My mom's tattoo," he cried.

"What? What tattoo?"

"The flower—*daisy*. My mom's!"

"Your mom—" Sam stopped. "Daisy had a tattoo there? Where he did that to Charlotte?"

Rufus nodded. He grabbed at Sam's arm as he said breathlessly, "I'm having a panic attack."

"What am I supposed to do? Rufus—" Sam must have moved wrong or too quickly because he swore and clutched his leg. "You've got to tell me what to do. Fuck this leg. Fuck this fucking leg!"

Rufus had to look away from the open doorway. He had to stop staring at the bloody flower carved into Charlotte's shoulder. That's when *What to Do When Anxiety Strikes*, Edmund Burn, PhD, Third edition, filtered to the forefront of Rufus's mind like smoke from an extinguished matchstick. He'd checked it out from the library based on the title alone—something in his gut told him he needed to study the contents. And Dr. Burn's self-help book on coping with anxiety and panic had been truly eye-opening, practically a guide to self-diagnoses. Rufus had checked it out a second time to read again.

Establish five objects you can see. Rufus slowly dragged his gaze from the body in the tub to the bloody tiled floor to the plush carpet of the bedroom. Carpet. And that pulled Rufus further—to the beautiful bed, couch, and drapes pulled open across the window.

Next was four things he could touch. So Rufus pressed his numb fingertips into the carpet. Then he rubbed them along the rubber ribs of his Converse, up the leg of his jeans, then his wool beanie.

Three things he could hear. That one was difficult. He could hear a high-pitched ringing in his ears, shallow breaths Rufus was fairly certain were his own, and then nothing. But nothing was a sound in and of itself, right?

Rufus allowed it and moved on to two things he could

smell. He touched the front of his shirt, raised it up over his mouth, and inhaled the scent of laundered cotton. Then he looked at Sam on his right. He could smell Sam, all clean sweat and masculinity.

The final sense to establish, to ground him in the here and now, was taste. Rufus put a clammy hand on the back of Sam's neck, pulled him in, and kissed his mouth.

When the kiss broke, Sam took his head in both hands and looked into his eyes. "Say something snarky so I know you're ok."

"You taste like cream cheese and barf."

Sam nodded. "Sounds about right. Can you stand?"

"I don't know. I feel like I'm dying."

"I can't carry you, Rufus. I need you to stand."

Rufus nodded. "Ok. All right. Hang on." He moved his hand to Sam's shoulder and used it as leverage to push himself to his feet. He felt shaky and tingly and too hot for how cool a day it was, but he managed to flash Sam a weak smile when the other man stood. "I guess this means you won't be carrying me over the threshold anytime soon?"

"Ask me when I don't have a knife hole in my leg. Let's go. And carefully—we don't want to fuck up this scene any worse than we already have."

Rufus had tunnel vision as they backtracked through the house. He kept telling himself, over and over, *One more step, one more stair, you'll be ok, you're almost there*. And then Sam was pulling the front door shut behind them, Rufus was wiping the doorknob with his shirt, and they exited the front gate and stepped onto the sidewalk.

"We need to call this in," Sam said as they hurried away. Then he shot Rufus a look. "Right?"

"Fuck. Sure, whatever. Call the police commissioner. The mayor. No—get Jesus on the line." He glanced back at Sam. "Not Erik. Not yet. I can't."

Sam made the call, reporting the facts in a few simple phrases that skated at the edge of Rufus's understanding. When Sam pocketed the phone, he did a double take of Rufus and said, "You need to sit down. Fuck, we both do."

Rufus walked north on Prospect Park West, passed a rack of Citi Bikes, sidestepped a group of college-age girls walking four abreast and all staring at their phones, and eventually came to a stop at an open bench near the Marquis de Lafayette memorial. He collapsed like dead weight and slid low into a position that resembled an overripe banana. He watched Sam, who'd been a handful of steps behind him, approach. Rufus weakly patted the seat beside him.

With a grunt, Sam dropped down next to him.

Rufus shoved his hands into his jean pockets. "I killed her. She was fine. She was living a good life. Then I poked, and the wound started bleeding, and I didn't stop, and now she's deader than Julius Caesar."

"You didn't kill her. A psycho killed her, the way he's been killing people for years."

Rufus's gaze was fixed on a faraway point. "Daisy's been gone longer than I ever had her in my life. Nothing's going to change that. Why'd I push Erik? Detective Larkin?" He took a short breath that broke a little at the end. "What the fuck does any of it matter? Daisy wouldn't even give a shit that I tried to do right by her. She wouldn't. This is the same woman who smacked me in the mouth when she didn't like what I said. The same woman who brought me into the Ramble at night instead of finding me a babysitter. The same woman who didn't care that by junior high, I was stealing and picking fights with other kids. She's dead and I'm still trying to get her approval. And now everyone I've asked for help—they're ankle-deep in shit or dead." Rufus took another soggy breath, leaned forward to rest his elbows on his knees, and shook his head. "It's my fault they're dead, Sam."

"You asked for justice because your mom deserves justice. The bitch of it is that, until somebody runs this psycho down, he's going to keep doing this because he likes doing it. The way you stop it isn't by backing down; it's by finishing what you started."

Rufus took off his sunglasses and passed a hand over his eyes. "What if Devon comes after you again? Or someone else?"

"Chalk it up to a bad night," Sam said with a hard grin. "Next time, I'm going to put a bullet between the fucker's eyes."

A smile ghosted across Rufus's face. "Never has a promise of violence made me feel better, but first time for everything, I guess."

A pigeon fluttered down in front of them and pecked at a graying piece of hot dog, its beak digging into the particles of meat.

"Good," Sam said. "Now let's go fuck someone up."

Rufus hung his sunglasses from his collar. "Why'd he cut a daisy into Charlotte's shoulder?"

"To taunt you."

"Aren't I already being taunted, though? It's weird. And sick."

"But—" Sam stopped. "I thought the compulsion was collecting body parts. Why a daisy? Because of Daisy? Did those old news articles mention anything like this?"

Rufus shook his head. "No, nothing." He turned on the bench to face Sam. "I think it's a little ridiculous and egotistical on my part to say he took precious time to cut that flower into her flesh simply to see if I'd cry. It's about Daisy. It's *always* been about Daisy and those girls."

"And Charlotte took Daisy's clients. Charlotte wasn't just a random girl. She wasn't just a source, giving you information about the past. Charlotte was the next Daisy, right? Kind of literally, in a way. Fuck, I would give a lot to be able to talk to one of her old johns right now."

"The next Daisy...." Rufus repeated, his brow furrowing. He chewed on his lower lip for a moment, then said, "Maybe you're right, when you say 'literally.' Like... what if he wanted Charlotte to *be* Daisy?"

"Like, go all Alfred Hitchcock and *Vertigo* and make her dye her hair and—" Sam gave a baffled twist of his lips. "What do you mean?"

"I sort of mean that, actually," Rufus said. "Serial killers have a type, right? We established that much— working girls. But what if the obsession were more exact? What if this guy was hyperfocused on Daisy, and... and now that she's gone, he's wanting a replacement?"

"So he cuts a daisy into her? I'm not disagreeing with your idea, but I don't understand that part. Why not make her wear something Daisy might have worn, or a wig, or Christ, anything else?"

"I'm a high school dropout," Rufus replied. "I'm not smart enough to answer that question. But I've lived this long by trusting my gut, and now it's saying do not overlook this."

"We know Devon couldn't be doing this on his own; he's not old enough to have been part of the original killings. I know everybody thinks I'm a clueless fucking rube, but I still say Mac is behind this shit. Either way, I want to talk to him. And Devon. Preferably right before I stick a knife in Devon's leg to see how he likes it."

"I wouldn't even know where to start looking for Devon. The little shitstain keeps finding *me*."

"What about Mac?"

Rufus shrugged. "Juliana didn't seem to think he'd be anywhere but that charming Bushwick slum. I've no idea where a washed-up pimp would be hiding nowadays."

"So?" Sam said with a shrug. "It's your city. You come up with a plan."

Rufus was quiet for a moment. He rubbed his hands together and dredged up Jake's voice from his memories.

You're smart, Rufus.

Rufus looked down and studied the untied lace of his high-top. He carefully redid the bunny ears. "Jake put Devon away for life. Even being released on good behavior, that wouldn't happen within two years. So that's a clue to me."

"What are the odds this guy would break out of jail and get sucked right back into your orbit? Why not run to Venezuela?" Shaking his head, Sam added, "And the life sentence, fuck. So how did he escape? I guess we could look it up online."

Rufus sat up straight. "Give me your phone."

Sam passed it over.

Rufus brought up a web browser and quickly tapped a few keywords into the search bar. He scrolled for a moment, cussed under his breath, then tried a new search. "Happening Now: FBI is looking for Devon Kelly, reported as having escaped from Sing Sing Correctional Facility on October 11. $5,000 reward." He turned the screen to Sam to show him a tweet from the FBI's New York City branch.

"Well, shit. I could use $5,000."

"You and me both." Rufus passed Sam the phone. "That explains that. I know there's been successful escapes from that prison since it opened in the 1800s, but nowadays? With security cameras and automatic doors and Big Brother breathing down your neck? Devon's a bad guy, but fuck if he's smart enough to dig a tunnel out of Sing Sing." Rufus leaned back. "Think someone could have organized his escape?"

"I think it's a pretty sweet fucking coincidence that right after you start looking into your mom's death, this guy escapes from a maximum-security facility, and then he decides to come after you."

Rufus cast Sam a doubtful expression.

Sam grinned. "I think it's time to get out of this fucking city."

CHAPTER
TWENTY-THREE

They took the subway back to Manhattan and got to Grand Central ten minutes before the 8835 Poughkeepsie was scheduled to depart on the Hudson line. Sam paid for the tickets—his leg hurt, and he wanted to get on the train and collapse more than he wanted to twist Rufus's balls about the money—and they boarded. The car smelled like cigarillo smoke, and the seats were threadbare, with holes exposing the old foam padding. Sam didn't care; when he finally got his weight off his leg, he almost sang hallelujah.

The ride upriver was supposed to take approximately an hour, but there was a delay outside Scarborough—someone, presumably kids, had pushed a shopping cart onto the tracks. It apparently took some kind of fucking genius to figure out that they needed to pull the cart off the tracks because the train just sat there, unmoving. On the west side of the tracks, the brown water of the Hudson River took on a blue sheen like steel where the sun hit it at the right angle. On the right, small frame homes alternated with parking lots of broken asphalt and stretches of oak and maple, fireworks of orange and red.

"Did that article," Sam said, "the one about the FBI and the reward, did it say how Devon escaped?"

"No, I found it on Twitter." Rufus held his hand out. "Let me check a few places. They might have posted that info somewhere where you can utilize more than 280 characters."

Sam passed over his phone.

Rufus opened the web browser again and began typing. "So you don't think he spooned his way through a wall?" he asked absently while clicking and scrolling.

"Since he's not a cartoon character, that seems unlikely."

A smile tugged at the corner of Rufus's mouth. "Asshole," he said lightly. He scooted closer after a moment and held the phone out between them. "FBI posted about the escape on their Most Wanted page."

The description of the escape was short and, unfortunately, the details that Sam had been hoping to find were scarce. Devon Kelly had escaped when a prisoner transport bus had been jackknifed by a tractor trailer. Kelly was one of five who had escaped, while the remaining prisoners were rounded up by officers who arrived on the scene shortly thereafter.

"There's got to be a juicier article out there," Sam said. "What about the driver of the semi? What was his name? Was he hospitalized? What was his excuse for barreling into the side of a bus? Maybe we can figure out where the accident took place at least."

Rufus shifted, bringing one foot onto the seat and

leaning his head against Sam's shoulder. "You want the world, don't you?" He typed some more, flipping back and forth between a few browser pages before eventually saying, "A tractor trailer struck a prison transport bus on Friday evening, after eight o'clock, five miles outside of Sing Sing Correctional Facility. The driver, identified as William Monroe, a contractor for a chain grocery, was transported to Phelps Memorial Hospital for minor injuries. Five prisoners escaped, among them Manhattan native Devon Kelly, found guilty of three counts of armed bank robbery and second-degree murder. He is considered to be armed and dangerous." Rufus tilted his head back to look at Sam from an awkward angle. "Sounds like the driver of the trailer just fucked up? Maybe he was drunk, or fell asleep at the wheel."

"If that's true, then the escape was luck. Bad luck for us and the driver. Good luck for Devon. Do you think that's what happened?"

"No," Rufus admitted. "I doubt it was sheer luck."

"I'd sure like to know what the fuck actually happened," Sam said. "I'd also like to know if Devon was talking about this before it happened, but I'm not sure where to start. Normally, I'd know enough about a guy to start picking at loose threads: the guys in his platoon, his girl—or his boy—his commanding officer, that kind of thing. But we're going to get a big, fat goose egg if we walk into Sing Sing and ask if we can please speak to whoever Devon Kelly might have been banging in the showers, please and thank you."

"Oh God," Rufus groaned as he dropped the cell in Sam's lap. "I do not want to think about the dick Devon might have had rammed up his ass."

Sam's eyes narrowed. "You're charming. Sort of. In a street-rattish kind of way."

"You keep talking this sweet to me and I'm going to

expect more from you," Rufus warned. "Maybe we can find a way to get his cellmate's name and talk to that guy. I mean, that seems to me the most likely candidate, yeah?"

"Yeah. How do we get the cellmate's name, though?"

"I don't know," Rufus protested. "Stick a fiver in a guard's pocket?"

"That's not a bad idea, actually. But maybe more than a fiver, and probably not at Sing Sing. I bet we can ask around, though, and find out where some of those guys go after a shift. Being a corrections officer is a fucked-up job, and I'd bet a lot of those guys just want a few drinks as soon as they're off the clock."

"Well, yeah, I won't argue with you on that. What's our angle, though? Two manly straight bros looking to buy a hardworking guy a drink?"

"Good God," Sam muttered. He grabbed his phone, opened Facebook, and began sending messages. After shooting off fifteen identical queries, he dropped the phone in his lap, stretched out, and closed his eyes. "Wake me when we get close," he said. "I want to see the prison from the train."

He'd barely closed his eyes, it seemed, when Rufus nudged him, and Sam blinked to clear his vision. The October day was drawing to a close, the sky purple to the east, a few stars—or, more likely, high-pressure sodium lamps—at the horizon. Sam had long enough to orient himself, and then they were passing through the prison proper.

Sing Sing had been built on an elbow in the Hudson, the water offering a natural barrier to escape on three sides. As the prison had grown, it had sprawled across the railroad so that now the tracks bisected it. It was an old place—Sam knew that much—and he could see the strata of periods and phases in the construction: the original, abandoned white-wash cellblock; red brick structures;

bleakly modern concrete buildings with asphalt shingles. He didn't see any inmates snipping through a chain-link fence or dodging a high-powered searchlight, but he figured there was still time. The closest thing he saw to a convict was a middle-aged man, potbellied, in overalls, doing a criminally poor job of raking.

And then they were through the prison, Sing Sing a bulk of shadows in the sunset behind them. They went another ten minutes up the Hudson, pulling into the Ossining station, when Sam realized he'd missed several messages on his phone. He scanned them, sent replies, and fought hard to suppress a grin when he got an immediate answer.

"Tin Dog Outpost," he said to Rufus.

Rufus stood from the seat and moved into the aisle with other passengers. "Are we playing *Jeopardy!*? I missed the category." He reached out to help Sam.

"Miraculous solutions Sam has provided." Sam swore as he put weight on his leg. "Do you have any Vicodin on you?"

"You know I don't. Do you want to find a pharmacy and pick up some painkillers? We'll have to google the nearest place. I've never been upstate."

"No, I'll manage. Until I can get a beer, anyway." Sam frowned as they made their way off the train. "What do you mean, you've never been upstate?"

Rufus shrugged and didn't say anything until they'd worked their way up the outdoor staircase and entered the station. "I mean, I've never left the city."

"Never never?" Sam said. The station was emptying quickly, and he checked the maps app on his phone for directions to the Tin Dog Outpost. "Let's get a taxi. Define never."

Rufus growled and said, "Manhattan, Brooklyn, Queens, Staten Island, the Bronx." He counted each borough off on the fingers of his free hand. "That's it. That's all I fucking know, ok?"

They made their way outside, and Sam flagged a taxi from the queue. "Wow. So this is kind of special, huh? Do you want to do something to celebrate? Are you ok? You're not freaking out, are you?"

Rufus moved to stand in front of Sam, staring at him as the taxi pulled up behind them. "Celebrate my journey to Bumfuck, New York? No, I'm fine, thank you. But are you going to tell me what the hell Tin Dog Outpost is? A Daily Double square or something?"

"The Tin Dog Outpost is a bar," Sam said, "where Private Jonny Linares, formerly of Charlie Company, Third Battalion, Nineteenth Infantry Regiment, is going to let us buy him shots of tequila and answer our questions about Sing Sing. Anything our little hearts desire to know." They climbed in the cab, and Sam asked for the Tin Dog. The driver nodded and pulled away from the curb. "Assuming he knows anything and isn't just trying to get free drinks."

"Uh-huh," Rufus muttered. "And did you, like… serve together or something?"

"Christ, no. The moron got a dishonorable discharge a year into his eight. I don't know for what—I don't want to know. I've never even met the guy, but the Army is a small world in some ways. I asked some friends if they knew anyone in the New York state corrections system."

Rufus nodded, but when he replied, all he came back with was "So Jonny wasn't into you?"

"He hasn't had a chance yet," Sam said with a shrug.

The Tin Dog Outpost, in spite of its Wild West-sounding name, had a Mexican decor: sombreros and bullwhips and colorful ponchos hanging on the walls, mixed in with black-and-white photographs of landscapes that might have been northern Mexico or southern Texas: hard, cracked, flatlands with scrub and sage; *vaqueros* astride scrawny horses; a woman in a long dress outside an adobe hut. The clientele was heavily Latino, and Sam had noticed, on the taxi ride over, that Ossining had a *churrasquería*, a *carnicería*, a *panadería*, and a family restaurant called La Cuchara. Several men in blue uniforms were sitting at the bar, exchanging a few desultory words but primarily focusing on the drinks in front of them.

"Want to pick out Jonny?" Sam asked.

"Why the fuck do you think I could pick him out?" Rufus hissed, looking around the place before pointing discreetly at the bar. "One of them?"

With a sigh, Sam said, "Very disappointing."

Rufus gave Sam's shoulder a rough shove. "I'll make a scene."

"That one," Sam said, pointing to the guy, probably in his midtwenties, who sat at the end of the bar. He had straight dark hair spiked up with gel, and he had sleepy dark eyes and an even sleepier smile when he talked to the girl tending bar. "I guess it would have been easier if I'd shown you the photo they sent me."

Rufus rolled his eyes. "You think?"

As they approached Jonny, Sam watched the young CO say something to the bartender. The girl's smile was plastered on, and she shifted her weight, obviously eager to move away from the conversation. Jonny said something else, and the girl shook her head, the smile cracked and crumbling now. She took a step, and Jonny reached across the bar and caught her arm.

"Are we interrupting something?" Sam asked as he and Rufus took stools at the bar.

Jonny dropped back onto his stool, and the bartender touched her arm, as though making sure she was free.

In the conversational void, the jukebox was playing Selena Gomez.

"We were having a chat," Jonny said. "And I'm saving those seats."

"No, you're not," Sam said, "because I'm the one you're waiting for." To the bartender, he said, "Do you have Dos Equis?" Then, to Rufus, "What about you?"

Rufus had been eyeing Jonny, disapproval of his behavior with the bartender painfully obvious in the redhead's expression, before he glanced at Sam and said, "G and T." Rufus looked at the woman and added, "Thanks."

"And nachos," Sam said.

The bartender slung a towel over her shoulder and moved to the end of the bar. Sam didn't think they'd be getting their food and drinks anytime soon. He turned his attention to Jonny and found that the CO was staring back with the same degree of scrutiny.

"You're Auden?" Jonny said.

Sam nodded.

"And who's Strawberry Shortcake?" Jonny said.

Rufus leaned forward on the bar top to look at Jonny around Sam's height and bulk. "Rufus," he said, smiling a fake smile. "That's Mr. Strawberry Shortcake, by the way."

Jonny rolled his eyes dramatically; it made him look ten years younger, and Sam was starting to understand why this asshole hadn't been able to hack it. Certain personality types were drawn to positions of force and authority—the Army, the police, corrections—and those same personality types often had major emotional problems. Being massive pricks, for example.

"So what's the deal?" Jonny said. "I got messages from Riggins and McGee asking me to talk to you. You've got ten minutes."

"Several prisoners escaped while they were in transit

last week."

"News flash," Jonny said and took a long drink of his Corona.

"We're trying to track down one of them: Devon Kelly."

"Well, he's not here. That's kind of the whole fucking point of a prison escape."

Selena Gomez was really putting her heart and soul into this one. Sam focused on the beat, counting it in his head, to distract himself from the idea of breaking Jonny Linares's nose on the bar.

After another pull on the Corona, Jonny glanced over. He must have seen something on Sam's face because he said, "Uh, I mean, I never knew the guy."

"His cellmate. Or any inmates he was friends with. We want names, and we want to talk to them."

"Yeah, I mean, I can ask around, but I can't get you special access or anything. You can come during visiting hours. If they want to talk to you, that's up to them."

"Then get us those names," Sam said. "Tonight."

"I'm not on duty until tomorrow."

Rufus leaned forward again and said, "I know you've got something wrong with your hearing, what with that nice woman having to basically tell you to fuck off a few times, yeah? But Auden said *tonight*."

"Uh...." His gaze darted from Rufus to Sam. "Yeah, ok, I'll text a buddy."

Sam wrote his number on a napkin and pushed it over to Jonny. Then he stood.

"What about your drinks?" Jonny said. "And those nachos?"

"Thanks for picking up the check," Sam said. "Make sure you give that girl a nice tip."

He was turning toward the door, beckoning to Rufus, when Jonny spoke again.

"I asked about you."

Sam turned back.

Jonny's dark eyebrows were arched, and his sleepy smile had sharpened. "When Riggins and McGee told me you needed to talk to somebody."

Selena Gomez faded out. The silence was a tide of blood whooshing in Sam's ears.

"That was a fuckload of dead soldiers at Benning."

The next song was Luis Fonsi, quieter, almost crooning.

Jonny was leaning forward now, Corona in one hand. "Lew Frazer was sure interested when I told him I was meeting you for drinks."

"You know Lew Frazer."

"Sure," Jonny said, the smile turning into a smirk now. "We're old friends. He was in the Seventy-Fifth too, just like you; I thought he'd know you, and I was right. He sure had a lot to say."

Sam considered this for a moment and then nodded. "We're done here."

"Lew said he'd pay cash if I told him where you were holed up. He's been looking for you for a while."

Suddenly, the throbbing pain in Sam's leg was gone. He felt light, buoyed up, almost drunk. He remembered what it had felt like to sight downrange, the first man coming into view, the six-pound trigger pull of the M4.

"Did Frazer tell you what I said I'd do if I ever saw him again?" Sam asked.

Something froze the smirk on Jonny's face.

"I told him if I saw him again, there wouldn't be enough left of him to bury. Remind him, next time you talk to him."

Jonny was trying hard to hold the macho posture, but the Corona sank down, and he leaned back against the bar.

"Ready?" Sam said to Rufus.

Rufus was staring at Sam. His voice was quiet as he said, "Yeah, sure."

CHAPTER
TWENTY-FOUR

Ms. Margaret appeared to be as old as sin, and her motel not far off. The one-story, eight room, nothing-special setup in the middle of nowhere needed a paint job a decade ago. The office was the size of a cubby hole. It stank of burned coffee, the Mr. Coffee pot in the far corner had probably been on since 6:00 a.m. that morning, and the vending machine of assorted soda, with a printout reading Out of Order taped to the front, buzzed ominously. Rufus did his best to ignore the sight and smell and sound as Ms. Margaret held his fake ID up to study through her bifocals and compare to the young man before her. Eventually, she sighed and slid it across the counter, and Rufus quickly pushed a wad of small bills into her gnarled hands.

"You know," she croaked, "I don't usually accept

cash."

"Cash is king," Rufus answered.

"I have one of those chip readers."

"I don't like Big Brother to be part of my banking."

Ms. Margaret was giving Rufus another look. She craned her neck to one side, stared out the glass window of the front door at Sam's looming figure waiting outside, then said, "This better not be some sex thing."

Rufus blinked a few times. "I'm sorry?"

"Had a film crew stay the night," she continued, waving an arthritis-ridden finger at Rufus through the plexiglass. "They humped all over everything. Had to send two housekeepers to clean up. Cost me money."

Rufus felt the tips of his ears burning. "It's not a sex thing. Which room?"

Ms. Margaret was still frowning as she slid a keycard under the plexiglass barrier and across the countertop. "103. I better not hear a peep, understand, young man?"

"Wouldn't dream of pulling on his hair," Rufus answered, jutting a thumb Sam's way. "Thanks, ma'am." He grabbed the card and slipped out of the front door. "Good Christ," he muttered. "Come on. 103. And we can't pull each other's hair tonight."

"No hair-pulling," Sam said solemnly.

Rufus unlocked 103, let Sam go inside first, then followed. He flicked the light switch on the wall, threw the door's deadbolt, then yanked his beanie off and tossed it to one of the two twin beds. "Hey," he said quietly. "Want to fill me in on what happened?"

"He's a piece of shit, but I think he'll get us some names."

Rufus moved past Sam, checked the generic bleach-scented bathroom, then reappeared in the doorway. He leaned against the doorjamb and crossed his arms. "You know that's not what I'm talking about."

Sam eased himself onto the bed, wincing as he lifted his injured leg onto the mattress. "It's not something I want to dredge up. Bad stuff happened. I got caught in the middle of it. They couldn't force me out, but I left anyway. That's the end of it."

"They've got these little travel-sized soaps in here," Rufus stated, indicating in the bathroom with the nod of his head. "Perfect size to wash your lying mouth with."

"Call me a liar again."

Rufus pushed off the door frame. "What're you going to do, fight me, Sam?"

Sam's face was unreadable, except for the set of his jaw—the set of his jaw was pure, unadulterated rage. "Yeah," he said. "You get to keep every fucking door in your life locked, and you get to say when you open them. But when I say I don't want to dig up the past, I'm a fucking liar."

"I've told you everything," Rufus countered. "You hear me? Things that no one else knows. I'm trying to return the favor, and this is what I get—a kiss-off. So fuck you."

"You're right," Sam said with a hard little laugh. "Fuck me." Then he rolled onto his side, his back to Rufus, and was silent.

Rufus shook his head and returned to the bathroom. He turned the tap on and ran the water until it was scalding hot, washed his hands until they were red, then dried them with a threadbare white towel. He tugged off his Chucks while walking to the beds. "Can I sleep with you, or are you going to shove me off the bed?"

The silence lasted longer than Rufus would have liked, and when Sam spoke, he was obviously trying to modulate his voice. "Yes. I'd like that. But just sleep; my leg is fucking killing me."

Rufus took a seat on the mattress and got comfortable. "So if Rosebud Jonny texts you by tomorrow, are we going to Sing Sing?"

"I guess so."

"You guess so," Rufus echoed, talking to the ceiling. He glanced at Sam. "I know you got rubbed the wrong way by that creep, but if you're going to take it out on me... I don't have the mental spoons for that."

Sam sat up, the movements stiff, favoring his leg as he stood. "I'm going to take a shower," he said, limping toward the bathroom.

Rufus sat up as well. "I know nothing about you, Sam. I asked one question, because I'm concerned, and you snap at me and shut down." He swung his legs over the side of the bed and stood again. "And just in case you weren't paying attention—my entire fucking life is on display right now, and it's embarrassing and humiliating. My prostitute mother and the abuse she doled out. My anxiety and panic attacks. My love-hate relationship with rooftops. The fact that I'm a drop-out with no skills beyond pickpocketing. I mean, fuck me, we're about to stroll into Sing Sing tomorrow. I spent eighty goddamn bucks on this chemically processed room. Ms. Margaret thinks my name is Tadd. People are dying and I'm scared because you're all I've got and I want you to be ok. But instead you're walking away."

"You're actually fucking unbelievable," Sam said. "I came halfway across the fucking country when you made one fucking phone call. I told you I was falling in love with you. Fuck this. I'm not doing this. I'm not going to feel bad because I don't want to talk about something that's dead and buried." He reversed course, heading for the door. "I'll get my own room. See you in the morning."

Rufus turned, hurdled over the second bed, and skidded to a stop in front of the door. He put his back against the locks and shook his head. "I love you too, Sam. I called you because I trusted you, and I was right to. I told you I want to get better, so that I can be that person for you too. So tell me what's wrong. Do you trust me enough to say that much?"

"Do I trust you? I went up against dirty cops with you. I went through hell with you. I came back, willing to do it all over again, because I knew you wouldn't ask if it wasn't important. And I asked you to fuck me, Rufus. That's about as much trust as I have to give somebody; you've got no idea what that's like for me, how it feels, how vulnerable I am. No idea. Just because I don't show it the same way as you doesn't mean I don't trust you."

"How the fuck would I know?"

Sam drew a deep breath. "Move."

Rufus's heart was slugging against his rib cage. He wiped his face and shook his head. "No. I don't want you to sleep somewhere else. I don't want you to wake up angry."

"Then stop pushing me to give you something I'm not ready to give."

Rufus's lip quivered, and the fact that he was about to cry made him angrier than everything that'd transpired between them. He bit his lip until he could taste blood, then shoved off the door, returned to the bed, and drew the comforter back. He sat down and stared at Sam's back.

For a moment, Sam stood there, hand on the doorknob. Then he turned and made his way into the bathroom. The hiss of the shower started, then the sound of clothes hitting the floor.

Rufus yanked the starched blankets over his head. He squeezed his eyes shut and prayed he'd fall asleep before Sam exited the bathroom.

Rufus had not been a fan of the plan to waltz into Sing Sing, even if it was no farther than the visitor's center. And sitting at a cold metal table beside Sam the next morning, watching the few other visitors and inmates in the room, he bordered on *hating* the plan. Rufus was intensely aware of himself, a petty thief with a record (albeit a scrubbed record) sitting only a hundred yards away from where he might very well have ended up doing the cell block tango, if not for the quick thinking of Jake Brower.

So Rufus distracted himself by staring at a woman two tables away in a leopard tube top. Her tits were practically falling out of the bit of fabric pulled tight across her chest. It had to be against some sort of dress code. Rufus tilted his head as she jumped from the bench and spread her arms wide to welcome an inmate being escorted into the room.

"I've never seen so much jiggling," he whispered to Sam. "Definitely real. Two bucks says she's smuggling tools underneath them. Girls in high school called it the pencil test." Rufus glanced at Sam, who had been quiet most of the morning. He wanted to say more, goad Sam into a conversation, but after the fight last night? Rufus bit the inside of his cheek and remained silent.

After a moment, though, Sam said, "Maybe she's got a file. Like the kind cartoon characters bake into a cake."

"That'd be strapped to her thigh, I think. Hey, does Sing Sing have conjugal visits?"

Sam frowned. "I'm not sure it matters; that woman looks determined to have a conjugal visit one way or another."

Rufus looked away from the happy couple and watched the security door open a second time. "Are you still mad at me?" he whispered.

"No. Are you still mad at me?"

Rufus shook his head. "No."

"Glad we figured that out," Sam said with a small smile.

A big man, at least Sam's size and height, but maybe a bit more doughy around the middle, entered the room. He had cropped silver hair and a matching bit of facial hair. He was directed toward Rufus and Sam, and when he reached the table, his brows knitted together, he asked, "You the clowns askin' 'bout me?"

Rufus leaned back on the bench. "Skip Roche?"

"I know who the hell I am." Skip gave Rufus a shrug off and then studied Sam. "Who're you?"

"Sam and Rufus."

"Packaged deal, are you?" Skip was still standing on the opposite side of the table. He rolled his meaty shoulders and kept staring at Sam.

"Buy one, get one free," Sam said.

"Stop jerking me around and tell me what the fuck you want," Skip answered.

Sam glanced around the room, catching Rufus's eye, and looked at the door marked OUTDOOR VISITING AREA.

Rufus got to his feet, stretching his arms above his head. "How about a walk, Skippy? Get some fresh air in those big ol' lungs." He reached into a back pocket and retrieved a cigarette.

"One fucking cigarette?" Skip countered.

"Calm down, I've got two," Rufus answered as he produced a second. "It's two more than you currently have, isn't it?"

Skip rubbed his facial hair, glanced at Sam, then nodded once. "Fine. Sure."

Rufus gave Skip the first stick, then led the way to

the access door. He stepped outside and held the door as Skip followed, with Sam taking up the rear. "So how long did you share a cell with Devon Kelly?" Rufus asked, producing a matchbox and lighting Skip's cigarette.

Skip's eyebrows rose. "You fuckers came all the way out here to ask me about *Kelly*?"

"Did I stutter?" Rufus asked.

"Watch it, Freckles." Skip took a step closer, looming over Rufus. "I could squash you under my thumb."

Sam cleared his throat. "Try that again."

Skip eyed Sam, took one step back, then had a long drag off the cigarette. "You two fuckin' homos?"

"Skippy is delightful," Rufus said to Sam before leveling his gaze on Skip again. "How long did you share a damn cell with Kelly?"

"About a year," Skip said before blowing a lungful of smoke in Rufus's face.

"Let me see that cigarette," Sam said to Rufus.

Rufus coughed and obediently passed the second stick to Sam, noting that Skip's eyes followed the motion.

"Matches?" Sam said.

Rufus tossed him the box.

"Hey," Skip said. "That's mine."

"Keep being an asshole," Sam said, "and I'll smoke it down to the filter. Play nice, and we'll see about getting you a whole pack."

"Camels. Not these fuckin' Marlboros."

"Baby, I'll even get you Virginia Slims if you want them," Rufus concluded. "Now tell us, did Kelly plan his escape?"

"I heard the bus was hit by a semi."

"So?" Rufus asked.

"So how the fuck do you plan that?" Skip glanced at

Sam and then backtracked. "As far as I know—no. He couldn't have planned it. He'd have needed someone on the outside to organize it."

"And Devon didn't talk about anything like that? Similar escapes? What he'd do if he ever had the chance? Even just joking around, bullshitting, nothing that sounded like he might have been planning something like this?"

Skip took another drag, tapped the ash, and said to Sam, "Come on, man. Everyone talks about what they'd do if they could get out. Kelly used to say that even Alcatraz had an escape."

"Wasn't successful," Rufus stated. "Most likely, anyway. They suspect the three men drowned."

"Yeah, whatever," Skip said. "I mean, that was Kelly's way of saying no prison was foolproof."

"But he didn't talk specifics? He didn't have a plan? What about friends on the outside, anyone he thought might help him?"

"We weren't friends," Skip answered. "We weren't homos either."

"Sam," Rufus said. "Grade A Gays must have foolproof prison escape plans. That's Skippy's Achilles' heel. We'll have to circle back and better organize ourselves. You know, just in case."

"The fuck is wrong with you?" Skip asked, staring at Rufus with his upper lip raised in a sort of animalistic disgust.

Rufus shrugged. "Where do I start?"

"He had some girl down in the city," Skip said at length. "One of many, but this one owns some mick bar or restaurant or something like that in Midtown. He said he'd always have a hole to hide in with her."

"What was her name?" Sam said.

"Give me that cigarette and maybe I'll tell you."

"Name first."

Skip narrowed his eyes. "Jessie. Give me the cigarette and you get her last name."

Sam held out the smoke.

Skip snatched it. "Murphy." He lit the end of the second cigarette with the burning embers of the first. "Anything else? Or can I enjoy this next smoke in peace?"

"Kelly ever brag about people coming to see him? Ever mention anyone by name?"

Skip took another drag. "Not names," he said on the exhale. "But he had something. Or he thought he did."

"Meaning?"

"Guys do it all the time. You hear everybody talk shit about snitches, and then the minute your back is turned, they run straight to the first guard and think they're going to get Johnnie Cochran to get their asses out of here. Fuck, I can't even say I blame them. The dumbass on the next bunk wants to spill his guts, why shouldn't you see if you can cut yourself a deal?" He puffed a few more times, eyes cutting across the yard and landing everywhere but on Rufus and Sam.

"Is that what you were thinking you'd do?" Sam said. "Let Kelly talk until you had enough rope to hang him and get yourself a get-out-of-jail-free card?"

"No." The word was too sharp, the way Skip angled his body too defensive. He waved the cigarette at them. "But Kelly thought he had one of those, what you said. He said he was going to make one call and walk right out of here. Just a snitch, like all the rest of these bitches."

CHAPTER
TWENTY-FIVE

The trip back to Manhattan was quick and quiet; the train left the Ossining station five minutes behind schedule, and Sam and Rufus passed the hour-long ride in a few snatches of conversation. Sam hadn't forgotten the sting of last night's fight, but he was also painfully aware that he hadn't handled things the way he should have. Rufus seemed willing to let the whole thing slide; if he was suffering any pangs about his own behavior last night, he didn't show them. Instead, he busied himself with Sam's phone, scrolling through search results and placing calls until he crowed with triumph.

"Got it?" Sam asked.

"Midtown Ale House. Owned and operated by Jessica Murphy."

When they got to Grand Central, Sam insisted he could walk the ten or so blocks to the pub, refusing to concede to any of Rufus's objections. After four blocks, he was limping badly, and after six blocks, he had to stop and sit on a bus stop bench, his injured leg stretched out in front of him. The October day was cool verging on cold, with arctic winds snapping down the cement canyons, but Sam was sweating. Five minutes later, though, he made himself get back up, and they finished the trek.

True to Skip's description, the pub had two Irish flags over the door. The exterior had been done to look vaguely European—perhaps even vaguely Irish, although Sam thought that might be a stretch—with mullioned glass doors, crimson trim, and gold-leaf lettering on the transom: WINE - BEER - COCKTAILS. In Kelly green, a wooden sign proclaimed MIDTOWN ALE HOUSE, complete with a four-leaf clover. In case you didn't get the message.

"How do you want to play this?" Sam asked when they were still half a block away.

Rufus slipped around Sam and studied the sidewalk ahead. "Well, there's always the balls-first approach. Walk inside and ask to speak with Jessie."

As Sam considered this, a group of men approached the door and went inside. They all looked like they were in their forties, all carrying extra weight, all with the air of guys who might like looking you in the eye and telling you to go fuck yourself, sir, and have a nice day.

"It's a goddamn cop bar," Sam said. "Devon Kelly is shacked up in a cop bar? You've got to be kidding me."

Rufus puffed his cheeks and blew out a long breath. "I did not see that coming." He glanced at Sam, grabbed his bicep, and gave a tug. "Let's go in."

They headed into the Midtown Ale House. The nod to a vaguely Irish appearance on the outside continued here: the lights low, provided by old-fashioned pendants; a long, scuffed bar, its stools padded with Kelly-green vinyl; tables and booths, with the room already half-full; the walls covered by photographs of stern-faced men and lithographs of poofters riding horses and hunting with dogs. The clientele looked to be about ninety percent men, all of them carrying themselves like cops. The staff was almost exclusively men too—the exception was a woman, her red hair pulled back in a ponytail as she slung drinks behind the bar.

"Jessie Murphy?" Sam asked, nodding at the woman.

"Considering the sausagefest going on in here," Rufus began, still eyeing the layout, "the odds are that's her." He pointed toward an empty booth a few feet from the door. "Let's sit for a minute. Your leg's about to buckle."

They took the empty booth, and Sam hissed in relief as he eased the weight off his leg. Rufus flipped through a menu, and a few minutes later, an older man with pouchy cheeks and a green apron stopped at their table. He dealt coasters like he was doing a card trick, and then he raised an eyebrow.

"Well?" Sam said to Rufus.

Rufus glanced at the waiter, offered a big smile, and said, "Jessie around?"

"Jessie?"

"*Yeah*, Jessie." He tugged his beanie off, showing the shock of red hair. "She's my cousin. Can you go get her?"

After a last glance at the coasters, maybe disappointed he'd wasted his trick, the waiter ambled toward the bar. He didn't move straight to the woman, which Sam thought showed an interesting degree of caution—the woman was the obvious choice, of course, and this was a cop bar. Instead, their waiter spoke to a young guy who was pouring something into a jigger. The guy nodded without looking up, finished mixing the drink—*a whiskey sour,*

Sam thought—and served it with a napkin. The waiter, meanwhile, had shuffled off to his next table.

"What are they playing?" Sam said. "Three-card monte?"

Rufus frowned a little and yanked the beanie over his head again. "I don't know. I thought the *if you've seen one redhead, you've seen them all* thing would work."

"It might. But they're acting like the first person walking through that door wouldn't know the only woman here is Jessie Murphy."

The tip-off, when it happened, might have gone unnoticed by someone who wasn't waiting for it. The young guy crossed the bar to fetch a bottle of what looked to be gin, and his path took him past the woman. He said something as his shoulder brushed hers. The woman—Jessie, presumably—didn't flinch, but her body did tighten: shoulders drawing up slightly, hand firming up around the tap. She finished pouring the beer, and as she slid it onto the bar, she looked up. Her eyes found Rufus and Sam immediately, and Sam realized he had misjudged. She wasn't scared; she was pissed.

Instead of more words, she shot another glance at the young guy behind the bar, wiped her hands on a towel, and headed down a narrow, dark hall. The young guy was pouring another beer, but now he wasn't making any effort to hide that he was staring at Sam and Rufus.

"Did we blow it?"

Rufus said, "For being a cop bar, they're all acting real suspish." Something about that comment made him chuckle to himself, and Rufus finally looked away from the bartender to study the framed photographs surrounding them. "*Amateurs.*" He then scooted closer to the wall and tapped one picture. "Even '70s fashion can't hide that this dude's a cop."

Battle jacket, stovepipe pants, an embroidered shirt

that Sam wanted to call a blouse. But yeah, the look was there in his eyes: cop.

"Probably doesn't play too well in good cop, bad cop, I bet."

Rufus made a sound of acknowledgment while leaning forward on the tabletop. He stared at a grainy image mounted between them. It was shot on film and slightly overexposed in the way that '90s aesthetic seemed to have a discolored fog over its subjects. In reality, based on the haircuts, it was more likely the early 2000s, coupled with a bad photographer. The picture looked like some kind of ceremony. The man in the middle—sufficiently handsome and imposing—was receiving a medal for bravery or valor or whatever, while flanked on either side by superiors.

Sam was about to say something about the '90s being even more shit for style than the '70s when movement at the corner of his eye drew his attention. He tapped Rufus's arm as the young guy from behind the bar approached their booth.

"Which one of you is supposed to be Jessie's cousin?"

Sam raised his eyebrows.

Rufus sagged back against the cushion. "Me. Don't we look alike?"

The guy shook his head and waved a bar towel toward the same narrow hallway that Jessie had taken. "Go on back to the office."

Sam glanced at Rufus, and when Rufus shrugged, Sam slid out of the booth. The young guy didn't want to make space; he stayed where he was, forcing Sam to either bump him—and, Sam guessed, hopefully start something—or to twist awkwardly as he emerged from the booth. Cop bar, lots of mustaches. Sam went for the awkward twist, even though it made his leg light up like a Christmas tree.

They maneuvered between tables, picking out a path past the bar and down the narrow corridor. It ended in two doors. One hung askew in its frame, and the smell of ammonia and wet mop floated out. The other was steel and obviously reinforced—cop bar or not, somebody at some point had probably had the very stupid idea to interrupt the night's count. Sam rapped on this door.

"Come in."

He pushed into the office, Rufus a step behind him. The room was about what he'd expected: bare plywood walls with a single layer of paint, an exposed bulb, filing cabinets, a *Kojak* poster featuring Telly Savalas with a toothpick between his teeth. The woman he guessed was Jessie sat at an IKEA-style desk, all white laminate and chrome, in the middle of the room. Her hands were hidden in her lap.

"Let's not do anything stupid," Sam said. "Those guys out there might buy your beer, but you don't want them coming back for this conversation."

"I've got plenty ideas on how to be stupid," the woman said, her voice thin with a tough veneer. "I'm still coming up with them." To Rufus, she said, "I've got twenty-two cousins, and you're uglier than every last one of them, so who the fuck are you?"

"God, lady, you're making me blush," Rufus answered. "I'm no one important. Just looking for a friend—Devon Kelly."

"I don't know any Devon Kelly. That all?"

"Did you know that less than two percent of the world's population has red hair?" Rufus asked. "So we might actually be related. What would your mother think if I told her you were lying?"

"My ma's dead, and that's the end of this conversation. Get out of my bar. Don't come back."

"If you think you're helping him," Sam said, "you're wrong. If you think he loves you, you're probably wrong about that too. He's a killer, and he's helping someone else do some pretty awful shit. So I'm going to give you my number, and when—"

"Get out."

"—and when he contacts—"

"Get out. Get out, right now. I don't want your fucking number, and I don't know what you're talking about. Get the fuck out before I start screaming, and then you can find out what a roomful of drunk cops will do for a pretty girl they watched grow up. Get out!"

Sam shook his head and turned.

Rufus, still standing, had clenched his hands into fists at some point—the knuckles so white, they looked ready to burst through his freckled skin. Sam could practically feel the coiled energy—rage, fear, frustration—ready to be unleashed from the redhead.

"My mother's dead too," Rufus said to Jessie in a clipped tone. "And your piece of shit Devon Kelly is part of that clusterfuck. I'm going to find him, with or without you."

Rufus was first out the door; Sam pulled it shut behind him, following Rufus's rapid footsteps down the darkened corridor. They emerged into the bar proper, into the smell of frying food and roasted malted barley, into the dim glow of the pendant lights, into the low hub of men's voices.

Rufus barely seemed to see where he was going; he tried to cut between the crowded tables, buttonhooked, and crashed into an empty stool. It didn't seem to register. He kept moving, his face pale and too bright in the pub's shadows. The young guy behind the bar was watching him. Their waiter, tugging his apron straight, was watching too. Sam straightened the stool and went after Rufus.

But Rufus stopped before he reached the door, jerking to a halt like he'd reached the end of a leash, his momentum still carrying him forward while something else yanked him back. As Sam caught up, he realized Rufus was staring at the wall of photographs again.

Rufus returned to the booths in the shadowed corner, put a knee on one cushion, and reached across to yank a frame free. He straightened, studied the award ceremony a second time, then turned to Sam. "This is him. Jimmy."

CHAPTER
TWENTY-SIX

"Jimmy Sirkosky," Rufus stated, reading the faded, printed names on the lower left hand corner of the photograph. He stood on the sidewalk outside of the pub, taking deep breaths of air that didn't feel like they were reaching his lungs. Rufus could feel a mild panic attack coming on. That tingle in his fingertips. That cold flush over his skin. He couldn't deal with that rush and crash right now. Not in public. Not in front of Sam *again*. Not after this realization—*Jimmy Sirkosky*.

Despite feeling robbed of oxygen, Rufus forced himself to take one slow breath. Then another. And another. The viselike grip around his lungs began to ease. He tapped into that yoga book from over the summer, about being aware and shit. And he almost snorted, because, yeah, he was *well aware* of how his legs and arms felt like tissue paper torn by a light breeze, but it helped.

When Rufus could breathe easier and didn't feel like he needed to upchuck into the closest trash can, he said more levelly, "Jimmy Sirkosky."

"You're sure this is the guy?" Sam frowned. One hand closed over Rufus's, adjusting the angle of the photograph. October light raked the glass. "Christ, he's a baby here."

"I'm sure," Rufus replied. "You know… you know that roller coaster feeling? In your gut? It feels like that. I know this is him."

"Fuck." Then, in a tone that took a moment to register as tense excitement, "Fuck. We've got a line on the fucker, Rufus. And he's a fucking cop."

Rufus's past was laid out before him just then—and it was up to him whether he remained in the abstract darkness forever or became a tangible thing in the present. Staring at the photograph of Jimmy was like popping open his Pandora's box and allowing a collection of long-forgotten sound bites to come tumbling out. The cry of Daisy being slapped and Jimmy ordering her to strip faster. The *hiss* of Jimmy zipping his pants on the way out the door. The smack to the back of Rufus's head, Jimmy saying on his way down the stairs, "See you next week, kid." And maybe it was that whack to the head—so vivid that Rufus could feel the sting even now, feel the way his neck jerked hard to one side—but it was like all the street smarts he'd been struggling to maintain over the last few months were suddenly righted.

Have you been paying attention? a little voice asked him.

Rufus looked to his right and saw Devon Kelly, Mets hat, Members Only jacket, strutting down the bustling sidewalk, half of his attention on a 7-Eleven slushie and the rest on the phone in his other hand.

Rufus dropped the frame to the ground. "*You!*" he shouted.

Of course, shouting *you* caused several passersby to look in Rufus's direction, but that included Devon, who certainly didn't seem prepared for Rufus to be waiting outside the pub. Devon chucked the slushie and bolted the way he'd come. Rufus dodged the sweet-and-sticky drink and shot down the sidewalk after Devon. Some unfortunate bastard behind Rufus had been beaned with the slushie and was now letting loose a string of obscenities in their wake.

"Come back here, you scrotum-sniffer!" Rufus called. He shoved a businessman out of his path, spun around a gaggle of tourists, and completely plowed through a construction worker who really shouldn't have fallen so easily, considering he was about three times Rufus's size.

Devon was all-out booking it to the corner of Thirty-Ninth and Eighth. He made a sharp left turn and crossed the street uptown. Cars braked and horns honked as he narrowly missed being run over. Rufus kept on his ass, dodging between two bumpers and sliding across the hood of a third car, its owner shouting at Rufus in Italian.

Devon approached Fortieth, crossed the street again, and ran for the 42nd Street–Port Authority subway entrance. He grabbed the pole around the barrier leading to the stairs in order to slow his momentum and maneuver himself in the correct direction, but he either let go too soon or overextended—it was difficult for Rufus to tell in that split second—and Devon's stocky body fell forward, his yelp of surprise cut short.

Rufus's chest was heaving, but he didn't stop to catch his breath. He ran to the stairs and hurried down into the subway. Devon lay on the landing, his body contorted, limbs splayed, neck so severely twisted up against the MetroCard reader that there was no coming back from it.

"*Fuck*," Rufus shouted. He crouched beside the body,

hastily reached into Devon's clothing, and removed the phone that had been pocketed before the chase began. Rufus ran back up to street level.

In spite of the limp, Sam had almost reached the subway entrance—he seemed to be trying to run, but with his injured leg, it was just an incredibly fast hobble, with the bad leg swinging out wide on each lunge. It would have been funny if not, well, for a lot of things. His face was bleached with pain as he snapped, "What the fuck—"

Rufus, hands on his knees as he took in several gulps of air, said, "He's dead."

"Are you ok?"

Rufus straightened and waved the phone. "Fine, but… let's go. Before someone fingers me for pushing him or something."

BlueMoon Diner was busy, as far as basic, slightly grubby diners went. Based on how Maddie conversed with several tables of folks dressed like office drones, they were early-lunch frequent flyers. Upon seeing Rufus enter, Maddie waved. He returned the gesture and took a seat in his habitual booth. Rufus slid across the old springs and cracked vinyl. His face was still flushed. He tugged his beanie off, covered the phone with it, then grabbed a handful of sugar packets, mostly out of reflex, as Sam sat across from him.

"Holy hell. That was unreal," he said, dumping the white granules onto his saucer.

"Are you ok?" Sam asked.

Rufus licked his finger and dabbed the sugar. "I think I'm angry. What a cheap way to go out, you know? After everything he's done… he trips on the fucking stairs and breaks his neck."

"Fuck," Sam breathed out, a little shakily. He dug a thumb into the corner of his eyes. "So much for getting Kelly's side of the story. Where the fuck is Maddie? I can't tell if I'm hungry or if I'm going to puke."

Rufus wiped his finger on his jeans and then nudged the phone toward Sam. "Here."

"Is that his? Kelly's, I mean?"

"Yeah."

Maddie strolled to the booth and ruffled Rufus's head lightly. "What have I told you about eating pure sugar, Freckles?"

"You my mom, Maddie?"

"If you don't watch it, I will be, and I can assure you, you will not enjoy it." She held up her pad. "Are we eating today, boys?"

Rufus looked at Sam again but reached for the sugar, seemingly unfazed by Maddie's threat.

"Club sandwich and potato salad. And a Sprite. And a Vicodin."

"Do I look like a pharmacy, handsome? But I got some Tylenol if you need it. This one giving you a headache?" Maddie asked, nodding at Rufus.

"I'd say a pain in my ass, but it's more like my thigh."

Rufus interjected, "I didn't do anything."

"Uh-huh," she said. "I'll file that away under Shit I'll Never Believe. What do you want, baby?"

"That depends on who's paying," Rufus replied, glancing at Sam a second time. "That motel was expensive."

"Yes," Sam said. "Obviously I'm in your debt." To Maddie, he added, "I'll take the check, just so we're clear."

"You're good to him," she said with a smile before smoothing down Rufus's hair.

"French fries," Rufus said. "A whole plate."

"And… a protein?" Maddie tried.

"French fries," Rufus reiterated.

She shook her head. "I'll be back soon."

Sam tapped the phone, and the screen lit up and displayed a series of app icons. "Unlocked," he said. "That's a nice change." He touched the phone icon, and two numbers appeared. Holding the phone so Rufus could see, he asked, "Is one of those for the Midtown Ale House?"

"This 212 one," Rufus said, pointing. "That's what was listed online."

"Huh." Sam laid the phone on the table and tapped the second number. The screen changed as he placed the call, a timer taking up much of the display. The phone rang. And rang. And rang. And then, at 00:08, the call went to a roboticized voicemail that simply repeated the phone number and requested that the caller leave a message.

"Well," Sam said, "if I were a serial killer using an escaped convict as a shit-poor assassin, I probably wouldn't leave a real chatty voicemail recording either."

"Are there any texts?" Rufus asked.

Sam tapped another icon. The list of messages was short: Kelly had texted only the unidentified number—the one Sam guessed connected him to whoever was orchestrating things.

"Whoever this person is," Sam said, "Kelly was pissed at them. 'I need money.' 'This bitch is crawling up my ass.' 'Why the fuck aren't you answering your phone?' 'Call me right now, motherfucker, or I'll start making some calls of my own.' 'Get me the fuck out of here.' 'What the fuck don't you understand about I own your ass?' On and on like that. Christ, if Jessie had seen these, she probably would have dropped his balls in the deep fryer." Sam spun the phone toward Rufus, dropping back against the banquette's vinyl back. "Not a fucking clue of who the mystery guy is, though, or what Kelly has on them. The way I see it, we've got two possibilities: Mac—and yeah, I remember that nobody else agrees with me—and this guy Jimmy."

Rufus powered off the phone and slid it back under his beanie. "I'm willing to entertain Mac as a suspect. He had a history with the original girls who were murdered, Daisy included. He wasn't above getting physical. He fought with George." Rufus's eyebrows rose as he remembered: "And that knife. But Jimmy? Because he was an asshole john twenty years ago?"

"And because everything about Kelly's escape suggests law enforcement was involved. That makes sense for the killings seventeen years ago too. Which is more likely? A pimp was chopping up girls in his stable and managed to completely avoid police attention, or a cop was killing working girls and knew exactly how to cover his tracks?"

Rufus shifted, and the springs squeaked under his weight. "It's more believable," he agreed. "Insider knowledge. Hiding in plain sight. That sort of thing. But if that's the case… he took seventeen years off and then started up again because I unknowingly poked the bear? What's the connection, or reason, between those murders then and the ones happening now?"

"I think that's part of it." Sam frowned. "I don't know much about serial killers, unfortunately, which is a sentence I never thought I'd hear myself say. We know this guy has a pattern, though, right? I mean, what he was trying to do to Honey—the wounds we saw. And what he did to Charlotte. There's some sort of compulsion, and when you started asking questions, it came roaring back—or whatever he was using to hold it off just wasn't strong enough anymore."

"What compulsions are you two troublemakers talking about now?" Maddie interrupted as she returned with plates of food.

"It's not for polite company," Rufus answered.

She leveled a look at him.

"Seriously." Rufus lifted his index finger and gestured by sliding it into his other fist.

Maddie snorted as she put their lunches down on the tabletop. "For that, I'm not bringing you extra ketchup. You get whatever's left in that bottle," she said, pointing to the condiments pressed up against the window. She patted Sam's shoulder, murmured something about his blessed patience, and was off.

Rufus grabbed the bottle and poured a glob of ketchup onto his plate. "He went after Charlotte. I think that's significant. She… I don't know… bridged the generations of murders. Which *would* suggest he knew her way back when, right?"

"Right. That could be either of them, though. Mac knew her. And they'd been in contact recently enough for her to get that knife to him. And when she took Daisy's guys, she got Jimmy—hell, she remembered him."

"Do you remember guys you slept with seventeen years ago?" Rufus was frowning. "Serious question."

"Some. Not all of them."

"Well, I don't. And I wasn't a sex worker. I mean, I'd think after a while, they'd all blur together or something. She remembered Mac, sure, except they had a long-established relationship. But she remembered Jimmy, and maybe that strikes as more strange to me." Rufus ate a few fries.

"Charlotte's death is strange," Sam said. "It breaks the pattern. The first set of killings all involved girls who were active in the life, and they stopped after Daisy was killed. The second set of killings targeted working girls— with the exception of Boy George, who was in the trade too. But Charlotte's different. She was out of the life completely, and the killer went to her house, got inside without raising the alarm, and killed her and her husband. I'm not disagreeing with you; the amputation, and the mutilation—the daisy tattoo—those make me think it was the same guy. But he also bent his own rules. He made an exception to go after Charlotte. Why?"

"Numa said she had a friend on the force, back in the day, the one who got her out of trouble," Rufus reminded. "If that was Jimmy, even if they hadn't seen each other in almost twenty years, I think *maybe* she'd invite him in for coffee or tea or whatever rich housewives offer. She owed her sweet life to him, doing her that favor. And Devon Kelly's been following us, I think. He could have told Jimmy who we've been talking to."

"I agree that if Jimmy was Charlotte's buddy, it makes sense that she'd let him inside. But would she answer the door wearing a lace teddy? Only if they had something else going already. A little something on the side that Norman couldn't offer. But why would Jimmy take the risk? I mean, he's known Charlotte for twenty years. She's got a certain amount of status as a public individual—hell, she's a major donor to the Fraternal Order of Police. She's not a street girl; people are going to ask questions. Even if Jimmy knows we talked to her, why risk that level of attention?"

Rufus dunked his fries into the ketchup on his plate and took a bite. "What if we've got it wrong with Mac? Charlotte *bought* him that knife. So, what if the teddy was for him too? She's expecting her old pimp, maybe new flame, at the door, and instead it's Jimmy. And he's got that compulsion after seeing her again. What if it wasn't even about Charlotte, really? Because he carved that daisy into her. Maybe that's what was wrong with Honey's shoulder too. What if... it's *always* been about my mom, but with her dead, these girls *now* are... substitutes?"

"That's… a fucked-up possibility. It makes a freak amount of sense, actually. It still doesn't give us our guy, but it might explain what the fuck has been going on."

"I need your phone."

After a savage bite, Sam slid the phone across the table.

Rufus dialed Erik's number and put the phone to his ear. "You're cute when you eat like a wild animal," he said to Sam as the phone rang.

Sam just grunted and mauled the sandwich again.

"You know what else I'd like you to aggressively— hey, Erik," he said when there was a click on the other end of the line.

"Where are you?" Erik said.

"Where is anyone, really?" Rufus replied. He stuck another fry in his mouth.

The sound on the other end of the call was a little bit like a cat going under a tire. "I'm going to ask you again, and I want you to tell me exactly where your freckled ass is sitting so that I can drive over there and personally kick the shit out of you. So. Where are you?"

Rufus furrowed his brow and propped his elbows on the tabletop. "Please don't talk about my freckled butt like you've been acquainted. I'm having lunch at a diner."

"Charlotte Davis is dead. Norman Davis is dead. And neighbors reported seeing a fucking Sherman tank and a redhead leaving the townhouse. So, Rufus, when I told you in our last conversation that I wanted to be kept apprised of all new information, did it not enter your fucking head that the murders of two respected citizens was worth a five-second fucking phone call?"

"It *was* called in," Rufus protested before his voice grew quiet. "I was… I was having a panic attack, ok? But Sam called it in."

"So what's this, right now? My lieutenant has a semi-permanent residence inside my ass chute because of these murders, so if you called so we could chat while you and your boyfriend braid each other's hair, I've got other fucking things to do."

"I didn't want to come to you empty-handed, Erik," Rufus explained. "But I've got a suspect now, and I think you should look into him. Jimmy Sirkosky. He's a cop. Well, probably still a cop."

From the other end of the call came the sound of movement: a chair scraping, steps, hinges that needed WD-40. Then Erik, in a furious whisper, said, "You'd better explain that very clearly and very quickly."

"I saw a picture of him. At a cop bar. He's the Jimmy who used to do business with Daisy."

Static crackled in the silence. "What the fuck," Erik said, "are you saying? Do you have proof that this guy, Sirkosky, that he had something to do with these girls? Beyond the fact that my CI, who any decent attorney would rip to shreds in fifteen seconds on the stand, vaguely remembers him as a john from twenty years ago?"

Rufus felt his cheeks warm. "Come on, Erik. I have Devon Kelly's phone. You can do a trace on the number he's been calling and texting. It's someone's burner and he was dangling something over the guy's head. Maybe that guy was Jimmy. Maybe Jimmy Sirkosky helped Kelly escape jail to do some dirty work on his behalf and ended up getting backstabbed by a stocky Mets fan."

"You've got a burner phone. And a number for another burner phone." Erik's breathing was ragged. "Don't fucking say anything. I knew this was a bad idea. I knew I shouldn't have done any digging for you. Now you've got this idea and you're like a dog with a bone."

"*Erik*," Rufus protested.

"No, we're done. If you've got something for me,

something legit, we can go back to how we were doing things before. But I'm not letting you drag me down the shitter with you."

Rufus pulled the phone from his ear and stared at the disconnected call. He glanced at Sam. "Erik dumped me."

CHAPTER
TWENTY-SEVEN

Sam had heard most of the conversation—for all his movie-star good looks, Erik sounded like an angry fishwife when Rufus started stirring things up—but he still asked, "Want to tell me what just happened?"

"Erik doesn't want to go down with a sinking ship." Rufus pushed the phone across the table.

"Ok," Sam said. "That doesn't really change anything, does it?"

"Changes my chances of ever getting another fucking paycheck," Rufus mumbled. He stuffed a few more fries in his mouth.

"No, it changes the next step. You've got a hunch about this; let's do the legwork and prove it. How do we prove

Jimmy Sirkosky knew Devon Kelly, helped him escape, and sent him after you?"

"Start with that bar photo, I guess. He's a cop. So, how high up in the ranks is he? What department does he work? We can probably learn something of the sort of strings he can pull based on that alone."

"So we start looking at Jimmy's life. We go through it with a backhoe if we need to. Everything he's done, everything he's owned, everything he's touched, starting with those killings in the '90s." Sam grabbed the last fries from the plate and shoved them in his mouth. "Why do I feel like this is going to be another trip to the library?"

Not much had changed since their last visit to the New York Public Library. People still crowded the lobby, the stone echoing with footsteps and whispers, the smell of sweat recirculating in the frigid air-conditioning. Instead of heading to the microfilm room, though, this time Rufus led Sam into a large hall. Tables filled the center of the room, while shelves lined the walls. Aside from a circulation desk, several of the public-use tables had PCs. A pair of young women, twins, in matching, shapeless hats pulled low over their foreheads, were actively using two of the computers, but several others were available. A sign said PLEASE RESERVE COMPUTER TIME IN ADVANCE.

"Did you reserve computer time?" Sam whispered to Rufus.

Rufus glanced up at Sam with a disbelieving look. "You take me for a public library rookie?" He inclined his head at a man seated behind the circulation desk, who waved in response. "I always have a computer at the ready."

They sat at adjacent computers, and Sam borrowed

Rufus's library card to log in; then Rufus logged in to his own machine. They each pulled up a browser, and Sam said, "How do you want to split this up? One of us looks for personal info, the other looks for professional? Or do you want to divide things up chronologically? Something else?"

"If you keep talking like that, I'm going to get a chub," Rufus whispered. "I'll take personal life. You check out the police medals that had him smiling so pretty for the camera."

Pocketing that tidbit—Sam knew he'd be coming back to that particular revelation sooner rather than later—he started his search with a simple phrase: *James Sirkosky awards*. The first result was a statement on the NYPD's digital newsroom, where Jimmy Sirkosky was identified as the recipient of the Medal for Valor and as a previous recipient of the Combat Cross. It included the same picture they had seen in the bar: Sirkosky receiving the Medal for Valor.

Sam opened a new tab and looked for descriptions of the awards. The Combat Cross, according to an online encyclopedia, was given for an act of heroism performed in personal combat, at risk of personal danger. The Medal for Valor sounded similar, although it was described as the department's third-highest medal, and it included a line about disregard for personal consequences in a moment of outstanding personal bravery. So, Sam summed up, at least two times, Jimmy Sirkosky had put himself in serious jeopardy and acquitted himself well. That was interesting.

Next, Sam started looking for the particulars. What had Jimmy done, exactly, to earn those awards? Jimmy Sirkosky's LinkedIn page described him as a lieutenant in the NYPD, and from what Sam could gather, he had come up through Vice. He was listed as a 2007 recipient for the Combat Cross and a 2010 recipient of the Medal for Valor. Neither page gave any details about what Jimmy had done to deserve the awards, but at least they gave Sam a starting place. He ran another search, limiting the results to the year 2007, with Sirkosky and police as the keywords.

The first result was an NBC affiliate's website with an article titled "Hero Cop Survives Shootout." Sam skimmed the article and then went back and read it again more slowly. According to Tricia Tuan, the reporter, Detective James Sirkosky had been serving a search warrant in the course of a robbery investigation. The person of interest had responded by opening fire on Jimmy and the uniformed officers accompanying him. Although one officer had been killed immediately, Jimmy had managed to drag the second uniformed officer, who was badly injured, to cover. In the firefight that followed, Jimmy had killed the gunman.

Sam left that tab open, opened another, and tried a similar search, but this time limiting the year to 2010. Once again, he hit pay dirt immediately, but this time, it was a Fox News article: "Liberal Media on the Hunt for Decorated Sergeant." Sharon Bailey, the reporter on this article, explained how members of the liberal press were conducting a witch hunt, with Sergeant James Sirkosky as the victim. Jimmy had apparently been seriously injured—according to Bailey—while defending a homeless woman from an attacker. Jimmy had killed the assailant and tried to save the woman, but she had died days later without recovering consciousness. Now "self-appointed liberal watchdogs" were demanding a full investigation into the events. Bailey ended by editorializing, suggesting that the city owed Jimmy not only its thanks but also recognition for his service. Recognition, Sam figured, that Jimmy had gotten in the next wave of political stunts.

He scanned both articles again, and then he ran a search for articles on Jimmy Sirkosky post-2010. He found one, and it only mentioned Sirkosky in connection with his wife, just names in a list of donors. Sam rubbed his eyes and tapped Rufus on the shoulder. "What do you have?"

Rufus swiveled in his chair to look at Sam. "Riveting stuff about good ol' Jimmy. His uncle died in 2009—funeral drew quite the crowd and they played a Frank Sinatra song. His wife—I shit you not, her name is Barbara—is on the PTA for Manhattan's Gifted Achievers. I guess she's a top fundraiser or something, which is stupid, because none of those kids need fucking scholarships." Rufus clicked his mouse a few times. "He's got a double life where he frequents a sex dungeon dressed as a dog." He looked at Sam and smirked. "I made that last one up. But the rest is true. What'd you find?"

Sam told him. When he'd finished, he said, "It's strange, right? I mean, I know he wasn't working as a candy striper, and maybe the first award, the one where he was serving a warrant, maybe that was legit. But the second one? With the transient woman who ended up dead, the alleged attacker dead, and no witnesses—that's a little too fucking close to home, don't you think?"

Rufus drummed his fingers on the desktop while staring at Sam. "So what, the cops cleaned up the mess and then pinned a medal to him for something that never happened?"

"Or he kills the john, starts having fun with the girl, and gets interrupted. Then the girl has to go too because she might talk. I mean, there's nothing, absolutely nothing, to suggest that's what happened. But I started thinking it, and now I can't stop thinking it."

"Did the article link the woman to sex work?" Rufus asked, scooting his wheeled chair closer to look at Sam's computer.

"No. Just identified her as homeless. I'm telling you, there's nothing in there except… except it's weird, and I don't like it. And after that, it's like a magic trick. Jimmy disappears. I mean, he makes lieutenant, presumably riding the wave from the Medal for Valor, and then he has a normal life. No more shootouts. No more Action Jackson."

Rufus nudged Sam's hand out of the way, took his mouse, and scrolled to the top of the article to stare at a dated photograph of Jimmy in dress uniform. He made a face and leaned back in his seat with a heavy sigh. "You'd think, once he made lieutenant, he'd keep going up the ladder. He clearly had aspirations for the top of the mountain and not working the trenches with all the detectives."

"Right. So what happened?"

"Daisy was killed in 2002. Within a handful of years, Jimmy's racing up the ranks, then his career caps in, what—2010?" Rufus scratched his cheek and then suggested, "I can ask Ophelia if she's heard anything juicy while standing around the water cooler?"

"Even if there's nothing official, there's always a reason guys like that stop moving up. If there's gossip—and there's always gossip—she'll know about it. Let's hear what she has to say."

When Rufus nodded, they logged out of the computers and headed for the stairs. Outside, the day was bright, the shadows crisp, and the smell of artificial cherry floated up from where a kid had spilled a slushie on the steps. They found a spot to sit near Patience the stone lion, and Sam handed his phone to Rufus.

Rufus dialed Ophelia's number and placed the call on speakerphone. "Hi, pal," he stated when the other end was picked up.

"Red." Her voice was cautious. "Why am I getting a sick feeling in my stomach?"

"You need to stop eating the dirty water dogs on First Avenue," Rufus answered. "Those things are probably soaking in toilet water."

"I'm hanging up now."

"Hey, come on. You're so sensitive these days."

"Five seconds. Four. Three. Two—"

"What do you know about Lieutenant James Sirkosky?"

The air brakes on a bus popped as it pulled to the curb. When Ophelia spoke again, the note of caution in her voice had doubled. "Ok, what the hell is going on?"

"That's why I'm calling," Rufus replied. "Do you know him?"

"He's a lieutenant in the Vice squad. He's supposed to be solid. Guys say he'll have your back. I mean, what do I know? I'm still hoofing it on patrol. Hold on. McCallum, I'm going to take a leak. Keep your panties on." Then came the sound of movement, and then in a quieter voice, she said, "Thank Christ that man has no idea how long it takes a woman to pee. I could be in here for four hours and he wouldn't even blink. I may have heard something about Sirkosky. Tell me why you're asking."

Rufus blew out a breath before saying, "I think Jimmy killed Daisy. I think Jimmy killed a lot of people. And we think it's suspicious that after 2010 his career seems to have stalled out."

"You think," Ophelia said. "Or you know?"

"Between us? I'm pretty sure I know it." Rufus glanced at Sam before continuing. "But I need evidence. So until I have something that I can point at and say, 'A-ha, Watson,' I'll have to think it."

"Shit. This is like the summer, Rufus. This is the same shit all over again." Ophelia was silent for a moment. "Do you know Barrera? Iyla Barrera, I mean. She's in Mounted. Probably not, I guess, unless you pulled your shenanigans and got chased down by a woman on horseback. Anyway, some of the women in the department, we get together every once in a while. Drinks, dinner, just, you know, a little solidarity. And after everything that went down last summer, Sirkosky had been sniffing around, talking to me, talking to McCallum, asking a lot of questions. I was complaining to the girls.

"Anyway, I'm getting off track. I was complaining, and then we all started talking about something else, and it all moved on. But at the end of the night, Barrera pulled me aside and said, 'Make sure he doesn't get you alone.' And I had no idea who she was talking about, so I asked, and she said, 'Sirkosky. Don't let him get you alone.' And we'd all probably had too much to drink because I said, 'An old guy like that?' And Barrera said, 'It didn't stop him from getting busy with that girl uptown.' Then it all came out: he got busted on a Vice sting, taking a working girl back to a hotel. They swept it all under the rug, but that's why he's stuck where he is. No bad publicity, you know, because he was a hero and he's a lieutenant and the department has enough shit to deal with. But no captain's laurels for Sirkosky. Ever."

Rufus stared at the phone. His eyebrows had inched so high, they were practically hidden under the beanie. "That girl he brought to the hotel—was she ok? I mean, she's still alive?"

"What? Yeah. I mean, I don't think they would have swept *that* under the rug."

"A guy's gotta ask," Rufus said, "considering all the murdered girls, past and present, were sex workers too."

"Look," Ophelia said. "You guys were right last time, although God knows I hope you're not right again. But just because Jimmy Sirkosky did some dumb shit in his life and is a misogynistic prick doesn't mean you're right. I'll ask around, see if I can find out where he was when these last two murders happened. Christ, if I can do that without painting a target on my back."

A pair of girls sprinted up the marble steps, giggling and laughing and pulling on each other's arms, trying to slow each other down. When they were past, the silence on the phone seemed to crackle.

"Let us know," Sam said.

"I don't even know why I'm saying this," Ophelia said, "but good luck."

The call disconnected.

"What now?" Sam said to Rufus. "I mean, Jimmy's even more of a piece of shit than we thought, but we're not any closer to tying him to any of this."

Rufus held Sam's phone, tapping the corners on either side with his index fingers as he watched the giggling girls vanish inside the library. "Do you think Ophelia loves me?" He looked down and started typing into the web browser. "She never wishes me luck. I should gently let her down before her heart's fully invested."

"Not while we still need her," Sam said. "She might do what she says she's going to do. If we're really lucky, maybe she'll actually dig up something on Jimmy. But we can't just wait around for Ophelia to tell us she came up empty."

Rufus nodded to Sam's response, but while he scrolled and typed some more, he muttered, "What'd I say that semitruck driver's name was…? William Mont—no, Monroe?" He tapped for another minute and swore. "Unless he's a ninety-year-old living in the Bronx, I can't find him listed in the White Pages. Might have been a fake name he gave the hospital."

An older man in a US Navy cap, a yellow Helping Hands vest, and sweats shuffled past them. He was towing an entire shopping cart's worth of Furbies—the tiny, furry toys were chattering and babbling to each other as they rattled against each other in the cart.

"Please tell me we're getting out of the city again." Sam scrubbed his face. "Ok, we've got to wait for Ophelia before we can do anything else with Jimmy. What about Mac?"

Rufus looked up. "What about him? He's a dead-end."

"I still don't like the knife. We don't know why Charlotte gave it to him or how he—oh fuck me. Where did the knife get delivered?"

Rufus had been midway to putting his sunglasses on when he froze. "I don't—Charlotte's, I guess. I mean, right?"

"Yeah, that's what I guessed too. But it's worth checking. Why don't you channel your inner punkin' darlin' and see what the people at the Forge can tell you?"

Rufus blushed, got defensive, muttered something about how convincing that call had been and Sam was jealous of his acting chops, and rang the poor receptionist at Out of the Forge because he'd plum forgotten the delivery address and needed to update his own records. She must have remembered Rufus, because he was only on the phone for a minute, tops, before hanging up and passing Sam the cell.

"No one says goodbye these days. Do you notice that? They just hang up."

"That particular cultural shift seems to happen extra frequently with you. Did you get anything?"

"I'm fucking charming," Rufus said and he poked Sam in the chest. "The delivery address was a place in the East Village. Nowhere near Charlotte's."

"Fuck." Sam eased himself off the ledge, massaging his leg. "Let's go take a look."

CHAPTER
TWENTY-EIGHT

Bryant Park to the East Village with an October chill in the air would have been a pleasant walk on any day that Sam didn't have a hole in his leg. So Rufus hadn't suggested it, even though it was the cheapest option. They were right near the Coney Island–bound F train, which would bring them down to Second Avenue, where they'd only be a hop, skip, and jump away from the address.

Of course, once Rufus got down into the subway, he realized Sam wouldn't be able to jump the turnstile either, and wasn't having to pay $2.75 a bitch? He dug his wallet from his back pocket, shoved his rarely used MTA card into Sam's hand, then jumped the turnstile himself when the rumble of an incoming train shook the platform. Rufus slipped into the car as the doors opened, leaned back against them so they couldn't shut, and flashed Sam a grin when the other man joined him. The doors shut as the woman in the booth had finally gotten from her seat and came out to yell at Rufus for not paying.

When they reached the East Village, Rufus led Sam down a quick walk on East Houston, then up and over to a walkup on Third between First and Avenue A. He skipped ahead as an older, grandmotherly type, pushing a stroller of two geriatric dogs, struggled to exit the building and hush the yapping rugs at the same time. Rufus grabbed the door and held it for her.

"Oh, thank you, young man," she said before shushing the dogs again and shoving the stroller onto the sidewalk. "Bless you."

Rufus gave her a salute. "No problem. Have a good day."

"Yes, you too. Hush, Bobby! Hush, now." The dogs continued barking as she toddled down the street.

Rufus turned and beckoned Sam to enter the building. "Kind sir."

Sam arched his eyebrows as he passed Rufus, but all he said was "Thanks."

Rufus followed, pulling the front door shut behind himself. He moved to the wall of mailboxes, studied the names, then tapped one. "1C. That was the apartment the Forge delivered to." Rufus slid around Sam and started down the long, narrow hall.

When they got to 1C, Sam glanced at Rufus, a question on his face, and Rufus waved for him to go ahead. Sam positioned himself in front of the door and hammered on it. He paused for a few seconds and began hammering again. In between blows, Rufus could hear someone moving on the other side, a man saying, "I'm coming, I'm coming," but Sam didn't stop pounding.

The door behind them opened first, and a slender,

middle-aged man with his toupee askew stood there, belting a kimono. "Excuse me," he said. "Some people work at night. Some of us are trying to sleep. Excuse me!"

"Fuck off," Sam growled and kept knocking.

"Well, really," Kimono Guy said. "I'm calling—"

Sam spun around so fast that Kimono Guy tripped over his kimono sash and landed on his ass, kimono flying up, exposing himself.

"Who are you calling?" Sam said.

"Nobody," Kimono Guy said. "Nobody!"

Footsteps were moving toward them from inside 1C.

Sam just stood there, staring at Kimono Guy. Kimono Guy flushed. And then something shifted, and he fluttered his eyes at Sam. Adjusting his toupee, Kimono Guy said, "How terribly rude of me. When you've finished your business with Mr. Stevens, you really have to stop by so I can at least offer you a drink."

"Stevens?" Rufus repeated just as a chain lock was sliding from the inside of 1C's door.

Sam didn't bother replying; he turned around as the door to 1C opened.

"The hell is all the noise?" Mac Stevens leaned into the hallway. He looked at Kimono Guy, then Rufus, then Sam. "This some kind of exhibitionist thing?"

Rufus stared at Mac for a singular second, but within that breath of passing time, his childhood, like a flip-book of hand-drawn figures brought to life through the persistence of vision, was right there in front of him again. And he had to decide, once again: was Rufus going to disappear into the shadows of the city's night, or was he going to finally be somebody?

Mac Stevens was a washed-up pimp from the '90s. A man who'd taken advantage of young, vulnerable women. A man who'd help shape Daisy into the woman she'd become and mold the life she was relegated to living. And when the unthinkable had happened—Mac had stood by and done *nothing*.

Rufus ran at Mac and slammed into him, knocking the middle-aged man backward into his apartment and crashing to the floor. "You piece of shit!" he shouted, leaning down to grab Mac by the throat.

The next minute, Sam was there, yanking Rufus up and off Mac. The bigger man interposed himself, a hand clutching Rufus's shirt to hold him in place. When Mac tried to scramble back, Sam put one boot on his chest and pressed down. Even through the wave of rage, Rufus could hear the *whoosh* of expelled breath.

"Sam—let me—you fucking waste of oxygen," Rufus hollered at Mac, trying to wriggle free. "All those girls. All those fucking girls!"

Mac's face was white, pasted with a sheen of sweat as he struggled under Sam's hold. "Wh—who the fuck are you two?"

"Do you remember when Shannon turned up dead?" Rufus asked Mac. "When Bunny went missing? When Daisy O'Callaghan called you, begging not to be sent to the Ramble because she was scared? Do you *fucking remember that*?"

Mac swallowed, licked his lips, and shot Sam a look before trying to lift his boot a second time.

"You are in some serious fucking trouble," Sam said.

"Fuck you, man. I don't know what you're talking about. How'd you get in the building? You'd better scram before I call—"

"The cops?" Rufus finished for him, smiling almost manically. Ripping away from Sam, he reached into his back pocket, retrieved his wallet, and began pulling out business cards, flicking them at Mac. "Who do you want to talk to? Detective Larkin? Detective Weaver? I've even got a beat cop who'd love to whack you upside the head, given the chance."

"Why wait for the cops?" Sam asked. He drew his foot back and kicked Mac in the side. It didn't look like the blow was hard enough to cause serious damage, but it drove the breath from Mac's lungs. When Mac tried to roll away, Sam pinned him with a boot again. "I want to get some answers now. See if he has a baseball bat. Or a pair of pliers. Anything, really."

Rufus eyed Sam, looked down at Mac next, then took a step in the direction of the minute studio kitchen.

"Wh-whoa, hey, wait," Mac protested. "Stop, come on. Don't—what do you want to know?"

Rufus returned and crouched beside Mac. "Did you kill my mother?"

"Who the fuck are you?"

"Daisy O'Callaghan," Rufus shouted again, grabbing a fistful of Mac's shirt and yanking him. "Did you kill her? Yes or no?"

Mac's breathing quickened, and he was visibly shaking now. "That was… that was twenty fucking years ago."

"Did you kill her?" Rufus demanded.

"No! Jesus fucking Christ, I didn't kill Daisy!"

"Then who did?" Sam said.

"How the fucking hell should I know?" Mac protested, only glancing away from Rufus for a second to address Sam. "Lots of girls got the axe. It wasn't me—I lost money because of it."

Rufus slapped Mac across the face. "She was a person, not a commodity, you piece of shit."

"Jesus, kid—"

Rufus smacked him again. "Tell us everything you know," he said, his voice cracking. "Or I swear to God, I'll commit a homicide of my own."

"I don't know who killed her," Mac said, more desperately. He looked up at Sam once more. "Tell him I don't know!"

"Tell him? Fuck you. You're going to give us something; you're up to your neck in this shit. Start talking."

Mac shook his head, sputtered more proclamations of innocence, but then he dared another look in Rufus's direction. "*Rufus* O'Callaghan?"

"I know who the fuck I am, you dumb shit."

"You're not… but you're supposed to be dead."

Rufus stood. "You must own a knife, right, Mac?" He started for the kitchen a second time.

Mac shot both hands out. "Kid. *Rufus*! Come on. I didn't—I was supposed to hit the fucking prison bus. That's it."

"Yeah?" Sam said. "Tell us about that. You were supposed to hit the bus? Why?"

"I was supposed to help Devon Kelly escape a prison transport bus upstate. I rammed it with a semi." Mac watched Rufus slowly return. "Kelly was supposed to gut this kid. Over a week ago. I was just paid to hit the bus."

"Yeah? You helped Kelly escape, and you knew he was supposed to kill Rufus, and—that's all, folks? We're supposed to believe you don't know anything else? Who put you in that fucking truck? Who sent Kelly after Rufus? Names, you piece of dog shit. And every fucking detail of the plan."

"It was Jimmy Sirkosky," Mac cried loudly. "Half up front, the rest after I picked Kelly up and got him back into the city."

"Yeah? Do you have proof? Texts, calls, messages, emails? Do you have dates and times?"

"Texts," Mac said. "From a burner Jimmy kept. Kelly had the same contact number." He shifted uncomfortably under Sam's weight. "Look, I had nothing to do with the plan to off *him*," he said, spitting the last word out while looking at Rufus.

"Yeah? It sounds like bullshit to me. An NYPD lieutenant decides to break a convict out of prison for a hit? And he gets you to help him? Fuck that. Jimmy Sirkosky could have driven past Rufus's place and taken care of it himself. You're full of shit, Mac. And you're wasting my time. Did you find pliers?"

"It's not bullshit! Christ Almighty. Kelly had dirt on Sirkosky," Mac protested. "Something about a video he had—Sirkosky fucking some bitch—"

Rufus kicked Mac hard in the ribs.

Mac howled and tried to curl in on himself. "Some *lady*," he wheezed. "Tried to kill her. I don't know, something like that. I never saw it. Kelly kept bragging the whole fucking drive back into the city that he'd been stringing Sirkosky along for years, promising to hand the video over for money. Only he never did—kept bleedin' Sirkosky for more cash. And when Kelly got locked up, he said he'd hand the video over to his lawyer, then *bam*— there I was, breaking the little fucker out. He was supposed to deal with Rufus for whatever reason, I didn't ask, but that shitbag probably has another ploy up his sleeve for milking more cash from Sirkosky."

"Not anymore," Rufus said. "The shitbag is dead."

"What about Honey and Chantalle and George?" Sam asked. "What did you have to do with that?"

Mac's face was twisted up in pain, and he shook his head. "Nothing. I swear to God."

"Sirkosky didn't want anything else?" Rufus asked.

"No, the truck and the knife. Just the truck and the knife, that's all."

"What knife?" Sam asked.

"It was just this knife one of my girls got me. I showed him one time. He liked it. I sold it to him."

"All right." Sam glanced at Rufus, his words still directed at Mac. "Phone. Right now. The one you used to talk to Jimmy."

Mac reached a shaky hand into his jeans and retrieved an unassuming cell. He held it up. "Here. Take it."

"You never met him in person?"

"Twenty years ago," Mac said. "When he was a punk kid wanting to fuck some—"

Rufus drew his foot back.

Mac held his hands out. "When he was a kid!" he corrected. "And—and then, I followed him home. A few weeks back. I didn't get a chance to speak with him. His fucking doorman was there."

"Address," Sam said.

Mac rattled off a street number. "The Village. A high rise."

With a grunt, Sam eased off Mac. To Rufus, he said, "Watch him." Then he disappeared into one of the back rooms. When he returned, he was carrying a bedsheet, which he took into the filthy kitchen area of the cramped front room. He cut strips from the bedding and brought them back to stand over Mac. "Want to do the honors?" he asked Rufus.

Rufus grabbed the strips and said to Mac, "Roll over."

"What?"

"I'm about five seconds away from actually killing you," Rufus warned.

Mac rolled onto his belly. Rufus crouched over him and tied his wrists together, then did the same to his ankles.

"Call Ophelia," Sam said. "Tell her to get her ass over

here before this dickbag causes even more problems."

CHAPTER
TWENTY-NINE

When they left the brick walk-up, Sam tried to shake off the encounter with Mac. The sky was milky white with a scum of clouds, and the air cool but with the tang of garbage and urine that seemed to follow him everywhere in this city. All of it, the whole performance in 1C, had been too close to the things Sam had seen at Benning, and suddenly the need for the wide-open spaces, asphalt and dust and corn burned white under the sun—it hit him hard.

"Can we sit down somewhere? Somewhere that's not a fucking stoop or a bench with a lawyer's ad. My leg is on fire, and I'm about to go out of my fucking head."

Rufus glanced toward the nearest cross streets and then up at Sam. "Can you walk about ten minutes? We aren't far from Tompkins Square Park." He reached a hand out, brushing his blunt fingers very lightly against Sam's bare arm.

Smiling—although it felt like a load of bricks—Sam took Rufus's hand and nodded. Rufus led them north, past brick apartment buildings bristling with window-unit air conditioners, under a sidewalk shed with a green canopy, past a still-drying patch of cement where someone, probably a prepubescent, had drawn a dick and balls with a concerning lack of pubes. They passed a store selling housewares, a cafe, a 24-hour gym, a nail salon, and a narrow storefront with an old-fashioned black-and-white letter board that said MAILBOX - OFFICE SUPPLIES - DELI SANDWICHES BUY BY THE SLICE, whatever the hell that meant. At Avenue A and Seventh Street, they jogged—well, hobbled—catty-corner to a park.

"We've been here before," Sam said, although he couldn't quite remember when. "What is this place?"

Rufus tugged Sam toward the nearest park entrance. "Maybe it looks different in the light," he answered, pointing toward the left. "We chased Marcus that way, after you had flirted with me at Bar."

"Right," Sam said. "That was a nice night. Except for Marcus getting murdered. And getting in that awful fight after." He gestured to a bench facing a sunny patch of lawn. "Can we sit?"

Rufus nodded and untangled his hand from Sam's so he could take a seat. He stood over Sam for a minute, smiling a little smile at him. The tips of his ears, visible above the beanie, were pink. "I liked it when you played with my hair."

Sam's next smile didn't feel quite so heavy. "I'll remember that. So we know Jimmy is behind everything, right? We just don't have anything but an old pimp's word and possibly a burner phone with texts from another burner phone."

Rufus deflated a little as he nodded. He moved to Sam's right and plopped down on the bench beside him. A breeze kicked up a mini whirlwind of leaves, rocking back and forth across the sidewalk in the shape of a three-foot tornado. Rufus rubbed his bare arms as gooseflesh pebbled his skin.

"Jimmy's as guilty as original sin," Rufus began, "but if we don't prove that, go to the city or, hell, even the FBI with tangible evidence of what he's been doing all these years, he'll walk." Rufus looked at Sam over the rims of his sunglasses. "Then he'll *definitely* come after me. Maybe Ophelia too. Fuck, even Erik."

"So we need evidence. Where do we get evidence that this lunatic has been killing women for twenty years?"

Rufus brought his thumb to his mouth and chewed on the nail. "Daisy had a tattoo. And remember how I told you, when I identified her remains, that her arm was missing?" Rufus rubbed his thumb against his thigh. "Charlotte had an ankle tattoo. The day we met her. I don't know if you noticed. But then her foot had been amputated. What if that's what he's been doing? Keeping parts of his victims? That would be a hell of a piece of evidence, don't you think?"

"What about Honey? Or Chantalle? Did they have tattoos?"

Rufus twisted his face up as he thought. "Honey did. It was a sloppy ivy vine on the back of her hand and around her wrist like a bracelet. And she had that chopping blow, but like he didn't get to finish."

"I bet Chantalle had something too. Fuck." Sam massaged his thigh. "Fuck me if I know what any of this means. He's taking parts—I'm sorry, I'm not trying to be disrespectful, but that's what he's doing. He's taking parts, and then what's he doing with them? That's the real question."

"But it's not just *parts*," Rufus corrected. "It's the tattoos. I mean, is he *collecting* them?"

"He's taking them for a reason. And I don't think he's just, you know, putting them down the garbage disposal. Guys like this—killers like this—a lot of them keep a reminder of their kills. Like a memento. A tattoo becomes a permanent part of you. A unique part of you."

Rufus held the back of his hand to his mouth and swallowed a few times. "If it was a memento, he'd keep it, right? So, if we found Jimmy in possession of… *those*… he'd be done for."

"All right. Let's think like a serial killer. A competent one. He's a cop. He's had a successful career until he shot himself in the fucking foot, figuratively. He's avoided suspicion for any of the killings up to this point, and he seems to even have a contingency plan. He's definitely trying to frame Mac with that knife. And the only reason we're on to him now is because he made two mistakes with you: he didn't get rid of you when you were a kid, and he put a moron like Devon Kelly on the job when you were an adult. Where's a guy like that—a guy with a wife, a family, loyal friends in the department—where's he going to stash his trophies? It's not like they're in the rumpus room and he can chat about them when the guys come over for a beer."

"And with a high-rise apartment," Rufus continued, "it's even more difficult to come by privacy. He wouldn't have a basement or attic, so logically he likely wouldn't or *couldn't* keep those sorts of trophies in his home."

"Ok, let's start there. Do you know where that address is, the one Mac gave us?"

"370 West Eleventh," Rufus repeated with a nod. "Opposite direction of where we are now."

"What are the odds Jimmy's keeping this stuff in a place like that?"

"I mean, he's ballsy, but he's not stupid. A family member would stumble across those sooner or later," Rufus answered.

Sam hesitated. "Would he keep them at work? You know, the last place you'd expect, that kind of thing?"

"God, I hope not. Erik isn't going to go snooping through Jimmy's desk drawers for me, even if I bent over and presented my ass for him."

"Which," Sam said evenly—he thought—"you won't be doing."

"Do I hear jealousy in your tone, Mr. Auden?"

"You hear the imminent sound of serious fucking trouble if you ever present your ass to Detective Erik Weaver."

Rufus was grinning. "Noted." He got to his feet and moved to stand before Sam again. "The way I see it, we've got two options. One, do nothing and run away somewhere where there's more cows and corn than people. Or two, break into Jimmy's place ourselves to find some evidence to use against him."

"One."

Rufus opened his mouth, closed it, then waved both hands. "Ok, but one wasn't a real option. You were supposed to say two."

"Fine," Sam said. "We'll save option one for later."

They walked north to Fourteenth Street and caught a bus across town. The walk at the end was only a few blocks, but it left Sam shaking and sweating in spite of the breeze knifing in off the Hudson. Jimmy's building matched Mac's description, complete with doorman. A Lincoln Town Car waited in front, and a woman in kitten heels, carrying a Bed Bath & Beyond bag as big as she was, was getting out of the back seat.

"I don't think I've ever had to get past a doorman,"

Sam said. "Do we go around back? What do you usually do?"

"I usually break into places without a doorman," Rufus answered, deadpan. "I can distract him and let you get inside first."

"The door won't be locked?"

"Nope, not places with a doorman."

"And how are you going to get inside?"

"I'll circle back after getting him away from the building," Rufus answered. "Come on. He's a bit pudgy and I run like the wind."

Sam nodded and let Rufus get ahead of him.

The doorman ushered the woman and her massive bag inside before walking back toward the middle of the sidewalk. That's where Rufus roughly bumped the man's shoulder and dipped a hand into his coat pocket. Sam briefly considered the action to be too obvious and heavy-handed for someone like Rufus, until he realized it was Rufus's intention to be caught. And just like that—

"Hey!" the doorman shouted. "You little shit!"

Rufus looked down at a big iPhone in his hand before waving it and asking, "Isn't this the model that's causing trypophobia? I'll take it off your hands." He skipped backward a few steps.

"I'm gonna kick your ass, kid!" The doorman broke into a run, and Rufus grinned before bolting, waving the phone over his head as he disappeared down the street.

Sam wasn't up to running, but he hobbled forward as quickly as he could. A fresh wave of nausea surged up inside him, and sweat stung his face, under his arms. At the end of the block, Rufus was cutting around the corner, and the doorman was chasing in a dead sprint. True to Rufus's prediction, the building's door was unlocked, and Sam slipped inside as a pair of older men, one in leopard-print pants and the other in a leotard—and only a leotard—passed him in the other direction.

"Well, hello," the man in the leopard-print pants said.

The man in the leotard growled and swiped a claw at Sam.

Sam stepped into an alcove, where one wall was lined with mailboxes. He ran his gaze over them until he saw Sirkosky - 6F. Then he hurried toward the elevators, ducked around a corner where he wouldn't be visible from the street, and waited.

Rufus burst through the front door less than a minute later, out of breath, his cheeks pink, but a decidedly victorious expression on his face. He did however, pause long enough to do a double, then triple take at the gentlemen. He shook his head and walked toward the elevators before finding Sam. "Miss me?"

"Oh no, I had plenty of company."

"I saw," Rufus said with a nod, jutting a thumb over his shoulder. He tapped the Up button next. "I could have had a brand-new phone. The one with the telephoto cameras and everything. Stupid thing was locked with a fingerprint scan."

"Do you find yourself needing to take a lot of telephoto pictures?"

"Maybe I'll start an Instagram account." Rufus slipped inside the elevator car as the doors opened. "Streets of New York, as seen by a street rat."

"6F," Sam said.

Rufus hit another button as Sam stepped inside.

They rode up to the sixth floor and followed the hallway to the front of the building, where a door was marked 6F. Sam put his ear to the door, but the damn thing looked solid, and he couldn't tell if the apartment was silent or if the door was just an excellent sound barrier.

"What are the odds the wife is home?" Sam said. "Fuck, what are the odds Jimmy is home?"

"Jimmy, probably not. Barbara, fifty-fifty." Rufus waved a hand. "Knock."

Sam rapped on the door. Five seconds, ten, twenty. He knocked again and checked his phone. When two minutes had passed, he made an *after-you* gesture and stepped aside. Rufus had the locks picked in under five minutes. Sam spotted a contact sensor in the doorframe, the kind that came with DIY home security systems, and for half a second, panic gripped him. No alarm sounded, though, and Sam traded a look with Rufus. After another half a minute, they moved into the apartment.

Either Jimmy or Barbara—or both—had taste. The living room, where Sam and Rufus stood, had classic furniture that they'd probably purchased decades before and that had kept its appeal with minor cosmetic updates: a chesterfield sofa with tarnished brass tufting, leather club chairs, teak bookshelves with a midcentury design that looked original rather than like a replica. The most obvious update to the room was the massive flat-screen television, but otherwise, everything looked like it had been purchased carefully and well maintained. Family money? Barbara?

Rufus was already moving through the room, snooping through the bookshelves, turning over the magazines stacked on the coffee table, digging behind the club chair's seat cushions. Sam limped past him, passed a small dining area and then a much larger—and expensively updated—kitchen, and followed a hall that ran deeper into the apartment. He passed a bedroom that obviously belonged to Jimmy's kid: a twin bed, a desk, dirty clothes on the floor, and every inch of the walls covered with Red Sox gear and posters. J.D. Martinez stared down from a poster; *It wouldn't kill the guy*, Sam thought, *to lend a fucking hand and pick up a sock.*

The next room was a bathroom, which Sam decided was exclusively the domain of the kid. He based that judgment on the toothpaste crusted in the sink and the toilet that looked like it needed first fumigation and then an exorcism. He kept going—if what they needed was in that bathroom, he'd make Rufus find it.

At the end of the hall was what was probably billed as the master bedroom. A king-sized bed dominated the space, and whoever slept on the far side of the bed—he was guessing Barbara—had to squeeze past a chest of drawers and a dresser. A tri-fold brass frame on the dresser held pictures of a young man and woman in wedding clothes. The mall bangs made Sam think early '90s. The room's best features were a picture window that opened up most of one wall, allowing in a flood of natural light, and an en suite bathroom.

Limping back toward the living room, Sam called, "Find anything?"

Rufus instead poked his head out of the kid's room. "Did you see all this fuckin' Red Sox shit?"

"He's got almost as much as I do."

Rufus's expression dropped. "You're a Red Sox fan?"

"God, your face. I'm just pulling your leg. Cubs."

Rufus let out a breath of air. "Don't scare me like that. Anyway, I found thirty-seven cents in the cushions. One of the pennies is a wheat-back." Rufus held it up. "Neat, huh?"

"Jinkies," Sam said, "that's super neat."

"All right, Velma. Calm down." Rufus stuffed the coins in his pocket. "Did you check the kitchen? They don't have any paperwork in the living room, but there's got to be a paper or money trail pointing somewhere." He brushed past Sam and then shouted, "Jesus Christ, this kitchen is the size of my entire studio."

Sam followed him. Rufus wasn't exaggerating; the kitchen really was the size of his studio apartment—if not bigger. Carrara marble (Sam guessed), miles of cabinets, a range hood big enough for Santa Claus. Rufus had already found a pair of double doors that opened to reveal a writing desk, apparently the location of the Sirkosky home office. He was pulling open drawers, piling papers on the desk, and trilling slightly off-key bursts of a song Sam thought was from *Chicago.*

While Rufus worked, Sam made his way through the rest of the kitchen, figuring out what rich people wasted their money on. Some of the things seemed useful—built-in paper-towel holder, for example, or the dedicated warming drawer—while others looked like bullshit—a touchless faucet for the sink. It took Sam a couple tries to figure out how it worked. By that point, it was kind of fun, so he tried it a few more times. Just to be sure.

"Ok, so two—*three* things," Rufus said from the desk. "The Sirkosky's don't go paperless." He waved a paper over one shoulder. "This is their bank statement—holy shit are he and the missus *loaded.*" Rufus put that aside and then turned around holding up what looked similar to a monthly statement, its logo and border an obnoxious bright orange color. "But more interesting, Jimmy has a storage locker. Three weeks ago, he paid an annual renewal fee."

"Well, that's pretty interesting. Any sign of how they got to be loaded? Big deposits? Does the wife have some kind of job raking in cash?"

Rufus picked up the statement again. "It doesn't look suspicious. These two deposits look like Jimmy's paycheck. Most of the money is in savings and an IRA account. I bet it's been there a long time." He looked at Sam. "Barbara probably comes from old money. Some stupid investment a great-great-great-grandfather made that she's still benefiting from."

"Well, God bless rich old white men," Sam said. "What about the storage unit?"

Rufus joined Sam and offered the statement. "He's got a closet in SoHo." He shrugged. "The middle unit. Access available 24-7, complete with AC to keep your questionable trophies in tiptop shape."

"Christ. This is some nightmare-level stuff. I didn't really dig around in the bedroom; do you think we need to see Barbara's stirrup pants and knock-off Madonna bra— the sharp, pointy one?"

"I'm gonna stop you right there, Sam. Because there is no way in hell I'm going through their underwear drawers to find out if Barbara is a granny panties or thong kinda gal." Rufus took the statement, folded it, then tucked it into his back pocket. "The unknown contents of Jimmy's locker would be more preferable."

CHAPTER
THIRTY

On their way to Wooster and Grand, Rufus and Sam stopped at a hardware store. Deez Nutz, which advertised as having been established in 2014 and boasted, per the sign in the front window display, WE HAVE ALL NUTS! EVERY NUT KNOWN TO MAN! (NO PEANUTS, HENRY. STOP ASKING. – THE MANAGEMENT). Rufus slipped inside and wandered up and down the congested aisles that he was absolutely certain Sam's shoulders would not have fit through. The tiling was old, stained, and missing chunks here and there, like something heavy had been dropped on it. Rufus briefly considered a display of mallets and sledgehammers, and then the damage to the asbestos-ridden floor made a lot more sense.

He eventually found a pile of miscellaneous tools in

the back of the shop—caulk guns, hammers available with a dozen different grips choices, even spud wrenches—but Rufus noted that he hadn't stumbled upon all these fucking nuts they claimed to have, which was some bullshit false advertising. Rufus grabbed some bolt cutters from a dusty shelf, paid for them, asked for a bag, which The Management replied to by sighing heavily before unearthing a loose plastic bag from somewhere under the register counter, and then he left.

Wooster was a pretty street and an example of the past meeting present. Cobblestone was partially paved over, one side of the street consisted of century-old walk-up tenements, the other refurbished storefronts for luxury shopping or pop-up modern art installations. If you asked Rufus, one maintained the charm of the city, while the other was like a benign tumor. And right there on the corner, nestled among the historical and contemporary, was Pack Yourself Manhattan.

"Closet on the second floor. Middle unit," Rufus said.

Sam nodded at the door. "And they let strange men with bolt cutters in a bag wander around inside?"

"Well, I'd hoped they'd give me a paper bag," Rufus protested. "But I guess the management at Deez Nutz wants to contribute to the climate crisis. Anyway, if we roll in like we're checking our unit, I can't imagine we'd be stopped."

"All right," Sam said, "let's try it."

Rufus grabbed the handle of the glass door and yanked it open. He handed Sam the bag, stepped inside first, and moved toward the counter as Sam walked in a few steps behind.

"Howdy," he said loudly.

The girl at the counter—and she had to be a girl; the poor thing was still rocking braces—glanced up from a magazine. She blew a bubble of gum, which then popped and got stuck in that mess of metal. "Shit," she mumbled, tugging at the gum.

"Uh… you good?" Rufus asked.

"Yeah. Happens all the time."

"I imagine."

She yanked a piece of pink from her front braces and flicked it into a trashcan. "Did you need something?"

Rufus shook his head. "Oh. No. I mean, just checking my unit."

"Ok." Still with a bit of gum stuck in those little colorful bits of braces, she opened a Trident pack that was sitting on the countertop.

"Is that sugar-free?" Rufus asked.

"Yeah. Don't want cavities." She popped it in her mouth and looked at Rufus again. "Did you forget where your unit was, mister?"

"No. Do I need to sign-in or anything?"

She snorted and almost choked on the gum.

"Never mind. This way?" Rufus asked, jutting a thumb over his shoulder in the direction Sam had already gone.

"Yeah, man."

"Cool, dude," he said dryly before leaving her to her gum and whatever heartthrob magazine teenagers read these days. He jogged around the corner, up the stairs, and met Sam on the second floor. "Oh my God. She called me *mister*."

"You know what you need? You need to really lay it on thick. Not just a beanie and torn jeans. Maybe a t-shirt from a punk band nobody's heard of. And spikes. You can use Elmer's Glue to spike your hair. Can we finish committing this felony before anybody wonders what we're doing here?"

"Kids these days *haven't* heard of the Dead Kennedys,"

Rufus said, patting his own chest and motioning to his shirt's logo. "Also, your sarcasm is noted, Mr. Banner. Don't Hulk out." He moved down the hall and motioned Sam to follow. Rufus stopped near the end of a wall of units and tapped one. "This is it. 215." He took off his sunglasses and hung them from his collar.

Sam unwrapped the bolt cutters and lined himself up with the stacked lockers. He set the blades against the shackle and compressed the handles. The blades snicked through the shackle, and the padlock sagged. He used the bolt cutter's blades to twist the lock and then, when it had pulled wide enough, he grabbed it and yanked it from the hasp.

"Want to do the honors?"

"You really know how to make a guy swoon." But Rufus wasn't smiling anymore, and the tease rang hollow. He took a very calculated breath—in and out—squared his shoulders, and gave the handle a firm tug. Whatever he'd been expecting—a cascade of human limbs to wash over them?—didn't happen. Inside were a dozen neatly stacked Rubbermaid containers on the shelf, just sitting there, as innocent as you please. Rufus reached inside, picked one up, and brought it close. There was a label made out of masking tape on the lid, with bright, crisp penmanship, like the notation had only recently been added before storage.

10/17/19 - turtle

Rufus popped the four snaps of the lid, took the top off, then barely managed to suppress what was a combination of a gag and a scream. He flung the container, and something brown—sort of like parchment, but thicker—smacked against the closet unit on the left, then fell to the floor with an odd *slap*ping sound. Rufus clutched both hands to his chest and took a step backward.

"Holy shit," Sam said, squatting. He shot back up

almost immediately. "Is that what I think it is?"

"*Skin*?" Rufus asked, the inflection of his tone going up so high, his voice nearly cracked.

"Fuck, fuck, fuck, fuck, fuck." Sam hunkered down. He gestured to the Rubbermaid and then back to the flap of skin. "A turtle. The tattoo. The date on the label makes me think that's from Chantalle."

Rufus pointed toward the shelf inside the unit. "Th- there are more in there, Sam."

Sam stretched up to examine the locker, shook his head, and started swearing a blue streak. "These are his trophies, the sick fuck."

Rufus stared at the Rubbermaids, but didn't move to touch them. "Do you think Daisy is in there?" His voice was very small.

"Maybe you should wait over there. I don't think you should see this."

Rufus shook his head. "I need to know. I need the truth, and I need to... to say goodbye. She wasn't perfect. But she was all I had."

Sam nodded, setting a hand at the small of Rufus's back as he came forward.

Rufus shuffled toward the unit again, then reached inside. He pushed containers aside, working his way toward the bottom of two neat piles. He tugged one free and read the faded penmanship—*01/05/00 – stars*—then put it back. Rufus grabbed the second from the bottom, this masking tape label yellowed from time: *02/24/02 - daisy*.

He popped the sides of the lid open, worked the top free, then looked inside. Rufus's eyes welled with unfallen tears.

"Fuck," Sam said, his hand still steady on Rufus's back. "I'm going to call Erik." Then, his voice softer, he said, "Maybe I should take that, Rufus. You saw it. You know. You don't need to go on hurting yourself."

"No." Rufus quickly snapped the lid in place and hugged the container to his chest. "I'll hold it. Call Erik." With his free hand, he wiped his eyes and cheeks dry.

Behind him, Sam spoke quietly into the phone. When he'd finished telling Erik about the locker, he ended the call and said to Rufus, "He's on his way."

"Ok." Rufus pointed at the rest of the contents in the storage unit. "Good thing he's a neurotic and labeled everything." He gave Sam a watery smile.

Sam hooked an arm around him and pulled him close. After a moment, he said, "What can I do for you? Christ, I can't even imagine what you're feeling."

Rufus put a hand against Sam's chest and gently pushed back. "I don't know if I'm capable of feeling anything right now beyond numb inevitability. Thank God I've got therapy coming. My psychiatrist is going to love me."

Sam squeezed him tighter.

Rufus didn't mean to crack a joke. It wasn't the time. It wasn't the place. It wasn't even funny. But he didn't know how to compute the Rubbermaid container he was holding against his chest without doing something very terrible to himself. So he shook his head, let Sam see the tears fall this time, and wrapped his hand around the back of Sam's neck before giving it a squeeze he hoped had conveyed one thing: *thank you for being here*.

Then Rufus saw a head of blond hair over Sam's shoulder, coming up the stairs. Then a face.

The same face he saw on the stairs every Monday as a boy.

Jimmy Sırkosky.

Rufus grabbed Sam's wrist, turned, and ran toward the

end of the hall, where there was a sharp, tight left turn into the next aisle. It dead-ended after ten yards. Rufus heard the shattering of brick to their right, at head level, before the echo of a suppressor shot followed half a heartbeat after.

"I always told you that I'd see you again, didn't I, Rufus O'Callaghan?" Jimmy called.

Sam's head swiveled, taking in the aisle in both directions; he had his gun in his hand. "How the hell do we get out of here? This is a fucking shooting gallery; there's no cover."

"Sam Auden, isn't it?" Jimmy continued, each word punctuated by the echo of shoe treads on linoleum as he moved down the aisle they had run from. "That's who you are. You were in the city over the summer. Digging into deep shit with this troublemaking punk."

"Let him talk," Sam whispered. He pointed at the ceiling. "I'll keep him busy down here. Go find Erik; that bag of dicks has to be good for something."

"You shouldn't have come back," Jimmy said, his voice now somewhere near his open storage unit.

Rufus looked toward the end of the aisle, then up. The units didn't have any headspace to climb across them, but the ceiling was shitty 2x2-foot drop tiles. He motioned up with a jut of his thumb. "Give me a boost," he whispered.

Grimacing, Sam holstered the gun. Then he set his legs and made a stirrup of his hands. "Quickly."

Rufus put his foot into Sam's hold, hands on his shoulders, and then propelled himself up. He reached overhead, moved the tile to one side, then hoisted himself up. Rufus reached a hand down and motioned for the bolt cutters.

Passing them up with one hand, Sam drew out the gun again with the other. His gaze was fixed on the end of the hall, where the sound of footsteps had stopped.

"Where is she?" Jimmy asked, the suddenness of his voice like a bullet cracking a mirror. "*Rufus?*" He was walking again, now passing his unit and moving closer to the end of the aisle.

Rufus carefully crawled across the frames of the ceiling. Too much weight for too long and he'd feel the structure dip, even under his less-than-impressive weight. Rufus wiggled across the tiles to where the tops of the storage units touched the ceiling, and that ominous dip and creak ceased. He moved along the length of the containers in the direction Jimmy was walking, dragging the bolt cutters in one hand.

Then a shot broke the stillness, a bullet chewing through metal so loudly that it drew painful gooseflesh all over Rufus's body. The sound reverberated off all of the storage units at a deafening volume. Rufus initially froze, curled into a ball, trying to make himself as small a target as possible as he thought Jimmy was shooting up at him. But no, there wasn't any sort of metal up here to make that god-awful... the shot had come from a Beretta.

Sam's Beretta.

Rufus scrambled forward, hoping that Jimmy was as momentarily deaf as he was, and when he neared the far end, he pulled a drop tile up and shoved it to the side. That's when the second round was fired—distinctly unique from the first. Not muffled in the sense that Hollywood portrayed, but Rufus could tell it was a gun with a silencer, and it sure as fuck wasn't Sam's.

That cry of pain that followed, though? That was Sam.

Rufus shifted so he could put his legs first and dropped down from the ceiling. He fell wrong on one foot, rolled his ankle, and slammed his knee into the linoleum floor. Rufus swallowed a string of curses, got to his feet, and limp-ran around the corner, still carrying the bolt cutters.

"—punkass kid puts up a good front," Jimmy was

saying to Sam, who was on the floor, a bloody hand pressed to his thigh. "But he's still just a fucking *kid*, crawling into some hole to hide while leaving you high and dry."

Sam's eyes were locked on Jimmy. His voice was tight with pain as he said, "He's not a kid. Not anymore. I bet you'll figure that out about five seconds before he takes off your balls with a pair of bolt cutters."

"Oh yeah?" And Rufus could hear the smile in Jimmy's voice as Rufus tiptoed closer from behind. Jimmy kept his weapon trained on Sam while making a sweeping gesture with his free hand at the empty aisle. "Where is he?"

"Behind you, you son of a bitch," Rufus shouted before he hit Jimmy across the back of the head with the bolt cutters. Blood spurted from the wound as Jimmy slammed hard into the opposite wall of units.

Jimmy was still holding his pistol as he staggered and turned toward Rufus. Rufus drew the cutters up and hit Jimmy across the face, slicing his cheek and nose open. Jimmy was screaming now. He dropped the gun, held his face in both hands, and slipped on the pool of blood underfoot. Sam was shouting as Jimmy fell to one knee, but Rufus couldn't make out individual words over the rush of unbridled rage pumping in his own ears. He cracked Jimmy over the back of the head a third time before the older man finally crashed to the floor.

Rufus was pulling back, ready to beat Jimmy to death with the bolt cutters, when a hand grabbed him and spun him around. "He's down," Erik was shouting. "Jesus Christ, Rufus, he's down. Drop the bolt cutters. Drop them. Drop them!"

Rufus only managed to drop the weapon after Erik shook him hard enough. His hands had gripped the handles so tight that his fingers were still locked in place. "Jimmy killed my mom."

"What the fuck?" Erik was muttering to himself over

and over again, his gaze moving from the bloody mess of Jimmy's face to Sam. "What in the fucking nine hells?" Then he grabbed his phone and shoved it into Rufus's hands. "Call for an ambulance." Drawing the cuffs from his belt, he moved toward Jimmy.

CHAPTER
THIRTY-ONE

The ambulance took Sam to Mount Sinai Beth Israel. When he woke from the surgery, he was in a hospital room. The room was small, but the hospital administration, with the blank defiance of reality that is the characteristic of bureaucrats everywhere, had found a way to make it shared—semi-private was the term, which to Sam made about as much sense as Jeannie McDowell, who had been captain of the girls youth league at Morgan Park Second Baptist, claiming to be a semi-virgin after she broke up with Cliff Ritenour. In other words, not a whole fucking lot. He was voicing this opinion to Rufus when Rufus put a hand over his mouth, and then he fell asleep.

When he woke, the room was dark. Rufus's body made a W over two chairs that had been pulled next to each other; somehow the redhead was passed out across the armrests. On the other side of the privacy curtain—semi-privacy curtain, Sam corrected himself—a man was snoring. The room smelled like canned chicken noodle soup. Through the window, the city looked like sea glass broken on a midnight beach.

The pain in his leg—in both legs, if Sam were honest—was bad, and he pressed the call button. The nurse came a few minutes later. He was a young guy with wiry brown hair, and he smiled a lot. He just couldn't have been more fucking pleased to hear about how much Sam's leg was hurting. After a few more minutes of listening and smiling, he left and came back with pills in a paper cup. Percocet. Sam took them. They made him feel like his skin was stretched too tight, like his head had gotten cut off and he was floating. But after a while, he slept again.

The next time he woke, it was morning, and Rufus was reading.

"What the fuck are you doing?" Sam asked, and then he cleared his throat and asked again more clearly.

Rufus's beanie was in the empty chair, his red hair a wild mess. He held up a pamphlet and said, "STIs. The nurses didn't have anything else to read besides some old copies of *O*, which I'm not really a fan of." He stood up and moved to the bed. "How're you?"

"I got stabbed in one leg and shot in the other one. How am I supposed to be?"

Rufus pursed his lips. "I didn't stab or shoot you—don't get cranky with me."

"Where's my gun?"

"Erik has it."

"Go get it. I need it."

"You don't need your gun. You're in a hospital."

"Why are you still here? Why don't you go home?

Why don't you get something to eat and have a shower?"

Rufus raised both brows. "I didn't want—do you *want* me to go?"

"That's not the point. The point is, you could have slept in your own bed, you could have changed clothes, you could have come back here this morning and—oh shit, I'm going to puke."

Rufus made it in time with a basin, but barely.

For a while, all Sam could do was hunch there, heaving and then dry heaving over the basin while Rufus rubbed his back. When it was over, he flopped back onto the pillow, covered in cold sweat, shaking. He wiped his mouth with the back of his hand.

"I'm sorry. I feel like shit, and I'm dizzy, and everything hurts, and—and how the fuck am I supposed to go anywhere, do anything, when I can't even stand up?" He covered his eyes with one hand. "What the fuck am I even saying?"

"I don't think you should worry about standing up and going somewhere," Rufus replied, calmly stroking Sam's other arm. "You were shot and stabbed, remember?"

Through gritted teeth, Sam said, "Yes, Rufus. I remember."

"I just mean, where's the rush?"

"What am I supposed to do? I can't go home. I don't have a home. I can't—I can't hop a bus. I can't crutch along I-70. I can't stay here; they're not running a fucking Motel 6." Wiping his face once more, Sam let out a slow breath. Then he dropped his hands and blinked up at Rufus: the wild red hair, the freckles, the Dead Kennedys shirt that looked like it needed a gallon of Tide. "Never mind. I'll figure it out."

Rufus fiddled with the sleeve of Sam's hospital gown, then drummed the railing. "I have a bed," he stated after a moment. "And a toilet. And a shower. And a fridge. Did you need anything else?"

Rufus looked very much like Rufus right then, maybe the most like Rufus that he'd ever looked to Sam—which a distant part of Sam's mind thought might be the Percocet talking. Strong and vulnerable and hurting, and underneath it all, very kind.

"A bed, a toilet, a shower, and a fridge. Is that right?"

"No laundry in the building," Rufus continued. "You have to walk your lazy ass down to the laundromat on First."

"Crutch."

"Whatever."

Sam licked dry lips. "Then the only thing I think I need is you. And maybe those BlueMoon pancakes."

Rufus smiled. "My treat."

Sam Auden and Rufus O'Callaghan return in:

A Friend in the Glass
(An Auden & O'Callaghan Mystery: Book Three)

Gregory Ashe is a longtime Midwesterner. He has lived in Chicago, Bloomington (IN), and Saint Louis, his current home. When not reading and writing (which take up a lot of his time), he is an educator.

gregoryashe.com

ALSO BY GREGORY ASHE

SERIES:
The Hazard and Somerset Mysteries
Pretty Pretty Boys
Transposition
Paternity Case
Guilt by Association
Reasonable Doubt
Criminal Past

Hazard and Somerset: A Union of Swords
The Rational Faculty
Police Brutality
Transactional Dynamics
Wayward
The Keeper of Bees

The Borealis Investigations
Orientation
Triangulation
Declination

Hollow Folk
Mr. Big Empty
All the Inside Howling
The Dust Feast
The Mortal Sleep

The Lamb and the Lion
The Same Breath
The Same Place
The Same End

**An Auden & O'Callaghan Mystery
(co-written with C.S. Poe)**
A Friend in the Dark
A Friend in the Fire

NOVELS:
Stray Fears

C.S. Poe is a Lambda Literary and two-time EPIC award finalist, and a FAPA award-winning author of gay mystery, romance, and speculative fiction.

She resides in New York City, but has also called Key West and Ibaraki, Japan, home in the past. She has an affinity for all things cute and colorful and a major weakness for toys. C.S. is an avid fan of coffee, reading, and cats. She's rescued two cats—Milo and Kasper do their best to distract her from work on a daily basis.

C.S. is an alumna of the School of Visual Arts.

Her debut novel, *The Mystery of Nevermore*, was published 2016.

cspoe.com

ALSO BY C.S. POE

SERIES:
Snow & Winter
The Mystery of Nevermore
The Mystery of the Curiosities
The Mystery of the Moving Image
The Mystery of the Bones

Snow & Winter Collection
Interlude

Magic & Steam
The Engineer
The Gangster

A Lancaster Story
Kneading You
Joy
Color of You

The Silver Screen
Lights. Camera. Murder.

An Auden & O'Callaghan Mystery
(co-written with Gregory Ashe)
A Friend in the Dark
A Friend in the Fire

NOVELS:
Southernmost Murder

NOVELLAS:
11:59

SHORT STORIES:
Love in 24 Frames
That Turtle Story
New Game, Start
Love Has No Expiration

Visit **cspoe.com** for free slice-of-life codas, titles in audio, and available foreign translations.

Join C.S. Poe's mailing list to stay updated on upcoming releases, sales, conventions, and more!
https://bit.ly/CSPoeNewsletter

Made in the USA
Coppell, TX
06 May 2021

55146636R00162